THE REDEMPTION OF
DANNY HARPER

a 60's novel

Doug,

Rather than attempt
to enumerate your many
Kindnesses and Virtues, I
shall merely accuse you of
being a friend.

2012

–

ISBN 978-0-9877054-9-5

http://www.amazon.com/-/e/B005VQ5EJA
http://dominuslumiere.blogspot.ca/

THE REDEMPTION OF DANNY HARPER

a 60's novel

JAMES HOCKINGS

CHAPTER ONE

A state of war only serves as an excuse for domestic tyranny.
~Aleksandr Solzhenitsyn

The passenger coach, a rolling relic from the golden age of steam, smelled like shit. To be precise, it did not smell exactly like fecal matter, but was in the same order of yucky magnitude. Tobacco smoke hung in layers like killer fog since the ventilation unit in this piece of rolling stock was dead and gone, and the stale/sweet scent of chewing gum in a multitude of flavors and a multitude of vintages wafted from beneath the seats, mixing with the omnipresent diesel exhaust.

This miasmatic combination sent a clear signal to Danny's stomach. "Rid yourself of last night's alcohol! Give 'er up, boy!" It was, fercrissake, only 6:30 in the morning; the booze from last night's revelries was still sloshing around un-metabolized in Danny's otherwise empty stomach. This morning, the Rock Island Rocket from Limmah, Illinois to Chicago Union Station was Danny's personal roller coaster to hell. The rocking motion of the car, so rhapsodic in folksy railroad songs, was running contrapuntally to the roiling in Danny's guts and composing a symphony of exquisite misery, rivaled only by the screeching aria of pain working its way to a high C in Danny's skull. The fact that Danny had a letter in his pocket that appeared to have been signed by the President of the United States himself, inviting him to Chicago, did not make him feel any better.

Of course, the train was not taking Danny to hell, merely to an earthly approximation of hell: Chicago in spring of 1969, and more specifically, the Selective Service Induction Centre for Northern Illinois, where officialdom wanted to poke and prod Danny to evaluate his fitness for service in the imperialist army of his great nation, presently engaged in conflict with some little yellow guys in black pajamas on the other side of the world - a conflict Danny had at one time mildly supported in theory, as long as "some other guys" were the ones fighting "those other guys." Danny felt he would be proud to serve his nation as assistant secretary of state or even in a post as boring as secretary of the interior, but he doubted the Selective Service System would offer him any post for which he would be well suited.

The spring countryside of Illinois slipped wetly by the rain-streaked window of the Pullman. The land was bare; Illinois' ubiquitous corn and soybean fields had yet to be sown. In the tiny towns and small cities on the route, the daffodils were dying and giving way to tulips in the sad muddy gardens of the poor and working class, who seemed, for some reason, to favor living near the tracks. Mostly, though, this stretch of Illinois was as unappealing to look at as the coach car was to smell. They both made Danny feel less than his best. He longed to be in his parents' house in Limmah, in his narrow bed, sleeping off his drunk.

Danny looked good, however bad he felt. He had showered and shaved for a change. Danny wore a starched and pressed white dress shirt with French cuffs fastened with fake gold cufflinks that a girl in high school had given him for Christmas long ago, a conservative maroon-and-blue striped tie, black wool cuffed dress pants, his favorite gray Harris Tweed sports jacket and polished black tassel loafers. In Illinois, nice people still dressed for travel. Danny came from nice people - not rich by any means, but nice. He had even slapped on some Old Spice Fresh Lime aftershave, which, in retrospect, had been a mistake. The fresh clean smell of lime Old Spice did not mix well with diesel fumes and a hangover.

Most of the nice people in Limmah worked for a nice company that made ordnance for the Army. Ordnance is a nice word for bombs and shells. Danny's dad made proximity fuses. The military uses a proximity fuse because it is more effective to have a shell go off just before it hits something than when it actually hits something. Proximity fuses detonated the first atomic bombs, but the nice factory in Danny's hometown had not been involved in making proximity fuses during WW II. Before becoming addicted to government defense contract work, the factory made wind-up clocks, but these had fallen out of fashion. Production of the new electric clocks had now shifted to foreign lands like Georgia and Alabama, where labor was not unionized. So the company made proximity fuses for the Army until it closed five years later, when the congressional district was no longer in the hands of the right political party. The company then moved its fuse production to those same non-unionized foreign lands that made electric clocks. The closure of the plant would catch 3,499 people in Limmah off guard. Danny's father was fated to be one of the 3,499 laid-off workers, spending his newfound freedom carving wooden toys with a jackknife and living on his dwindling savings, to die of a broken heart at the age of 57 … less than a year after being laid off.

Danny was traveling with the son of the plant manager. The scion's name was Skippy Wright. He and Danny got on well, despite the difference in their social stations. They were both intellectual existential heroes, if only in their own minds. They were probably two of only a handful of students who had come from the local high school who could even spell "existential." That in itself made them special. Danny and Skippy were so very special that the dumb Pollock and Dago jocks - who could not spell "existential" and had no interest in learning how - had regularly threatened to pummel both of them. This common threat forged a common bond between Danny and Skippy. There is nothing like a shared enemy to bind together the members of a social group, if two can be termed a "group."

Skippy was not as well dressed as Danny, despite having a more extensive and expensive wardrobe. Skippy was a year ahead of Danny in school, and had just graduated from a fancy eastern college where fashion was influenced by itinerant folk troubadours. These troubadours were, in reality, mostly just Skippy's peers who had dropped out of the same exclusive eastern college. They had taken to imitating the Okie accents and the worn and torn, working-class clothing of the real folk troubadours of a previous generation, who rode in boxcars, ate half a can of beans (on a good day), and would have traded their homemade guitars for a chance to get a good education at a prestigious college with a meal plan. Skippy wore jeans that he had ripped in strategic places, and a neatly pressed checked flannel shirt that he had been unable to keep out of the hands of the Wright family's compulsive Polish housekeeper, who insisted on ironing everything. Fortunately, it was raining, so at least Skippy's new workboots looked muddied and authentic.

Danny lit a smoke and asked Skippy, "What if they draft you right out of your physical?" Skippy was going to his induction physical and Danny to his pre-induction physical.

"I hope they do. I'll get a free plane ride to Vietnam, where I'll defect to the other side." Skippy always had a pat answer. He was going to be a lawyer.

Danny thought this was foolishness. Danny knew the little guys in the black PJs only ate a few moldy rice balls and an ounce or two of rat meat a week and Skippy was a chubby chow hound, but he didn't want to burst Skippy's defection balloon. Instead, Danny asked Skippy a more frightening question: "Does your father know what you plan to do?"

"No, he doesn't need to. They won't draft me, anyway. I have asthma and flat feet and I've been accepted at Harvard Law." Bingo! Everyone knew they didn't draft lawyers. Lawyers had drafted the draft laws. "I'm going to fight for the rights of black men on death row."

Danny asked again, nearly the same question: "Does your dad know that?"

"No, not the part about the Negroes ..."

Danny was impatient with this discussion and withdrew into his pain. Stubbing out his seventh cigarette of the trip in the tiny overflowing ashtray in the arm of the seat, he asked no one in particular, "I wonder if the bar car's open?" He closed his eyes and fell asleep.

I feel good and I feel sleepy and I feel real strange. My pee pee has the tingles. I open my eyes and see her. She has her hand on it and is rubbing it. She looks real tall sitting next to me on the bed and her head has a halo around it from the ceiling light. She has on a white almost see-through night gown. Her blue eyes are shining with an unnatural light. With the halo around her head she looks like pretty angel Dad puts on top of the Christmas tree. I try to talk and she says, "Shsssssssh," and keeps rubbing it. It's big now, like it gets sometimes when I have to pee in the morning, but I don't have to pee now. She moves her head down near my legs and I see the chuck wagons and branding irons and doggies on the bedroom curtains. I love cowboys and want to be one when I grow up. My eyes wander away from the curtains and I can see her boobies inside the loose nightgown she is wearing. It has flopped open as she bends over near my pee pee and pulls down my blue Roy Rogers jammy bottoms and takes me pee pee in her mouth. Does she want to kiss my pee pee? I close my eyes. I think I'm dreaming or dying or something. I'm real excited, like when I see a puppy I want to pet or when I eat my favorite food—fried chicken. But more excited than that. Excited like I never felt excited before and dreamy, like when they gave me that smelly gas when I got my appendix out when I was 3 and a half... And about to explode in my belly and between my legs.

Then the side of my face explodes in pain. She slaps me harder than I ever remember. "You filthy little boy. See what you made me do and see the mess you made."

I think I peed myself, but when I reach down to feel it, the pee is all sticky. I'm crying. I don't know why she hit me, except maybe 'cause I peed in bed.

You think I hit you, don't you. Well, I didn't hit you but I will if you ever open your big trap about the bad thing you did tonight. I'll hit you so hard your head'll spin, if you tell anybody.

Who did she think I was gonna to tell? She was my mother.

Danny awoke to a jolt and a bang as the train hit a switch in one of the dank tunnels the Rock Island Main Line took through downtown as it neared Union Station. Danny was drenched in sweat and shaking; it was not just the hangover making him sick. He unconsciously checked the side of his face for stinging. He surreptitiously checked his underwear for sticky. The train stopped with a final jerk.

CHAPTER TWO

Violence can only be concealed by a lie, and the lie can only be maintained by violence~Alexander Solzhenitsyn

Danny and Skippy debarked onto the always cold and damp cavern that was the Union Station platform. The world-renowned beaux arts iron pillars and cantilevered ceilings were festooned with cotton candy-like tufts of gray detritus that dated from the age of steam trains, with some newly belched contributions from the Iron Horse Diesels. The smell was like damp gunpowder mixed with used motor oil, and was unmistakably the smell of a train station. The light here, under the city, was the same dim gray as the detritus. This cold dead light sucked all the color out of anything it touched including Danny, who - suffering from booze flu and the ever-dreaded dream - had little color to begin with.

Chicago was not a city Danny loved. His last visit had been to the 1968 Democratic National Convention police riot, although Danny had not rioted or even seen any rioting that he could remember. Chicago's finest had nevertheless seen fit to kick in Danny's head as he exercised his constitutional right to peacefully sleep off a bad acid trip in the doorway of a downtown pawnshop. He still had a noticeable divot in his left temple. It made for a good story, one which he told various versions of to various people at various times.

Richard J. Daley, the mayor of Chicago, was the last of the big-city Democratic bosses. A measure of his power was that he was a white mayor in a black town. He ran the city like his private fiefdom. The Chicago police acted as Mayor Richard J. Daley's private army. If you were on his good side, you got the pothole in front of your house filled or had your lakeshore high-rise project approved. Of course, greater tribute was expected for the greater favor. A mere vote would buy you a filled pothole. Being on his bad side - by having long hair, ragged clothes or a good education - would get you a free beating. Danny had triple qualified to receive his just deserts on August 29 of '68. He bore the scars with some pride.

Danny and Skippy's destination in this benighted city was a charmless three-story red brick edifice just three blocks from the train station. It lacked charm in the way that only an old government building could. A goon squad of Chicago police surrounded the building, patrolling behind a razor-wire barrier and cradling short-barreled Remington riot guns, restraining snarling German shepherds on short leashes and all displaying that "flat cop" stare calculated to terrorize unarmed boys in their late teens and blacks of all ages. Mounted officers patrolled outside the wire. What a welcome! Only the horses appeared friendly, with their soft brown eyes and fuzzy faces. But the chilly welcome outside only presaged the even lower temperature inside.

To gain entry to the center, the boys had to show their papers to a giant economy-sized be-sidearmed and be-nightsticked military policeman. The papers read, "You are required under penalty of law to present the accompanying documentation at the designated Selective Service Induction Centre along with your Selective Service Registration Card, Form SS213-B, and a valid piece of identification. See the reverse for the list of valid types of identification. Failure to do so is a federal offense, punishable by a fine of up to $10,000 and a maximum imprisonment of no more than 10 years." It was signed by the President of the United States.

The boys moved a few yards into the building, past the MP, and were confronted by a purple–faced and pockmarked man with gold lieutenant's bars and bad breath - so bad it was offensive even at a distance of six feet. He achieved such remarkable range with his killer breath by shouting every word in an apparent rage.

"Climb the stairs, shitbirds, and take a fuckin' basket from the clearly marked and indicated basket location to your left and insert your draft card into the draft card slot conveniently located at either end of the basket near the top of one of the short sides of the basket!"

Danny amused himself with mental pictures of what a "shitbird" would look like.

At the top of the stairs, near the "clearly marked and indicated basket location," Danny and Skippy located the baskets and inserted their draft cards into a "draft card slot conveniently located at either end near the top of one of the short sides of the basket!" They encountered another greeter just past the basket location who yelled with surprising enthusiasm for 9 in the morning, "Ladies, take off all your clothes except your panties and shoes and deposit the rest of your clothes in the basket your government has so conveniently provided for this purpose. You'll then give the basket containing your clothes to the soldiers manning the clothing basket depot located to your immediate left in this hallway to your left. LEFT! Left is *that* way, ladies!" The greeter pointed left, firmly and repeatedly.

Witnessing this performance by an assuredly demented and probably demonic 250-lb. man in a wrinkled and sweat-stained uniform sporting a five o'clock shadow at 9 in the morning cured Danny forever of his fantasy about stewardesses pantomiming

12

instructions at takeoff. Danny hung his head, beaten and bested by a man who could so effectively flaunt his superior testosterone level as early as 9 in the morning. Skippy, however, perhaps practicing to be the kind of attorney who could free a black man from an Alabama death row, attempted to look defiant - as defiant as an overweight Caucasian leftist can look wearing only jockey shorts and shoes.

Being a keener about even this demeaning task, Danny shuffled his way to the left, followed by Skippy, and offered up his basket of outerwear to a corporal and a private at the basket depot window. The private smiled warmly, all the time lovingly appraising Danny's snow-white underpants. He continued on down with his appraisal, taking in Danny's snow-white legs and ending in Danny's polished black Bass Weejun tassel loafers. The private was not a white person.

In fact, only the officers were white persons. Skippy and Danny were the only candidates Danny could see who were white persons aside from a few judgment calls who might have been Mexican.

It was at that point that Danny noticed that the black guys of all shapes and all sizes did not look at all vulnerable in just their skimpies and shoes; they looked fierce, fiercer even than the unduly loud men in uniform.

Danny scanned this room full of fierceness with hooded eyes, hiding a look of terror tempered by resignation - the very mien of a wildebeest brought down by lions. "We're screwed."

Skippy whispered back, "No, the ruling classes are screwed. No one can defeat a united proletariat."

Danny turned his body to face Skippy with his head still hanging. "Skippy, you're not a member of the proletariat. I am, but I don't wanna be."

"Oh … right." Skippy often forgot his privileged roots and Danny had to remind him.

Their conversation was rudely interrupted by a uniformed representative of the ruling cabal who shouted, "During your stay, you'll be escorted to a number of 'stations!' At each station, you'll be required to present yourself for examination. Those of you who co-operate will probably be finished by early afternoon and can leave. Those of you who don't take this seriously will be asked to return to Station #1, and begin the whole process over again. You might be in this building for days on end until your behavior improves. If several of you don't co-operate, your whole group will be asked to repeat the process from the beginning. You're encouraged to help your fellow 'teammates' co-operate so that you can all leave sometime before the summer!"

Danny intuited that Station #1, since it was #1, would be the station examining that part of prospective inductees which would be the most accurate anatomical predictor of the candidate's suitability to serve in the Army of the Republic.

"Bend over and spread 'em, ladies."

"Spread what?" Skippy squeaked weakly, his nascent lawyerly pugnacity gone, and perhaps also his dream of being accepted by the proletariat.

"Open your ass cheeks, fat boy."

Skippy and Danny became separated after Station #1. Danny feared Skippy may have presented his examiners with something suspect on or about his rectal region, but dared not ask the rough military minions of the ruling class a question this delicate in nature. Instead, Danny and his band of black brothers trudged in surly silence to Station #2.

At Station #2, the medics, if that is what they were, examined the manhood of each candidate, or in Danny's case, his relative lack of manhood when he compared himself to his colored companions. The "medics" were not satisfied with a mere modest glance to assure themselves that no women - driven, no doubt, by a desire to kill their fellow humans - had sneaked into the Induction Centre. No, the latex-gloved medics insisted on cupping the balls of each candidate for slaughter and asking him to cough.

Danny was not used to the tender attentions of his own sex, and the difference between his manhood and that of his colored comrades became even more strikingly apparent after this tender touch of latex. The thought crossed Danny's mind that given a few drinks and some sweet words, he might have come around a little, rather than shrinking into near invisibility.

Stations #3 and #4 were dull by comparison to Stations #1 and #2 - just heart and lung tests. Danny could still feel the warm glow of that gloved hand on his nether regions.

At Station #5, Danny had a chance to display his knowledge of ophthalmology. He told the doctor, "While I may have adequate vision to serve my country, I don't possess true depth perception, as I have a strabismus, which causes a virtual nerve blindness in the central portion of my right eye whenever my left eye is open. And, since I'm right-handed, this disability prevents me from being a good judge of distance while shooting a rifle."

The doctor answered him with that particular tone of grave respect in his voice that Danny was sure he reserved for his learned colleagues. "Uh-huh. I see. Yes."

Reassured that the doctor accepted his self-diagnosis, Danny concluded, "So, I'm probably unfit to safely and effectively fire a rifle and perhaps not even be a very good typist, as I wouldn't be able to accurately judge the distance from my fingers to the keys."

The eye doctor looked thoughtful. He squinted up at the eye chart and then back at Danny. "Son, the Army welcomes boys with only one eye. Our marksmanship instructors can teach you to shoot with your left hand." He marked Danny "Passed." "You know, son, your country needs you more than ever in these troubled times."

Sadly, Danny knew the doc was right. These were troubled times. Danny understood troubled times only too well.

Station #6 offered Danny the chance to divulge his feelings about his own troubled times. Station #6 offered Danny the chance to talk in semi-private to a real psychiatrist. The psychiatrist offered Danny a seat across from him at a small table. Ropes and stanchions held the other members of Danny's group back at a distance of almost 6 ft. Danny felt very safe with this member of the healing profession; he radiated that kind of vibe.

"Son, is there anything bothering you? Anything you want to talk about?"

Danny looked into the psychiatrist's soft brown fatherly eyes, and knew he was with a man he could trust with anything. Danny began to speak his heart, slowly and haltingly. "Doctor, I'm barely holding it together anymore. I dropped out of school. I'm drunk every day and all night, too, if I can get enough speed to keep me awake. My girlfriend is pregnant. I don't even know what kind of drugs I'm taking most of the time, I take so many. I'm losing weight. I have no appetite. My parents hate me. I have terrible dreams and wake up screaming. I sometimes can't tell what's real and what's not. I hear people whispering, telling me to do the most appalling things. I think they're trying to kill me. I want to hurt myself."

The doctor heard the pain in Danny's voice and saw the tears welling up behind Danny's clear blue eyes. He seemed to look into Danny's soul. He put his big warm hand over Danny's and said, "Son, it's going to be alright, I promise. The Army can help you get through all this."

The psychiatrist opened Danny's folder and marked him "Passed."

Station #7 was where the Selective Service System separated the sheep from the goats. "Any of y'all who's been arrested or convicted of a criminal offense will go to the left and enter that door with the big red sign that says 'Offender Interviews.' Y'all see which door I mean?" The uniformed dupe of the ruling classes who was speaking pointed with his arm to the marked door, and held his arm on point until all of the self-identified "goats" in the group stood and began the march of shame to the Offender Interviews door. Danny was a goat. So were three-quarters of his group.

Danny seated himself in the front row of desks in the Offender Interviews room because that row was empty. The other rows were almost completely full. Military police with batons and sidearms stood at the sides and back of the room. Some absentmindedly slapped their batons across their palms. All the MPs were practicing their "flat cop" stare, although none of them seemed to need much practice.

An officer addressed the throng of offenders. "I'll ask each of you to describe the nature of the crimes you were charged with, and the sentences you served for those crimes. Based on what you tell me, you'll either be allowed to proceed back to your group outside, or you'll be questioned further in a separate facility by one of the MPs at the back of the room. We ask you to be honest. Uncle Sam is counting on all of you, and needs all the help you can give us in these difficult times."

There it was again, thought Danny. The Army understood difficult times. At that instant, Danny felt warm, almost as warm as he had felt when the medic cupped his balls. He decided he would tell Uncle Sam everything about his criminal past - honestly.

Danny was nearly moved to tears by the confessions of the other men. Danny now considered them to be men, not the mere boys who had entered the center just hours before. These men, products of deprivation and discrimination, told heroic tales of their struggle for justice and a way out of inner-city poverty through brave acts of armed robbery, robbery with violence, pimping, grand theft auto and drug trafficking.

Danny thought these lost souls deserved a second chance, even the ones the MPs handcuffed and dragged out of the room through a back door.

Danny had never before confessed his sins in public while clad only in underpants and shoes. He knew it would be difficult, but he was determined, as a matter of honor, to do so in a bold and forthright manner. He was through with deceptions that ultimately disappointed people. When his turn came, Danny spoke his confession in a strong clear voice. "Sir, I was arrested for internal possession of an alcoholic beverage in the state of Iowa while a minor person. I was convicted and fined $80 and served two hours in jail."

The room fell silent, and the officer at the front stared at Danny in awe - exactly the response Danny felt he deserved for his clarity, brevity, and bold Lincoln-esque honesty.

"What the hell? Are you fuckin' with me, dickbrain? Get your pansy ass out of here before I kick it so hard you'll be tasting turds for a week. Out! Now!" The officer pointed to the exit door.

Danny had obviously disappointed him, and was being sent back to the sheep. He noticed that the sheep outside were now clothed, and Danny asked one of the lighter-toned black men where he might find his own clothing. "That way, motherfucker!" Danny thanked the man, for he knew that in ghetto-speak, the man had probably expressed his approval of Danny, if not his actual affection for him, by using this rough-and-tumble appellation.

Station #9 was lunch. Danny managed to find Skippy without much trouble in the crowded cafeteria. Skippy stood out like a snowball in a coal pile. Danny sat with him. They both began to talk at once about their respective experiences. Skippy's recounting quickly took on the tone of a polemic. "I feel there was an Hegelian influence on Trotsky that ultimately led to his assassination and the eventual grave disappointment that communism became under Stalin after the glory of the revolution, and this leads us to envision a similar situation vis-à-vis the politics of China and her client state, Vietnam, and that's why we're here today being humiliated by the imperialist lackey running-dog capitalists in the Selective Service System and the U.S. Army."

Danny was impressed, but not in a good way. "Keep your voice down," Danny whispered, looking around fearfully. "Are you some kind of commie now? Jesus, I just wanna smoke a joint."

Station #10 was a very large classroom fitted with student desks. Danny immediately felt more comfortable than he had all day surrounded by this room's academically inspired decor, and was preparing to take a nap when the imperialist lackey running-dog capitalists began to pass out test papers and bark orders about how to fill them out.

It seemed the Army wanted to test intelligence. At last, Danny had a chance to make up for the disappointment he had caused the Army earlier in the day. He seized this opportunity like a terrier would a rat. Danny knew how to take tests and do very well on them, indeed.

Danny finished the two-page, multiple-choice test in 4.5 of the 30 minutes allotted for its completion. He was so bored during the next 25.5 minutes that he even checked his work. The question about whether the object shown in question 33 was a picture of a right-handed screwdriver or a left-handed screwdriver or both or neither seemed a bit of a no-win to Danny, as he felt that it was neither "both" nor "neither" but simply a good example of a question being deficient in both clarity and logic. He chose to answer "both," which was correct in a sense, but Danny felt cheap about condoning this type of sloppy thinking in his testers. Danny thought, "How can they possibly expect to win a war when they're such sloppy thinkers?"

After the 30 minutes had passed, the imperialist lackey running-dog capitalists picked up the test papers. They told the assembled multitude to shut the fuck up and stay the fuck in their seats. This seemed like a wise thing to do, since moose-sized MPs were glowering at the candidates from every corner of the room. Danny believed his high-school hall monitors could have learned a few things from the Army about keeping order. Or perhaps just arming high-school hall monitors with .45 automatics would be sufficient to achieve a similar level of control.

After shutting the fuck up and staying the fuck in their seats for another half-hour, the testees were addressed by an officer from the front of the room.

"I know some of you tried to fail this test on purpose. I know some of you think this is funny. I know some of you heard Ringo Starr failed the English army intelligence test and now you want to be just like that long-haired pussy fag Limey cunt and avoid service in the Army of the United States. Well, fuckheads, it's not going to work. We have the legal right to keep you here all day and overnight and all the next day for weeks on end, if we determine you need further testing. You could be right here for the duration of your country's need and I assure you, we won't make it pleasant for you. DO YOU UNDERSTAND?

"Before we send those of you who failed this test to another room, where I assure you that you'll either pass the test or be here until you're very old, I want to present for your edification someone who should be an example to you, someone who'll be an officer someday and lead you into combat, someone who not only passed the test but had the only perfect score in this room. I want my future brother officer to stand up. Daniel No-Middle-Initial Harper, will you stand up now and show these fuckknuckles what a leader looks like?"

Daniel No-Middle-Initial Harper dutifully stood, but only for about 11 seconds.

The room swam in Danny's vision as he looked around. Eyes! He saw 1,000 black faces turn toward him, and 2,000 black eyes lock on him like Sidewinder missiles coming in for the kill. These eyes were the eyes of angry young men who had seen and done it all. Most of their seeing? Scenes of oppression and violence. Most of their doing? Illegal acts.

Danny imagined himself in the jungle. He knew he would be the kind of leader who leads from the front. He saw himself walking on point in tall elephant grass, moving one slow step at a time, fear like vomit in his mouth that he couldn't expel, with a platoon of armed black men behind him and an unknown number of armed yellow men somewhere in front of him, none of whom had the slightest interest in his welfare or longevity.

Danny fainted.

Two concerned MPs dragged him to a small first-aid post and laid him gently on a cot, with his folder of test results on his chest. The medic, who had so tenderly cupped Danny's balls earlier, said tenderly, "You'll be okay. You just stood up too fast and were too excited at being told that you could become an officer. You've passed all your tests, and this fainting business wouldn't show up on your record; I won't make a note of it. You'll be able to leave and rejoin your group after a few minutes of rest. Rest now, little soldier."

He laid his hand on Danny's hand. "You're going to love the Army. You'll meet a lot of great guys with similar interests. I certainly have."

Danny closed his eyes and tried to visualize where Toronto might be on the map.

CHAPTER THREE

War paralyzes your courage and deadens the spirit of true
manhood~Alexander Berkman

After being released from the custody of the Selective Service System, Danny and Skippy met each other in the reception hall just inside the main doors, as they had agreed to do. Skippy was looking downcast, perhaps still chafing from the humiliation he had suffered at almost every station. Danny knew enough not to rub it in. Although he was bursting with pride, Danny didn't gloat about his perfect score on the army intelligence test - the only perfect score in the testing room and perhaps in the entire history of the test. Now was not the time. It was time to bond with Skippy in discreet silence and let Skippy get something to eat. Danny knew that fat boys could not survive on a lunch of boiled cabbage, instant mashed potatoes and mystery meat.

Skippy's eyes were filled with food lust. "Our train doesn't leave for another hour or so. Let's go to that German restaurant around the corner. Remember? Bergerdorkenhutzsteinholtengarten or something like that ... It was kinda down some stairs to a lower street."

Skippy had a sense of humor when he was not yammering political nonsense. Danny wondered, however, if Skippy - with his penchant for displaying useless erudition - was not just stringing together the names of a few obscure German philosophers to subtly test Danny's knowledge of the history of 19ᵗʰ-century German philosophy. This got Danny thinking about Friedrich Nietzsche. Then he thought about Nietzsche's Superman, then about the Superman Comics he had collected as a child, then about how his mother has thrown out his comic books collection as punishment for some imagined failing on Danny's part. This thought made Danny rage inside. Danny was stoned on a combo of speed and sleep deprivation, his thinking branching out onto finer and finer limbs, until he finally fell off the last little branch like a squirrel with bad judgment. He came back to "reality" with a disappointing thud, and said absently, "Fine with me. The German place ..."

Danny knew it was always best to defer to a fat boy's choice of restaurant, just as he knew not to make suggestions when the fat kid was ordering pizza. Fat kids never seemed to pick a loser. Danny was feeling good now despite the rage at his mother for throwing out his comic books- great, in fact - and not the least bit hungry. Danny was being charitable in offering to eat with Skippy. Danny's hunger had fallen victim to stimulant drugs and adrenaline from his rage. When Danny had picked up his clothes before lunch, he had tapped three tabs of Dexedrine out of one of the collar stay slots in his white dress shirt and popped one. Then later, just before meeting Skippy, he had swallowed a second dexie in the can and crushed the third one and snorted it, just to get the rush.

Skippy led the way to the restaurant. They walked and walked but could not seem to get there. Danny surmised it was the speed making him lose track of time and distance, so he just gabbled and jabbered about nothing as they made their way to dinner. A speed-induced motormouth ...

Finally, Danny got curious. "Skippy, where the fuck are we going? It was only three blocks from the train station to the Induction Center and that German place has to be somewhere between the two."

"Right, but it was kind of down a side street," Skippy explained.

"Cool." If you couldn't trust a fat kid to find a restaurant …

The two walked more than a few minutes.

"You fucked up. Now we're lost." Danny had the speed jangles and was losing his patience. The adrenaline from the drugs and anger was taking over his more charitable side.

"Uh, maybe. Sorry. We could ask somebody."

Just then, as fortune would have it, they saw a young black male walking toward them. He had a huge Afro and was dressed like Jimmy Hendrix. "Cool," Danny thought. "Maybe I can score a joint to perk up my appetite." The only drugs he had dared take to the Induction Center, fearing dope-sniffing dogs, were the tabs of speed in his shirt. German shepherds were not trained to smell prescription drugs.

As he got closer to Danny and Skippy, "Jimmy" smoothly reached into his pocket and just as smoothly unlimbered a 6-in. switchblade, which he brandished with some obvious skill. Jimmy raised his eyebrows in salutation and smiled a goofy kind of smile. Danny knew "Jimmy" was high on something, or possibly many things. Without thinking, Danny elbowed Skippy hard in the ribs. Skippy, who had no physical skills and no sense of balance, fell off the curb into the street. Danny ran full speed right at "Jimmy", who stabbed Danny in the chest for his trouble. Danny stood still and looked down at the knife stuck in his chest. He lifted his head and saw the psychedelic mugger running full tilt in the opposite direction. Danny rocked the knife back and forth a few times and jerked it out of the hardbound volume he was carrying under his shirt.

Skippy was on his knees in the road, crying and staring at Danny's back, having just witnessed the most traumatic thing imaginable: the stabbing death of his friend Danny, a man who had just sacrificed his own life to save Skippy's.

Danny turned around. He spied Skippy in the gutter and held the knife up in the air like a spear and gave a war whoop, like Hollywood Indians attacking a wagon train on the big screen. Skippy's eyes bulged. His jaw dropped. He peed himself. The warm wetness on his leg brought him back to earth just long enough to croak, "Are you alive?" before he fainted, cracking his head on the curb as he went down.

Danny started shaking. He shook so badly he could barely hold the knife, but he remained standing. He dropped the knife on the pavement. He took a step and found he could walk, if he did it carefully. He began walking over to Skippy, and for some reason, he counted his steps aloud through chattering teeth. "One. Two. Three. Four. Five. Six. Seven. Eight. Nine. Ten. Eleven. Twelve. Thirteen. Fourteen." The counting calmed Danny enough for him to be able to kneel down and try to revive his fallen intellectual existential hero-comrade. "Wake up, asshole. Fucker, wake up!" Danny then slapped Skippy in the face for good measure; he knew from watching movies that's what you do when people faint. It's what Danny's mother always did to him to bring him back to her way of thinking.

Skippy opened one eye in response to the slap. "Did I die?"

"No, you pissed yourself." Danny said with mild disgust undisguised in his voice.

"Oh, shit, I did. Am I bleeding?" Skippy whined.

"From a non-fatal head wound."

Skippy put his hand to his head and it came away covered in red.

"What happened?"

"On the way out, I made a snap decision and stole the ops manual from the table behind the MP at the door."

"What?"

Danny opened his sports coat and unbuttoned his shirt to reveal a slender hardbound volume with a green army cover. The cover had a knife wound dead in its center and was entitled *Operational Manual, Induction Center U.S.A. Restricted # AOM 2317b sub. 878, 1965, 66, 67 rev.*

"You attacked that guy."

"Shit, I don't know what the fuck I did. We'd better find the train station and get you cleaned up. Fuck eating. I need a fuckin' drink."

CHAPTER FOUR

Distorted history boasts of bellicose glory . . . and seduces the souls of boys to seek mystical bliss in bloodshed and in battles.~Alfred Adler

Four years before his Selective Service pre-induction physical, Danny was dozing in the front row of chemistry class in his senior year of high school. Old Man Preller, who taught the class, made no attempt to rouse him from his slumber. He had given up on Danny early in the year. He knew Danny would pass his class, no matter how much of it he spent sleeping. Preller knew Danny would not need chemistry where he was going: some small junky college where he would get a small junky degree in an easy subject area, and then go on to teach this easy subject in some small junky high school. With luck, Danny's students would pay Danny back for his sins by sleeping in *his* classes.

What Old Man Preller did not know was that Danny was not idly sleeping but actively dreaming. Danny was moving his lips and his eyes were rapidly darting to and fro behind his eyelids. Preller, if he had been observing anything other than the legs of the girls seated on the raked tiers of the chemistry lecture theater, could have easily observed that Danny was in a REM state of sleep. But Preller was inattentive. Preller's inattentiveness was physically manifested in his hands. He had only eight and a half fingers; the other one and a half had been lost in some chemistry lab accident in his salad days as an inattentive undergraduate. He seemed proud of this loss, and was fond of holding up his fingers while hypothesizing about fractions in front of the class. "Let's postulate that we have three and a half moles of hydrogen ..."

While Preller was scanning the nylon-clad legs of the nubile nymphets he deliberately assigned to seats at or above his eye level in the raked lecture hall, Danny was scanning an ocean inside his eyeballs for his three favorite cowboys: John Wayne, Gary Cooper and Henry Fonda. They had been momentarily hidden behind a swell. He saw them again, to his relief, bobbing in the warm, bathwater-benevolent ocean, dressed in their full frontier regalia of 10-gallon hats, boots, chaps, duster coats and gun belts, replete with matching sets of Colt Peacemaker single-action revolvers. The three cowboys were bone dry. Since it was a dream, Danny did not question this miracle. They did not have horses with them. Danny did not question why they had no horses. Dreams are like that.

Danny heard the strains of the Beach Boys' hit *Surfin' Safari* playing softly, almost sadly, in time to the roaring and splashing of the waves. The song had a lot more reverb than usual, and seemed to be in an eerie minor key. The cowboys were grim-faced, as cowboys should be. They betrayed no emotion as they bobbed up and down in the heaving sea. Danny felt this solid and silent threesome, these exemplars of the epitome of manliness in Danny's daytime world, were somewhat reassured but certainly not seduced by the narcotic effect of the golden glowing sea and Brian Wilson's heavenly harmonies. Only the call of justice and truth could seduce these three.

To Danny's horror, he saw a huge angry wave approaching his heroes from far out at sea, appearing in dream reality to be both a woman in a sheer nightgown and simultaneously an ordinary killer wave. He realized these stoic plainsmen were in mortal danger. Danny wanted to call out a warning, but he had no voice, as often happens to dream bystanders. The killer wave grew nearer and Danny was afraid for his heroes, but also worried about having lost his voice. Just as the wave was about to crash into and crush this all-star posse, he saw the three cowboys rise up on top of the monster wave itself on carnival-bright surfboards, each an eye-popping candy-colored masterwork. The trio looked neither left nor right, nor down at the killer wave/woman in a sheer gown they were riding, but fixed their steeliest stares on the beach. They hooked their thumbs on their gun belts - a signal they were ready to draw their fancy Colt .45 Peacemakers. They planted their beat-up boots firmly on their boards and bent their knees for the ride to the beach, atop the mountain of woman/water that had so recently threatened them. Their jaws were clenched and their chins set defiantly.

Without warning, heavy weapons fire erupted from the beach and geysers from shells sprouted all around these brave men. Yet still they rode defiantly toward the beach, perched on their surfboards, riding a huge black wave. They never wavered or flinched. The Beach Boys fell silent, their sweet haunting minor-key harmonies replaced by the thunderous rolling din of war. Danny saw indistinct figures, small and black like ants in the distance, running on the beach. Danny heard a loud crackling voice and the ants disappeared, the cowboys disappeared, and the din was done.

The announcement announcer repeated all his announcements twice, anticipating correctly that the first announcement would merely be sufficient to wake the students, and a second one would be required to sink home the message. In Danny's case today, that assumption proved correct. Danny was sleeping the first time the message came over the wood-clad loudspeaker with the gold cloth grill mounted over the official classroom clock. "Would any interested junior or senior student wishing to meet a representative from Huldrych Zwingli College please report to the guidance office now?" Danny immediately recognized three important things in this announcement: the name Huldrych Zwingli; a non-punishable way to get out of class; and that he, Danny, was an "interesting" senior student - except that he got the last part wrong. The announcer had said "interested," not "interesting." This mistaken hearing on Danny's part would not prove fatal, but Danny's meeting with the Huldrych Zwingli College representative would, however, prove to be fateful.

Danny recognized Huldrych Zwingli as the name of the "Third Man of the (Protestant) Reformation," along with Martin Luther and John Calvin. Danny's mother, knowing Danny to be guilty of repeated Mortal Sins, forced him to attend church services, Sunday School, Daily Vacation Bible School and confirmation classes. Try as Danny might, he couldn't get Pastor W.W. Leifhebber or his minions to let him sleep during any of these events. As a consequence, Danny was steeped in what he considered to be sappy American bullshit middle-class religious doctrine, history and tradition. Zwingli was part of that history.

Pastor Leifhebber had chosen the Zwinglian doctrine of the Eucharist as his PhD thesis. The good pastor had failed to complete his PhD, but still harped endlessly to the bored, confused and horny 14-year-olds in his confirmation class about this arcane topic. His lectures on the Zwinglian doctrine of the Eucharist fell on deaf ears except for Danny's. Danny never wanted to know anything about Zwinglian anything, but his ears and mind grabbed, stored and filed everything, whether he wanted to grab, store and file or not. His memory was phenomenal, although there was much Danny wanted to forget. Because of his accursed memory, Danny never studied for a test, not even once to try it out, and never took notes in any of his classes. He did not abuse his textbooks with those horrid florescent highlighters. He didn't have to do any of that. He was a genius with a gift for listening.

Danny did not know he was smart. He was aware that there were a few really, really stupid kids in some of his classes (they drooled on their books), but he just assumed the rest of his mates had the same mind he had, but chose to study and take notes and highlight things because they were filthy conformists. He loathed conformists. He had no idea his mates needed to do all that bullshit studying crap to grasp the school lessons that Danny considered mostly nonsense. Danny's unawareness of his own brilliance is a good example of how stupid some smart people can be.

With thoughts of Zwingli dancing in his head, Danny danced out of his chemistry class and into the guidance office to see the college recruiter. Danny saw the recruiter and fell in a kind of love. Danny was no homosexual, but he recognized and was awed by beauty when he saw it. The recruiter was the prettiest man Danny had ever seen, apart from Danny's father who looked like Clark Gable, only better. The man Danny would forever think of as the Pretty Man was dressed like a male model. His smile put the sun to shame with its warmth. His handshake was firm and dry. Danny was nearly speechless. Danny was almost never nearly speechless, but he was then.

The men in Danny's town never looked half this good even at weddings and funerals. The Pretty Man had the look and tone of the fine man with the cologne smell who sold Danny's parents a carved leather-bound set of *Wonder Book of Knowledge* encyclopedias, that he said would "help your child get a head start on the road to academic success, and which can be purchased for only $1 per week and $1 down." As far as Danny knew, his working-class parents were still paying for this set of books, nine years after Danny had read and reread them cover to cover and moved on to more challenging material.

"I hope I didn't park my car in anybody's spot," the Pretty Man said, pointing out the guidance office window to the front lot of the school.

Danny looked out the window.

"It's the new British Racing Green Ford Galaxie Convertible. It's got four on the floor and a police interceptor engine." As if Danny could see under the hood to differentiate his Galaxie from all the other British Racing Green Ford Galaxie Convertibles out in the lot.

"You mean the one parked in the principal's spot?" Danny exclaimed with glee.

They turned to each other, locked eyes and laughed. The Pretty Man was a shit disturber. No one ever dared park in that spot. With that, the deal was struck even before the courtship began. Danny was going wherever this man led. The Pretty Man was not an empty suit; he was a rebel in a suit. And Danny, being a great rebel himself, occasionally liked to relinquish this role and follow an even greater rebel - one worthy of his respect.

The courtship itself involved looking at loose-leaf books filled with glossy color 8x10 photos of a tree-covered campus with winding footpaths and ivy-covered buildings. It was always summer in Northeast Iowa, and the sun always shone on the college.

"You play sports?"

"No."

"What's your grade point average?"

"I dunno. Maybe an A-, maybe an A."

"What do you do for fun?"

Danny was not tempted to tell the Pretty Man what he really did for fun, which included frequent masturbation at the top of the list, but he knew what the Pretty Man expected him to say. "Writing, reading, acting, public speaking, hunting, fishing, helping others ..."

At the words "helping others," the Pretty Man locked eyes with Danny and kept them locked. The Pretty Man had a mandate from the liberal Christian college he represented to find kids who wanted to help others, especially if they had a straight-A average.

No other students showed up to see the Pretty Man recruiter, as no one else knew Zwingli from a hole in the ground. Most of the people in Danny's hometown were Catholic, and the rest came from Protestant churches whose pastors did not have shattered academic aspirations that led them to harp on Zwingli's dim place in church history in their confirmation classes. After a fairly long time locking his eyes with Danny's, the Pretty Man broke contact and left the outer office to confer with Miss Evers, head of the Guidance Department, who was one of the two teachers Danny lusted after. Evers had very large, pert breasts on a small frame, and wore tight sweaters to let everyone see her bounty. Danny stared at the rise and fall of Evers' breasts as she talked to the Pretty Man about Danny in her glass-walled office. Danny hated guidance sessions with her. It hurt his eyes and his neck to have to look at her face for the agonizing 30 minutes he spent in her office serving out his thrice-yearly mandatory guidance appointment obligations.

After his chat with the full-breasted Evers, and having somehow escaped falling victim to her charms, the Pretty Man felt moved to start closing the sale with Danny. "How'd you like to take a ride with me up to Zwingli next Thursday and stay for Homecoming weekend, all expenses paid? You can bunk down in the freshman dorm with one of our student guides."

"I can miss school on Thursday, Friday and Monday?" Danny could not disguise his enthusiasm.

"Of course."

With that, the sale was closed, and they shook on it. Mr. Daniel No-Middle-Initial Harper did thus plight his troth with Zwingli College.

CHAPTER FIVE

At least we're getting the kind of experience we need for the next war.~Allen Dulles

Danny packed his coolest clothes, the ones he bought for himself--the ones his mother hated, and left for college in the British Racing Green Ford Galaxie Convertible with four on the floor and the police interceptor engine. Danny was offended to see two other people in the car with the Pretty Man. He had assumed the car ride would be like a date with the Pretty Man - just the two of them. Also in the car was a great tall boy hogging the front seat, presumably needing the legroom. Harvey was a high-school track star from a nearby town who would become a college track star at Zwingli and, finally, a track star with the U.S. Coast Guard Track Team after graduating from Zwingli with a 3.98 average. Harvey thus contributed four years to the Vietnam War effort by running track, the way in which he was most able to serve. After the war, Harvey would build a successful career selling insurance in his hometown.

There was also a mousy girl with funny teeth in the back seat with Danny: Sheryl, who smelled of mildew, would drop out of Zwingli in her first semester because of panic attacks, die of cancer in her late 20s in Kentucky, and be survived by two children and a strong, silent carpenter husband. She picked her nose energetically, without shame or subterfuge, for the bulk of the ride. Danny could not stand to look at her, so he tried to look out his little side window. It was raining and the heater was on. The side windows were fogged over. Convertibles do not excel in the rain. The heater had little effect in the back seat except to fog the rear windows, too. The heater didn't heat the back-seat passengers. Danny settled in for what would be seven hours of hell. Sheryl settled in for seven hours of nasal mining. The track star kept up an inane seven-hour running conversation with the Pretty Man about sports, starting with baseball and proceeding to basketball, then football, and into sports Danny had never even heard of like lacrosse, jai alai and curling. Danny interjected at one point early on, while they were still on the topic of baseball, by commenting that his mother was a Cubs fan. The front-seaters pretended not to hear, so Danny shut up for the rest of the trip.

There were no four-lane highways to Dekorum, Iowa, just arrow-straight two-laners surrounded on either side by endless flat fields of drenched corn stalks and soggy soybeans, broken by small farm service towns every 20 miles or so. The countryside began to roll by as the fancy Ford with the police interceptor engine approached, crossed, and finally followed the Mississippi River. The roads here were twisty. Danny could see little snatches of shiny river through the fog-frosted window. Once or twice, Sheryl craned her neck to see the river on Danny's side of the car. Danny winced, lest one of her boogers drop on the spray-starched white shirt his mother had pressed the night before, and had so forcefully told him to wear to "make a good impression."

Danny had to amuse himself with his own thoughts, since he did not follow sports. Sheryl's presence prevented him from fully engaging in the sexual fantasies that were his mind's default setting, so he had to skip to something a little more high-toned. He thought about college. He imagined the classrooms in the ivy-covered buildings at Zwingli.

The antechambers in the temple of learning would not smell like old lunches gone bad and sweat socks like his high-school classrooms did; no, they would smell like "learning," which Danny imagined to be a combination of old books, a hint of pipe tobacco and the elusive scent of the bung plugging an ancient barrel of Scotch whiskey. The teachers would not have old acne scars and bobbing Adam's apples like the loser teachers who taught high school, for these college chaps would not be mere teachers, but professors - older, wiser, bearded and be-tweeded, stopping every so often in the lesson to adjust their pince-nez for subtle emphasis at some critical juncture in the web of logic they were in the midst of spinning. Danny was intoxicated by the idea of learning, while maintaining a healthy hatred for school. Lost in the ivy-covered buildings and the winding paths between them in the college of his mind, Danny fell asleep.

The fantastic Ford with its foursome and four speeds came at last to the little town of Dekorum, Iowa. The town sign said "Home of Zwingli College - One of the Top 100 Small Colleges in America." Just as the car passed that sign, the rain ended and the sun broke through the scudding black clouds that had dogged the travelers for the entirety of their seven-hour trip. The sunrays through the broken clouds pointed like the fingers of fate to the main clock tower of Zwingli College. Seen through the fog-bound plastic convertible window of the Pretty Man's car, past the finger-infested nose of the girl beside him, those magical rays looked to Danny like divine road signs to his future.

The Pretty Man deposited the two boys at the freshman dorm. It would be their home-away-from-home for the next three days. Danny walked an intimidating gauntlet of real men (fresh-men!) to the room of his "Student Body Buddy," Tom Tomlinson. After a few polite words of greeting, and a brief but careful appraisal of the cut of Tom's jib, Danny asked his first hesitant question of a Real Zwingli Student: "Where can I get some beer?"

Danny would remember little of those three days.

He returned home less a conquering hero and more the sole survivor of a massacre. He had a red Zwingli College nightshirt in his bag that he had purchased on his first day on campus from the college bookstore. It had a fierce little belligerent-looking Protestant warrior figure embroidered on the breast. Much of the remainder of the shirt was decorated with puke. He hid that shirt under his bed at home, unwashed for weeks, ostensibly so his mother would not find it and punish him in some way. But the mostly unconscious reason for his hoarding of this smelly piece of polycotton was because it symbolized, for Danny, his first foray into the world of wisdom and a life of freedom. It was also his first foray into the wondrous world of heavy drinking on consecutive days. This kind of drinking easily joined the panoply of his favorite things in life, which included guns, writing and sex. But even daily drinking would never surpass sex as his primary obsession.

His sexual obsession, an obsession perhaps more accurately described as an obsession with sexual *failure* than with sex itself, began innocently enough in high school the day Danny answered a question on an English test Miss Palmer gave about Hawthorne's negative view of the Transcendentalist Movement. The answer Danny wrote to the test question was a poem. The poem was not about Hawthorne or the Transcendentalist Movement. Danny had not read the assigned material by Hawthorne. He was incapable of reading Hawthorne. Danny believed Hawthorne to be guilty of abusing their common native tongue. Hawthorne's language confused and angered Danny. A lot of things confused and angered Danny, so there was nothing personal in his hatred for Hawthorne.

After class, as Danny lingered in the room mooning about his failing grade on the test, Miss Palmer called Danny to her desk. "Daniel, you know I was forced to fail you on this test. Do you care?"

"Some." Danny was reluctant to speak to her or even meet her eyes up close. Miss Palmer was the other teacher after whom Danny lusted.

"That's not exactly the answer I want to that question." After a moment searching Danny's blank face, she went on, "But that's not why I asked you to stay after class. I wanted to tell you that I think your poetry is beautiful. Rough in spots, but passionate and beautiful ... You know, I write poetry too. I have for years, but I don't have your raw talent and certainly not your fire. I think my talent is for teaching. I think ... This is just my first year, but ... Has anyone ever told you that you have a gift - a very precious gift - and that it's your obligation to use that gift?"

"No."

"Well, Daniel, I'm telling you now. Look, I'll make you a deal. If you write me one poem or short story every week, and at least promise to *read* the books I assign you, I'll give you an 'A' in this course no matter what else you do. I could get in trouble for this with the principal, so this is our little secret. Okay? Can you keep a secret?"

Danny shrugged.

Miss Palmer ignored the shrug and went on, "And for your part of the deal, in addition to what we agreed, I want you to go back and read the Hawthorne piece I assigned last week. Do we have a deal?"

"Okay."

"Okay, what, Daniel?"

"Okay, Miss Palmer."

"No, I don't mean that you need to call me Miss Palmer. I mean, do we have a deal and can you keep a secret? In private like this, you can call me what my friends call me, Amy. That can be our secret, too."

"Yes." Danny's heart was starting to beat so fast he could barely speak. "Amy," he said gingerly, trying out the name, "I can keep a secret and I'll read Hawthorne, too. I'll do that for you." He emphasized the word "you." What Danny really wanted to say was, "I'll do anything for you."

Miss Palmer had given Danny permission to use her given name. No high-school students in this school, or for that matter, any school in this decade, ever dared call teachers by their given names, even in private. If Amy (the thought of even thinking of her as "Amy" gave Danny shivers) thought his writing was passionate and beautiful, then he would write all day, every day to impress her. Amy was a dream. Amy was his dream alone, for he alone in the whole school had the key to her private persona - the Amy persona. She was not some boy's movie-cowboy dream, she was a man's dream. And Danny felt his manhood rise at the once-forbidden thought of their future together. Danny had never seen a more sexually attractive creature.

Amy Palmer had a primitive, almost masculine face, with a big head and strong jawline, sharply defined. She had almond-shaped eyes that were widely spaced. Her eyes were an unearthly shade of lavender. Her eyes were set deep in their sockets. Lips fat as figs ... Her voice was throaty and deep - a mature woman's cigarette and whiskey voice, more suited to a black woman singin' some hurtin' blues than a white woman teaching English. Amy was big-boned and thick, but nowhere was she fat. Her body shape projected a power that her gentle demeanor denied. Danny had spent a lot of time in class undressing her in his mind and knew every line and curve of her body, seen from every angle. He worshipped her every line and curve singularly, and the totality of her form as well.

He knew her smells - the sultry seductiveness of her sophisticated choice of perfume, the mixed messages of her breath (cigarettes, coffee and mint). Danny tried to catch the scent of her damp musky womanhood as she walked by his seat on her way down the aisle to check the students' workbooks. He longed to know what secrets his nose might uncover inside that tight skirt as she sat on her desk droning on about gerunds and subjunctive clauses to an uncaring class as her skirt rose up a little on her thighs, almost to the point of reveling a garter, but not quite.

As of the day Miss Palmer became Amy, Danny wrote a poem a day and a short story every weekend. He gave these verbal offerings to Amy with the tenderness a father might have in passing an infant child back to its mother. The poems were ballads of longing and love, and the short stories were tragic tales of heroes too heroic for their own good and too tongue-tied to express their love for the heroine, and therefore moved to redouble their efforts in the "noble deed" department. Cowboys in shining armor …

Danny read these poems and stories aloud to his beloved Amy after class and after school. Every so often, Amy would accidentally brush against Danny or her breath would whisper against his ear or cheek. Accidentally … When this happened, Danny would instantly become engorged and have to squirm to hide his tumescence.

On an unusually warm Saturday in early spring, Danny met Amy at Fran and Joe's Dairy Bar. They had met there before on the odd Saturday to discuss the short stories that Danny wrote on weekends. Danny sipped tea, which he disliked, but preferred to coffee, which he hated. It seemed more adult to drink tea than a milkshake or soda, and Danny had felt compelled to act in a more adult fashion since he began his relationship with Amy. She was watching her weight, drank black coffee and smoked constantly.

Amy cut this particular "Fran and Joe" meeting short. "Daniel, would you like to go on a picnic? It's simply glorious outside."

"Sure."

"I have a blanket in the car, and we can get a sandwich or whatever you want to take with us. I have some of my favorite poems of yours I've saved in a binder, and I'd like you to read them to me outside, under the sky, so they can soar to the heavens."

"Sure."

Later, just outside of town, on the blanket in a deserted corner of a deserted park under a clear blue sky, Danny read some of his poems aloud. As he read one of his most soulful pieces entitled *The Silence That Sings Her Name*, Amy grasped one of Danny's arms and then the other. Danny fell silent at her touch and became still. He was held captive, more by her lavender eyes than her hands. She pulled Danny's face slowly to hers until their breath mingled in the few inches of air between them.

Danny entered a state he had never been in before, timeless and transcendent. Amy invaded his body through every orifice and pore. He no longer belonged to himself. He belonged to the universe, and the universe was Amy Palmer.

Danny's memory could never re-enact the first sight of her naked, straddling him, sweating and calling his name. It could not replay the feeling of ultimate completeness he felt when he first thrust inside her. The experience was beyond and above his memory's capacity to capture and replay.

Danny would, however, remember her words from later that day. *"I first fell in love with your writing, and then I realized it was really all of you I loved."* He would remember her uttering these exact words while he was naked on his back and staring at the sky. The early spring sun had slipped behind a cloud and a little gust of wind blew across his belly. The wind still had some winter chill in it.

He would remember being too afraid to look again at her nakedness after they had been together, as she lay next to him on the red wool blanket that smelled of rubber and gasoline from being in the trunk of her car. He was afraid if he looked at her, she would disappear.

What happened on that blanket on that day could not be described by any definition of "sex" that was present in Danny's limited vocabulary of sexual experience. What had happened was not high-school sex at a drive-in movie, where getting a little outside-the-blouse feel made for a successful night. This was not the sex that guys he knew got after going steady with a girl for six months, which merely consisted of getting jerked off once a weekend if they were lucky. It wasn't like the sex Danny had jerking off in tandem with his cousin, Little Moose, in Moose's sister Sally's room while going through her underwear drawer. This was the real sex thing. Danny didn't have to beg for it, and it didn't involve promising to marry Amy first, although Danny was sure he and Amy would get married when he got out of college. Danny knew that, and knew that she knew that, and therefore they didn't have to discuss such obvious details.

Teacher and student mated like rabbits gone rabid, in the evenings when Danny could slip out of the house on his bike for a "ride" and on the weekends, when Danny's parents left him alone while they retreated to their fishing cabin on Roundhouse Lake, several hours away.

Danny was obsessed. Nothing else mattered but Amy. Teenage testosterone, combined with a natural penchant for dreaming in the daytime as well as the night, combined to produce a 17-year-old who was, to all intents and purposes, certifiably insane with love. Danny, comparing himself to Shakespeare's Romeo, thought Romeo was callow and shallow in his love for Juliet, compared to his own more complete and mature love for Amy.

As Danny's last year of high school came crashing to an end with his grades in the toilet, his testosterone temple also came down with a crash so mighty it stunned him into the same silent place he had visited once before, when he and Amy first kissed on the red blanket that smelled like rubber and gas as they lay on the grass on that glorious spring day. Amy delivered the world-ending words to Danny's ear in a hesitant whisper, in an intimate moment, as the couple lay together under the periwinkle sheets in her old pine bed. "Daniel, I'm going to have your baby."

As the summer wore on, Amy no longer seemed so beautiful to Danny. She had newly minted hormonal acne and an ever-thickening midsection. Danny sensed she no longer saw him glowing with otherworldly intelligence through her increasingly sad eyes. She turned inward, perhaps shifting her attention to the new life growing inside her. Danny knew, without being told, that she saw him now for what he really was - just a silly and bewildered 17-year-old boy who wrote sophomoric verse and self-indulgent prose.

On the 29th of July in the summer before Danny entered college, Amy told him that she was going to Chicago for a few days to see her old roommate and catch some theater. On the last day of July, Danny tried to call her, only to discover that her phone had been disconnected. He did not see her little red Mustang fastback behind the house she rented. He rode his bike up to the windows of her apartment. They no longer had curtains. He looked inside the naked windows and saw the interior of her apartment stripped to the bare walls. Danny couldn't ask anyone where she had gone; she and Danny were both guilty of crimes and misdemeanors a small town could never forgive or forget.

He had promised her 10 months before that he could keep a secret. That was the start of it: one little secret. Danny now had to bear many secrets, none of which was little. That was the end of it. The light went out in Danny's eyes.

A week and a half later, Danny got a letter postmarked from the British West Indies. It had no return address. Inside was a note that read:

My Dearest Daniel,

We should never have started what we started, but what's past is past. I'm not sorry so much for myself as for you. You deserved better, and someday, you'll understand why you deserved better.

I was, first of all, in love with your writing and I love it still. If anything remains of us, let it be the writing. Never stop writing. Remember me once in a while, when you're famous.

Affectionately,

Amy

Danny read the letter and felt nothing. He had felt nothing for days. It was an odd feeling, feeling nothing, but he knew it felt better than what he could have been feeling, if he could still feel. That seemed logical. Logic told him that. Danny began behaving in a logical fashion. He knew it was logical to smile once in a while, so as not to alarm those around him. He ate, but did not taste the food. He went to bed at a decent hour and closed his eyes, but did not sleep for fear of dreaming the dream he most dreaded. He brushed his teeth and listened to his usual radio station. Aside from his inability to make light conversation - which did not alarm his parents, as he had long practiced the art of being monosyllabic - Danny did not appear depressed.

The morning after the letter arrived, Danny slipped out of the house well before dawn, his RCA quarter-inch reel-to-reel tape recorder under his arm, his father's Colt M1911 in .38 Super Caliber tucked in the front of his pants, and a notebook full of poetry in his back pocket. Both the tape recorder and the pistol were loaded. He walked five blocks to the city's Centennial Park and through the park to a picnic gazebo in the remotest part. There was an electrical outlet in the gazebo, and it was live. He plugged the recorder into the outlet, turned it on and tested it. He took the Colt out of his pants and dropped the clip into his hand. He cycled the action and no shell ejected. He replaced the clip and cycled the action again, putting a round into the chamber and under the hammer. He removed the safety. He put the hammer in the half-cock safe position and laid it on the picnic table next to the tape recorder. He laid the notebook of his poetry next to the Colt.

He turned on the recorder. The birds were beginning to sing, and the sky was just showing light in the east. He opened the small black notebook of poetry with the intention of reading it aloud, but no words came. He stared at the open book and the moving tape reels and the big black Colt automatic. He waited.

When the first rays of the sun entered the gazebo and fell across the notebook, Danny picked up the Colt and pulled back the hammer to full cock. He stood back a few feet from the notebook and emptied the whole nine-shot clip into it. He turned off the recorder, unplugged it and tucked the machine under his arm, stuffed the Colt into the front of his pants, and felt the hot barrel burn the tender skin on his belly. He picked up the biggest chunk of notebook that remained after the execution and deposited it in the nearest trash barrel. He walked home. Summer ended with a bang. Summer ended with a whimper.

CHAPTER SIX

Nothing except a battle lost can be half as melancholy as a battle won. ~Duke of Wellington

In early September of Danny's saddest and best year on the planet, he traveled to the northeastern corner of Iowa to begin his wanderings in the wilderness of academe. The trip was full of agony. Danny's parents occupied the front seat of the 1956 Nash Rambler Custom station wagon. They were more excited than Danny at the thought that he would be the first of his generation to be exposed to a tertiary education. Neither his parents nor any of his 18 aunts and uncles had done more than graduate high school. Mom Harper chirped mile after mile about the wonders Danny might encounter at college, while all the time warning about the type of women he might encounter there. She seemed to need a response from Danny—especially about the women. None came from Danny. Danny's ears were still ringing with the sound of the big Colt pumping round after round into his poetry book, and his nose was filled with the smell of fire from the pyre upon which he had placed the remainder of his poetry, all of his short stories and essays, along with numerous unsent letters to the mother of his child. Danny could not speak without screaming, so he grunted or remained silent.

Danny had never been away from home for more than a day or three, except for the summer camp he had attended several years before. The camp scholarship was a prize that Danny won from the local American Legion Post for writing, and then dramatically reading, the most patriotic Armistice Day essay in all of Lamoille County that whole year. The Legion also gave him a new silver dollar in a plastic case. The summer camp scholarship prize allowed him to attend a paramilitary "leadership training" project run by the Legion every summer, on the grounds of the State Police Training Academy. A boozy retired infantry brigadier ran the camp and took pride in the authenticity of the military brutality he inflicted upon the lucky campers.

Danny didn't take too well to "leadership training" but made a few bucks selling the *Playboy* magazines and vodka he had the foresight to smuggle in with his luggage. He tripled his investment by selling these items at inflated prices, while depriving himself of ethanol oblivion and sexual stimulation. Delayed gratification, he found out, was one of the basic tenants of good leadership and the foundation of a capitalist economy; so the camp experience, while brutal, was not totally wasted.

Danny's imagination stalled when he tried to imagine what lay in store at Zwingli. As the first member of his family, and one of the few from the spectrum of society in his working-class town to go to college, Danny had no access to oral mythology about college days - the kind usually told around campfires in one's youth. The movies didn't help much either, except to imply that college girls were generally busty and bubbly, and college professors old and crusty. Beyond that lay uncertainty … It was the overwhelming uncertainty brought on by his experience with Amy that had driven Danny into what psychologists of a later age would call a "reactive depression," what Danny's parents called "that mood again," and what Danny thought of as a preview of hell.

There was no real alternative for Danny aside from college, or even this particular college, because the military draft could pluck up any young man, at any time, who was not shielded by the student deferment the Selective Service System granted men who enrolled in college and continued making "uninterrupted progress toward an undergraduate degree at an accredited institution of higher learning," which meant "carrying a full academic load" and not failing very many courses or "losing a semester." While Elvis Presley seemed to be having a passing fair time in the Army in *G.I. Blues* - the 1960 semi-autobiographical musical film which supposedly recounted Elvis' service in the Army in Germany - Danny suspected that Elvis would not be doing a sequel about fighting in the festering jungles of Asia. Danny had no interest in serving there, either. Zwingli College in Dekorum, Iowa may have seemed frightening, but Danny knew there were worse places. He chose Iowa.

This college, in particular, seemed particularly interested in Danny. It may have had a hard time filling its quota of over-bright disaffected underachievers that year and so had to reach out all the way to Central Illinois to find one. It gave Danny a scholarship, which luckily was not based on his last semester's grades, which had fallen with Danny into the black pit of Amy-lessness. It gave him a "grant-in-aid." It gave him a promise of a job on campus. It told him a lot of supportive crap that he did not believe, but his parents did. He failed to respond to this supportiveness or flattery, but then, he was depressed. He failed to respond to much of anything.

Faced with the reality of being drafted if he were not making "uninterrupted progress toward an undergraduate degree," Danny chose the lesser evil. The jungles of Vietnam seemed harsh punishment for a little goofing off. He knew that if he took even one semester off or failed too many courses, the military draft could blow him all the way to the killing fields. Before he met Amy, the thought of being able to use guns to legally kill other people had seemed like a fun idea. He had seen all of John Wayne's war movies, and he, like "The Duke," believed in defending America. Danny loved guns, and he loved America.

The Vietnam War didn't bother Danny. It was simple: America was never wrong. Danny truly wanted to fight for freedom someday. He had been raised and trained to be a red-blooded bellicose American boy. Danny subscribed with his own paper-route money to William F. Buckley's snobby right-wing *National Review* magazine, and was on the John Birch Society mailing list and proud of it. Moreover, his hero, John Wayne, publicly supported the war, and Gary Cooper and Henry Fonda couldn't possibly have been against it.

Danny thought the war in Vietnam was okay in theory. He just didn't want to be bothered going there anytime soon, especially not in the infantry as a private. Danny wanted to go to Vietnam, but only on his own terms, in his own time, preferably as an officer, preferably in the navy, preferably on the bridge of a giant battleship sending 16-in.-high explosive greetings to crappy commie sampans or junks somewhere waaay over the horizon. All real Midwesterners have a knack for salt sea sailing, probably from seeing all those miles of flat land covered in cereal crops waving in the wind.

Danny was no chicken peacenik. Amy had talked to him once about Gandhi and Martin Luther King, but Danny was not greatly moved by what he considered sissy liberal crap. But the mere experience of loving Amy had touched something inside Danny that hinted that there were probably more important things than guns and killing. Danny had tasted love, and would never be the same, even if love tasted sour this fall.

As a result of learning to love, killing and guns fell down a quarter-notch on Danny's list of favorite things. Lately, booze had come up a notch or two on the list, as a way to cope with the loss of love. Drugs would trump everything on the list in due course, except love.

Upon arriving at Zwingli, Danny's parents helped him unload the car's contents into room 427 of the Men's Freshman Dorm. With that done, they made Danny suffer the humiliation of taking a walk with them around the winding, tree-shaded paths of the campus. Danny believed that if they saw him walking with his parents, his peers would mark him for all time as "that kid with the parents." Real college men did not have parents - they were alienated existentialists who wandered alone in an ivory tower, pondering the hopelessness of it all. Danny convinced his parents to leave as soon as the walk was over. Danny shook his father's hand and gave his mother a stiff hug, trying to avoid the feel of her breasts. Danny saw a look in his father's eyes that conveyed wistful envy mixed with some other sadness. Danny had learned to read his father's eyes out of necessity, since his father was an intelligent man of deep emotion but few words. Mr. Harper read real literature, but only in private. That kind of guy … Danny loved him like a god.

Danny watched the Nash Rambler Custom station wagon meander down the pretty campus lane. He was alone, and the college monster was about to eat him.

He hadn't shed a tear after Amy deserted him with his child in her belly. He didn't moistly mourn during the brutal execution of his poetry notebook and the burning of the other writing. But he felt the weight of it all now, on the sunny sidewalk in front of the Men's Freshman Dorm. He stood there without moving and made no sound. He hung his head as though praying. His arms hung limply at his sides. The tears came and threatened never to stop. The world spun away, leaving Danny alone in a cold weightless vacuum of emotion.

The tears, of course, did eventually stop. Danny looked around at the hubbub of arriving students, departing parents and sibling goodbyes, and realized he looked a hell of a mess. He was afraid his new peers might mark him as "that kid who was crying in front of the dorm." Danny ran away from the dorm and ended up in a natural bowl in the earth near the lower level of the science hall across the street. The building had an outdoor water tap. Danny walked to the tap, turned it on, and splashed cold water on his swollen eyes. He caught his breath. He walked across the street toward his dorm, but detoured well to one side in order to circle around to the back stairs, thus avoiding the arriving throng. He ran up the back stairs and retrieved the mirrored sunglasses stowed in his shaving kit.

Danny needed a cigarette. His parents smoked, but did not let Danny smoke. They never caught him smoking, since they could not discriminate his smoke smell from their own. Danny had been smoking regularly in secret for several years and was addicted. The seven-hour car ride had thrown him into nicotine withdrawal, which added to his other several general and specific anxieties. Danny realized to his dismay that he hadn't hidden any cigarettes in his luggage, and what was worse, he had no idea where to buy them. He had no idea how to get from the campus to downtown, where there would be stores selling cartons of cigarettes. He'd not been paying attention on either of his two trips through town, either with the Pretty Man or with his parents. Danny figured that if he were to be eaten by the college monster, he should at least go down like a man: with a cigarette between his lips.

As Danny walked aimlessly around the campus, secure now behind his mirrored shades, he saw an older guy walking toward him and summoned up the courage to ask: "Excuse me - do you know where I can buy a carton of smokes?"

The older guy, who Danny thought must be at least a junior based on his cocky walk and confident smile, replied by stopping and tapping an unfiltered Lucky Strike from his pack. "Here."

"Thanks, but I smoke Parliaments."

"I'm low on fags, too. You wanna walk downtown and get some?"

Danny was amazed that this world-weary young man would stoop to accompany him to a downtown he didn't wish to admit he could not have found himself.

"What year are you?" Danny did not say "sir," but his voice carried the tone of respect he reserved for "sirs."

"First year," the man said from behind his B&L Ray-Ban Aviator glasses.

The man had fooled him completely, and maybe the B&Ls had helped by hiding his eyes, but he had such an air of truly masculine confidence and such an artfully composed disheveled elegance about his person that Danny would have believed he was 35. He was cowboy cute, with a strong defiant jaw, thin chiseled face and a lean lanky look. He was even wearing cowboy boots and jeans, as though he had dressed expressly to impress Danny. The faded denim shirt and the red bandanna around his neck were a style of dress Danny was thoroughly unfamiliar with seeing on his peers. Danny was wearing polished wingtips and a white shirt under a nice sweater.

Danny would later learn the "man" he was walking with was only 17 – they were both the same age, having come early to college because of late fall birthdays. Danny, with his schooling in leadership at the Legion boot camp, could recognize all the qualities of a leader in this magnetic man, who called himself Dick. Danny was in need of leadership.

Danny had a million questions. "So, how come you know your way downtown, if you're only a freshman?" Dick offered him an unfiltered cigarette, which he refused, but Danny's natural reluctance to admit further weakness was overcome by the feeling of trust that offering had imparted. Danny thought Dick probably wanted Danny to feel like, roughly, his equal.

"Both my parents did their undergrads here. All my grandparents did their undergraduate work here, too, and live here now or are dead here. Mostly, my family did their graduate degrees at Harvard or Yale. I'm in this town a lot, unfortunately." But Danny knew Dick was not from here. He had a Boston or New York accent, or one of those funny ones from the East Coast. "My paternal grandfather and great-grandfather were both presidents of this place, and my maternal grandfather was a dean. I hate it here."

Danny continued to pepper Dick with questions. He found out that Dick had left his hometown honey to come here. "She was okay, but kinda immature." Danny could see that it was only right to leave a girl behind who was kinda immature. Danny did not mention that the girl he left behind had, in fact, left him and was kinda too mature at the ripe old age of 23. Danny did not mention she was kinda pregnant, either.

Danny just said, "Yeah, I left one behind, too." Just saying that little bit, even though it was mostly a lie, made him feel better. He trusted Dick.

If Dick had cried at being dumped off at this small college in the middle of God's Iowa, it didn't show on his face. Of course, he was wearing dark glasses. Dick had little expression at all beyond a tiny, secret smile. Dick exuded the laconic, sexy style of a tightly wrapped young rodeo cowboy or a tongue-tied, shuffling, head-down boyish Bob Dylan, although Danny did not like Bob Dylan because Bob was a commie, despite being gloriously rich and famous.

Danny immediately felt he could read Dick's silences the way he was able to read his father's silences. He knew Dick's silences, much like his father's, were filled with grand ideas. A nod of Dick's head could mean volumes or a Zen-like nothing. Danny knew Dick needed him to interpret those golden silences to the rest of world. Danny fell in love right then and there. He had a purpose in life. Danny would be the Boswell to this beautiful Buddha boy.

After a few blocks of walking in silence, Danny felt Dick really open up to him. Dick said, "I can get us some beer later. My cousin Trixie is a senior and she likes me."

Danny felt he wanted to open up to Dick as well, but he couldn't just yet. Dick would understand, because Dick was wise, but also, he knew Dick wouldn't care, because Dick was above it all. That was obvious.

What Danny really needed to open up was a case of beer and a pack of Parliament kings. And so it would come to pass, that afternoon, that Dick and Danny would find the smokes and beverages they were looking for and, in so doing, forge a bond that would keep them together for several years.

CHAPTER SEVEN

Wisdom is better than weapons of war.~Ecclesiastes 9:18

As might be expected at a small Christian college, classes in religion were obligatory, at least for the first two years. The religion Zwingli served up to the simple Midwestern small-town kids who entered as freshmen was a very strange dish indeed! It was nothing at all like the "Sunday School religion" with which Danny and most of his fellow students were already familiar.

The Religion Department at Zwingli had undergone a bloodless coup two years before Danny's arrival. It was led by a Harvard Divinity magna cum laude grad by the name of Oliver Wendell Woodman. The old head had quit in reaction to this man's hiring by the college board, against his recommendation. Sensing a power vacuum, Oliver Wendell Woodman had inveigled to have himself named the acting head of a radically changed department. Other Religion Department veterans and even a few newer professors in the department had quit, following the lead of the old head. The few junior department members who remained were forced to change their theological tune or face career stagnation without tenure.

The new official Zwingli College brand of theology was an offshoot of Christian atheism, salted with a sprinkling of associated doctrines that attempted to reconcile Christianity, science and psychotherapy. Add in some Gospel of Social Change, and Zwingli had a theological stew none of the benighted freshmen had ever tasted. Of the three CORE program subjects freshmen were required to take in the first two years, CORE religion was the most talked about and the most controversial.

Religion was the hot topic of hundreds of late-night bull sessions in first-year dorms. Television viewing and Internet surfing had not yet replaced the college dorm bull session. There was no Internet, and the only TV was a small black-and-white set bolted in place, high on the wall of the dorm's lobby lounge. That TV only received two channels on its rabbit-ear antenna, and one of the channels was mostly fuzz. The bull session was the only form of entertainment aside from studying - which only nutcases considered entertaining - and sex, which was as hard to find as a pig with wings, for all freshmen (and fresh-women) lived in segregated dorms with strictly enforced curfews.

Religion was interesting to Danny because its illogic seemed to come easily to his poetic brain. The professors in religion tutorials were beginning to take note of Danny because he always sat in the front row, always made eye contact and always had his hand up. Danny also attended some religion classes in which he was not enrolled, and did the same thing. The professors in the classes in which Danny was not enrolled were aware that Danny was not enrolled, but they could not find it in their hearts to throw him out. He was the most fully engaged student in the room, and set a benchmark for the dullards sleeping in the back rows.

The whacky new brand of religion that the Reverend Doctor Oliver Wendell Woodman brought down from Mount Harvard to the benighted peoples of Zwingli appealed mightily to Danny, because it was so different from the style of religion his mother used as a club to beat him into submission, after hitting him in the head with a wooden spoon had begun to lose its effectiveness. Her favorite commandment was good old #5 - "Honor thy father and thy mother: that thy days may be long upon the land which the Lord thy God giveth thee." Danny no longer cared how long he lived, as long as he didn't have to listen to his mother's bitching. She had attempted to inculcate in Danny, if not a respect for religion, at least a fear of religion. Understanding religion was Danny's ticket to freedom from fear. Danny's mother had tossed him the hot potato of guilt from her nocturnal visits to his cowboy bedroom and used religion to produce a fear of throwing it back.

Religion, for Danny, was an area of study that had the potential to explain some of the Great Mysteries of Life. Foremost among these, but certainly not standing alone next to his mother, was the question of why Amy had left him and taken his child.

It pleased Danny no end to write home to his mother about what he was learning in school. In a letter, she couldn't interrupt his thoughts or hit him. He gleefully wrote about his new religion that in no way resembled the Biblical instructions he had received at the end of her wooden spoon. Despite his new book learning, Danny was still the wretched end product of that old Jesuit saying: "Give me a child until he is seven, and I'll give you the man." He still believed deep down in the superstitious crap religion of Sunday School and in the God-Who-Agrees-With-My-Crazy–Mother, no matter what his logical mind told him.

It was late, but it was always late when these bull sessions happened. This night's edition of the college bull session was in full swing in Dick and Danny's room. Dick was there along with a few others. The topic tonight was miracles. Danny, for his part, recounted seeing a real ghost once and having been the subject of a miraculous cure for his public-speaking phobia. Danny wanted to believe that if miracles existed, then maybe, somehow, if he only believed strongly enough, Amy would miraculously come back to him. Amy sat at the back of his mind, always, like a patient vulture seeking to devour the parts of him that died every day he spent without her. Danny thought of Amy and became carrion.

The discussion went back and forth, to and fro.

"There've never been any miracles."

"There were miracles in the olden days, but there are no miracles anymore."

"There are miracles all around us, but we just don't see them."

"There are miracles but different kinds now from the ones in the Bible: like penicillin, f'rinstance, and Sputnik ..."

And Danny's final contribution: "There are only miracles if we *believe* there are miracles."

This last statement had a significant impact upon the tribe gathered in Danny's room.

Dick, who had been silent for the last hour, added his considerable weight to Danny's statement. "We could make miracles happen now, if we had enough faith."

Danny thought, "Bingo! Well, there you go now. Dick has the obvious answer. Dick is the Buddha."

"Okay, Dick. What kind of miracle?" Danny asked, wanting to draw Dick out.

"An easy one, like walking on water ..." Dick's voice never showed hesitation or fear or uncertainty. That's why he was a leader, although Danny sometimes had to interpret his pronouncements. Dick could be inscrutable at times. Dick was the Buddha.

Acting as John the Baptist to Dick's Jesus, Danny called for action. "Well, then, why don't we go try it out right now?"

As most of the boys had, at some point in the evening, been smoking weed and/or drinking adult beverages, the proposition that the group should try to walk on water seemed eminently reasonable to the tribal mind.

Still, the enormity of their commitment suddenly hit them. It silenced the group for a moment. But this challenge had struck a chord they were all waiting to hear. These spiritually beleaguered boys were all the victims of a deliberate conspiracy on the part of the college to strip them of their religious schoolboy faith and replace it with the cutting-edge religion brought down from Harvard by O.W. Woodman. His "cutting edge" department was keen on supplanting their simple faith with a more intellectually fashionable crypto-atheism. This newfangled religion didn't sit well with the boys' corn-fed basic Midwestern Evangelical Protestantism. They would have all secretly liked to return to the comfort of being pure Sunday School stupid - Danny among them.

"Now," the group mind thought, "if we could only walk on water, we could, in all good conscience, turn back from these newfangled teachings, without the necessity of openly mounting any direct logical or scholarly challenge to the learned men our parents are paying so dearly to teach us."

None of them dared to say this aloud. However, they all solemnly agreed with Dick to form a plan in order to execute this requisite miracle. To assist with forming a plan, they decided to pray. This in itself was a step in the direction of the Old Tyme Religion. The boys bowed their heads in silent prayer, except for Dick, who kept his eyes open and smiled a mysterious smile. The Buddha ...

The collective decided that it would be a good idea to gather at "The Transformer" and pray more there. "The Transformer" was a tiny brick building with a steel door on the way to the chapel. The door said "Transformer" and "Keep Out." The building itself hummed and sometimes clicked. Dick and Danny had dubbed it "The

Transformer" with capital letters to imply that it was imbued with magical powers to transform. Dick and Danny's followers now spoke of it in hushed tones, for Dick and Danny were themselves gaining a reputation as being magical collegiate medicine men.

None of these boys had ever before dared touch the door to this temple of transformation. They all averted their eyes when they passed The Transformer on their way to chapel or the field house. No one else at Zwingli knew what this group knew - that every student had to enter this building alone someday before he or she could graduate. After that, so their myth went, no one would recognize those students anymore, not even their closest friends. The students who entered would be "transformed." Such was the magical story of "The Transformer" that Danny interpreted from Dick's enigmatic silences and cryptic remarks.

The bull-session boys gathered this night in the darkness at The Transformer's door. Danny asked them to touch it, as he knew Dick wanted them to do. They did so gingerly with one finger or two. The steel door vibrated under their touch and seemed to hum at a higher pitch as each boy said his silent prayer for personal purification before this holy task. The boys prayed that their belief would be strong enough to allow them to walk across the Upper Winkasheen River that flowed through campus, now menacingly swollen with early fall rains.

It had rained for 40 days and 40 nights, or at least drizzled every day, which was a record rainfall for this part of Iowa that stands to this day. This Biblical record rainfall, Dick had hinted, was a sign that the boys were on the right track to making a miracle.

After their prayers, they left "The Transformer," having indeed been somewhat transformed, and silently walked to the banks of the Upper Winkasheen River like early pilgrims schlepping to the Holy Land. Danny's prayers were muddled and filled with images of Amy, some sexual. Danny hoped the prayers of the others were purer and would make up for the lack of piety in his own devotions.

The tribe of searchers trudged to the muddy bank of the Upper Winkasheen River. They stood watching the roiling river for a bit. Danny advised, "Take off your shoes." The disciples and Jesus probably took off their sandals before they skipped across the wave tops on the Sea of Galilee. It just seemed fittingly Biblical to Danny that his boys be barefoot, too.

They all removed their shoes and socks but no one moved. No one spoke. They stared at the river and avoided looking at each other.

Because Danny suspected that someday he might be called upon to lead a flock of believers to the Lord in his life-role as a minister, or perhaps onstage playing a minister, he decided to go first.

Danny said, "I'll go first."

And he did.

He immediately sank up to his knees in the cold muddy water. He waited a moment, because he felt this sinking was just a test of his faith. He knew he would soon be elevated to the top of the water and that his good fellows would follow, their eyes glowing with the light of the Lord. Danny knew he could walk on water partly because of his faith in God, more so because of his general faith in miracles, and mostly because of his faith in Dick.

Danny waited and waited for deliverance, looking out to the river and then up at the leaden night sky. His eyes were shining and his heart aglow. No deliverance came. His feet and legs became numb. His feet remained on the muddy bottom, fixed there by gravity and other assorted laws of physics the Divine One had chosen in His Wisdom to not mess with on this particular evening. The wetness crept up his pant legs and soaked his underwear.

When Danny turned to his faithful followers, all he saw were their backs in the distance as they trudged up the hill to the main campus, shoes back on their feet, with Dick in the lead.

Danny climbed out of the flooded river. He felt the wetness in his underwear and felt a sting of embarrassment like a slap across his face.

He put on his shoes.

He followed them.

None of them ever spoke of that night or miracles ever again.

CHAPTER EIGHT

Violence is an admission that one's ideas and goals cannot prevail on their own merits.~Edward M. Kennedy

There was a hearse. It was a 1948 Henney-Packard hearse with a straight-eight engine, a two-barrel Carter carb, and three on the tree. It was finished not in black but midnight green. The "passenger" section was upholstered in deep maroon velvet with matching curtains on the rear windows, held back by corded gold satin rope. The driver's section was deep gray mohair. This fine October day, the passenger section was filled with five very alive Zwingli boys and the driver's section held two others.

The Zwingli boys, who collectively owned this relic, belonged to a social organization known as the Muffers. The Muffers were an ancient but unrecognized fraternity at Zwingli. All of the fraternities at Zwingli, with the exception of the Muffers, were unrecognized in terms of national affiliation, but still officially recognized by the college administration as "brotherhoods" and the sororities as "sisterhoods." The Muffers were not officially recognized by anyone as anything.

The Zwingli "Community of Faith and Learning" viewed the Muffers as outcasts - boozers and losers. There was a saying in the community that summed it up: "Tri-Omegas piss in the sink, Zetas piss on the floor, and Muffers piss on their shoes." All seven Muffers in the hearse, and another seven in more mundane vehicles, were heading to three days of pissing on their shoes at the biggest annual drunk in the region: Oktoberfest in La Crosse, Wisconsin.

Danny had supplied all of the Muffers with fake draft cards and fake Wisconsin Age of Majority cards. Danny had lovingly forged these documents in his father's photographic darkroom on a product called Kodak Lightweight Document Paper. He then laminated them at Limmah City Hall on a laminating machine in the lobby that took a quarter. These cards cost less than 40¢ to produce, and Danny sold them for $10 each. He plowed the profits back into booze to help him forget Amy. Danny loved free enterprise and the American Way. Danny loved forgetfulness even more.

Danny, in the spirit of brotherhood, even though the brotherhood he belonged to was an unrecognized brotherhood, brought 24 Bud tallboys for his friends to sip along the way. Danny knew Dick was holding some Dexedrine and probably some pot, but did not begrudge him his secret stash. Being the Buddha, Dick sometimes needed a different type of fuel.

The Muffers planned to arrive in time for the ceremonial tapping of the Golden Keg. Dick, the usual wheelman, kept the Packard at maximum speed. The lumbering old Packard could only do 45 mph on the twisty two-lane roads along the Mississippi, and only 30 on sharp curves. The president of the G. Heileman Brewing Company, headquartered in La Crosse, tapped this golden (well, spray-painted golden) keg from atop a huge farm wagon draped in beer advertisements. A team of draft horses of no real distinction pulled the creaky wagon. No one mistook them for Budweiser Clydesdales, or the wagon for the handcrafted elegance of the one in the Anheuser-Busch commercials.

As the driver whoaed the horses in a cordoned-off parking lot downtown, the company's CEO, dressed for the occasion in ill-fitting lederhosen and a jaunty Tyrolean hat, tapped the Golden Keg and dispensed beer, free to all and sundry supplicants eagerly thrusting their big official plastic Oktoberfest cups in his direction. It was like a beer communion ceremony. Hold the wafers. No pushing.

Although the CEO didn't have a fancy hand-carved Budweiser wagon, and the nags pulling it were not up to snuff, the beer was free for awhile and the atmosphere was like Mardi Gras, except that the settlers in this area were not the fun-loving blacks and Cajuns of the Mississippi Delta but emotionally repressed and hardbitten Scandinavians and Germans. They had settled this more northerly, colder and hardscrabble end of the Mississippi with their Protestant work ethic and their belief in delayed gratification. N'Awlins was the Big Easy, but the Big Responsibility was more descriptive of the lifestyle along this northern end of the Big River, except at Oktoberfest, when the natives went - well - native. These sturdy folk looked on drinking like everything else in their world: hard work to be carried out with earnestness and commitment. The Muffer boys from Zwingli were mostly from this same genetic stock and carried the same sense of commitment to most things.

Danny and Dick soon lost the other Muffers in the crowd, but being inseparable, did not lose each other. Day One of Oktoberfest, they determined, was a day best used to settle into the rhythm of a long-distance drunk and establish a dignified pace for the mayhem. The Oompapa Tent was where they started. This tent was full of the older and more established drinkers in town, and these older men provided an example of how to survive a three-day beer marathon. Drink, sit, eat, drink, sing, eat, drink, drink, dance, eat, drink, sit, sing, drink - all at a mature pace.

However, a few hours of this sedate drinking was enough to bore the boys. Danny wanted to hit the Rock 'n' Roll Tent, as he hated the sound of the accordion in the Oompapa Tent and could only take so much of it. The Rock 'n' Roll Tent was full of Danny's age peers, none of whom had the slightest idea how to "distance drink," except to drink and repeat and drink and repeat and drink and repeat - a series of sprints, really, more than a marathon plan. This rather mindless rhythm of "drink and repeat," combined with the pounding rhythm of the "devil music" being played by a hired-on-the-cheap local rock band - who compensated for their own growing beer-induced incoherence and natural lack of talent by turning up the volume - led to the tent's male inhabitants becoming asinine dead stupid mean drunk within hours. Young men that drunk feel compelled to exercise their God-given right to not be so much as glanced upon by other males without punching their lights out. The punching started small and grew like a testosterone avalanche. In the melee, the inseparable Dick and Danny became separated.

By nightfall, there had been so many fights in the Rock 'n' Roll tent that the city cops, backed by state cops, backed by helmeted kids in the Wisconsin National Guard, took it upon themselves to clear the tent by force. The National Guard troopers, being kids themselves, looked enviously at the sea of beer that they could not themselves drink. They also glanced nervously at the ugly mob they faced. The National Guard kids had not been issued ammunition for their rifles and had never been trained in crowd control. They nervously followed the example of the two police forces, who were trained and had live ammo.

The three armed groups never fired a shot, but by sparing no gratuitous brutality with clubs, cattle prods and rifle butts, had very little trouble subduing 500 weaving teenage drunks armed only with plastic cups and male hormones.

The armed representatives of law and order dragged and kicked the worst brawlers into squad cars, paddy wagons and even city works vans they had pressed into service for the emergency. Those drinkers unable to stand or walk were given rides as well. The rest of the kids were herded un-gently to the jail on foot, driven in one big herd like longhorn cattle. The county jail proper had, of course, had been filled to overcrowding hours before. However, the authorities, showing real ingenuity, cordoned off the courthouse lawn with road-construction sawhorses. The cops herded and heaved the revelers onto the lawn, then told them that they were in jail and couldn't leave until they were sober. Cops and guardsmen patrolling outside the sawhorses, batons at the ready, were ordered to keep the rowdies in until they were sober enough to leave. They were also ordered to keep the peace inside the "sawhorse jail," if trouble broke out there.

Danny shuffled around the lawn in a boozy haze, but he was still able to stand and speak. Danny saw Craig, one of his Muffer brothers, walking around doing an amazing imitation of a prisonyard shuffle and screaming curses at no one in particular. Danny approached Craig and told him to shut up and be quiet and stay close. "Craig, I can get us out of this joint in no time."

Danny believed he could talk his way out of anything. He had, after all, been the captain of his high-school championship debating team. He didn't believe that his slurred speech would negate his logic, once he brought it to bear. Craig went the extra mile beyond the quiet Danny had asked for by actually passing out for several hours. Craig fell like a sack of dirt at the foot of a bronze statue of Arthur MacArthur Jr. of the 24th Wisconsin Volunteer Infantry Regiment, who, as a 19-year-old brevetted colonel at the Battle of Missionary Ridge in the Civil War, won the Medal of Honor for rallying his men to victory with a cry of "On Wisconsin" - now the title of the University of Wisconsin's fight song. Arthur MacArthur was the father of General Douglas MacArthur. Danny amused himself by reading the plaque on the statue and throwing up a rich mixture of bratwurst, buns and beer on his shoes. He later cleaned his shoes by pissing on them, good Muffer that he was.

After several hours, and with the night still young, Craig regained consciousness and Danny, once again in a conspiratorial whisper, cautioned him to shut up and stick close by. "Just observe me, and be amazed."

Danny hailed a National Guardsman who looked way younger than Danny or Craig. "My friend here has to get back to his car to get his insulin shot because he's a bad diabetic. He's probably gonna die in about half an hour if I don't help him get to his car."

The poor kid in uniform said, "Yeah, okay, I don't wanna kill no one, but youse gotta wait 'till my sergeant over there by that van goes for a coffee or a piss. Then I'll let youse out. That fucker's drunker than youse guys and mean as hell."

Getting into his role now and trying to establish rapport, Danny asked, "So how is being in the Guard?"

"Not bad, except for that prick of a sergeant. Bein' in the Guard here is better than bein' in the Army over there in Nam and getting' my ass shot off. Is he really a diabetic?"

Danny confessed, "Nah, we just have to meet a couple of girls over at the Circus Bar."

"That's cool."

When the sergeant disappeared, Craig and Danny "broke out" of the sawhorse jail under the watchful eye of their friendly National Guardsman. Danny looked at the kid and said "On Wisconsin!"

The National Guardsman just looked at Danny funny. Danny guessed that local military history was not on the syllabus of the Wisconsin National Guard training program.

Danny pointed at the kid and pointed at the statue of MacArthur and said, "Read the statue." Which earned him another funny look. And, with that, Danny and Craig disappeared into the night.

The two Muffers found the Circus Bar. They stayed until closing, and never did see the girls they had met in one of the tents. The two left to look for the hearse to get some sleep, and to search for any tallboys of Bud that might be left alive under the dirty sleeping bags that littered the back. All drunks think they need a nightcap. They began aimlessly weaving their way around town to find the hearse, with Craig singing and yelling.

Craig was a smallish guy but he had a big mouth when he was drunk, and his face bore some evidence of the consequences of his mouthiness. Craig had a black eye and a cut lip. Oktoberfest was less than 12 hours old, and Craig had already been beat up, at least once.

As ill luck would have it, on other side of the street, three large black guys appeared, coasting along. Craig, seeing them, took immediate objection to their existence and started yelling "nigger" this and "nigger" that at them. Craig had a death wish when he was drunk.

Danny screamed in his face, "Craig, shut up!" But Craig just yelled all the louder and waved his fists in defiance.

The black guys sauntered across the street like they had all the time in the world. Their hands were in their pockets and they were smiling. Danny read in their body language, "Knife! Gun! Brass knuckles!" The black gentlemen came to a stop in a loose semicircle around Craig and Danny. Craig and Danny had their backs to a brick wall and could not run.

Danny shouted over and over, "Craig, shut up, shut up!" Finally, in desperation, Danny grabbed Craig by his shirt front and shouted right into his face, "Shut up!" Craig didn't shut up. Danny shook him until his head hit the brick wall. He still wouldn't shut up. Danny sensed he was on the right track to a resolution of the crisis. He slammed Craig's head into the wall again and again, and when he'd cold-cocked him, Craig finally did shut up. Danny held Craig as he slid down the wall, slowly, like a gob of spit, leaving a wet red trail on the brick. Craig finally puddled onto the sidewalk.

The black guys were still just standing there doing nothing. One of them said, "Nice work, white meat; we couldn't a-done any better ourselves." He smiled and nodded slightly at the other two "brothers," and they just walked away.

Danny sat down on the sidewalk beside Craig. Danny heard him moan, but poor Craig didn't wake up. Danny was relieved he hadn't killed him. He hoped Craig just had brain damage. No one would notice brain damage, because Craig was so fucked up anyway. Danny's mouth was dry, and he needed a smoke. When he tried to get a cigarette out of the flip-top box, his hands shook so badly that he got six out at once instead of just one. When Danny tried to light one of them, he couldn't get the match to line up with the end of the cigarette. "Fuck it! Fuck you, fuckin' Craig! Fuckin' niggers!" and he threw all six unlit cigarettes into the gutter and cried.

Miraculously, just then, Danny saw the Muffer hearse come weaving very slowly down the middle of the street. The driver stopped when he saw his two Muffer brothers. With help from some guys in the back of the hearse, Danny threw Craig inside the coffin bed.

The driver called out as Danny walked away from the hearse, "Where the fuck are you going? Doncha wanna ride?"

"I gotta … I dunno. Fuck it." Danny walked away, waving a goodbye arm in the air, but not looking back at the hearse. Danny looked like a man on a mission. He needed to find some female companionship.

†††

Craig Johnson; age 24; 27 September 1971; helicopter crash;
Vietnam; Lutheran; unmarried; Gleason, WI; draftee

CHAPTER NINE

Is it security you want? There is no security at the top of the world.~Garet Garrett

Danny bobbed slowly to the surface of that oozy black lake that sucks down a drinker after two or three days of drinking and is often confused with sleep. He had fur on his tongue - not just the coating of filth laid down by too many cigarettes and much cheap beer, but real animal fur. A smelly gray cat had bedded down on top of his head while Danny was unconscious. It was rhythmically flopping its tail over Danny's lips, which is probably what had caused Danny to open his eyes. The cat sat smugly atop the worst headache Danny could ever remember. Danny shook the cat off his head and looked around.

Danny saw that he was on a scratchy maroon sofa that sagged in the middle. He was in a living room that looked like everything in it had been bought used, then used harder, never cleaned and put into a bag, shaken, and poured back in the room at random. In short, it looked like students lived there. The room was lit by a single, small, filthy window that leaked a little lead-colored light.

It may have been Saturday or Sunday or even Monday. There was evidence everywhere that there had been many people in this room drinking and smoking and eating pizza in the recent past. Danny's blackout refused to give him any other hints about the recent past.

Danny speculated that he was in La Crosse, Wisconsin - possibly in the morning, but the morning of an unknowable day. Danny maneuvered himself into a shaky upright position. Each time he moved his head was another hammer blow to the anvil of his hangover. He ambled down the hall at a brisk stagger to find the loo. His bladder was near bursting.

He opened the first door to the right ... Wrong room ... Three naked people were passed out on top of a bed. Nice ass on the middle one! But no one he knew, and no toilet ...

Second door ... Wrong again ... One person asleep on a rug, long hair, face down. Not such a nice ass ... Hairy ...

Third room ... Gold! Piss gold ... And Danny had gallons of golden piss to unload! Danny cracked his first half-smile of the day in the cracked mirror that hung over the cracked toilet bowl. On the underside of the seat, someone had written, "It's so nice to have a man around the house."

When Danny had finished and zipped up, he noticed a sound. It was the sound of a trickle of running water. He turned around and noticed a shower behind him, and from his years of training in a household run by parents who grew up during the Great Depression, knew it was his duty to turn off the tap and not waste water. He pulled back the curtain.

She was dead, and there was blood everywhere, except where the trickling water had eroded it away. She was a mottled gray and purple and yellow, but not any color a live human should be. Her lips were coated with pink frosted lipstick, but a bluish hue showed through underneath. Her eyes were open and she seemed to be smiling.

Danny took hold of her hand and lifted her arm. He did not know why he did this. He saw that she had cut the veins in her arm the long way - elbow to wrist and not across. Danny had studied the way to do this properly if you were serious about it, and he saw she had done it the right way. Cutting along the vein meant the emergency doc couldn't sew it shut again. Danny dropped her arm and looked at her eyes.

Her eyes! She had one lavander eye and one blue eye. The blue eye was the same shade of blue as his mother's. The lavender the same shade as Amy's. Those strange cold dead eyes burned their way through Danny's brain until they arrived at his core. Once there, they spread a coldness throughout his body that reached into every cell. Danny's chest tightened and he fluttered and flailed to the tile floor on his knees, like a flying duck falls when shot in one wing. Danny scuttled to the toilet on his knees. This time he threw up over and over again, until only dry heaves were left.

Danny had to get out of wherever it was that he was. Danny had to find his jacket. Danny had to find the exit door. Danny had to find his cigarettes. Danny had to find his shoes. Most of all, Danny had to find Dick. Only Dick would understand. Only Dick could make it better.

Searching in a controlled panic, Danny found his jacket and shoes on the floor by the sofa. Under the jacket he found, miraculously hidden, a full warm six-pack of 16-oz. cans of Budweiser. He grabbed the jacket and the Bud, snatched a few of the longer butts from an ashtray and headed out into the city.

Danny felt suddenly and inexplicably light in the snappy October air, the hangover having turned from pain into a kind of cloudy, dissociative euphoria. He felt the way he had when a car hit him, head on, when he was on his little red Schwinn 20-in. two-wheeler when he was five. He didn't hurt at all, and he didn't want to go the hospital with the men in the flashing truck. He yelled to see his stuffed bears, Big Teddy and Teddy Junior, to tell them what had happened first.

Danny wanted to see the bears more than anything. "No hospital. NO! I have to see my bears!"

He wanted to curl up with them under his cowboys and chuck wagons bedspread, with a silver six-gun in each hand. He loved his silver six-guns ... "Oh please, Teddy, I want my silver six-guns!"

Danny became logical as well as light. He gravely intoned instructions to himself as he walked. "First, I have to find the road out of town. I know the Mississippi River borders La Crosse on the West. I know the river will probably be downhill from anywhere in town. I know the bridge back to school crosses the river from downtown. I think the light over there is the rising sun behind the overcast. That way is east; it's morning. If I turn my back to the light, I should be walking west, and I should be walking downhill, and I should find the river." Danny said this between sips of warm beer while trying to find matches with his free hand to light one of the longer butts he'd scrounged from the ashtray.

As Danny walked through the deserted downtown of what he believed to be La Crosse, Wisconsin, his back to the light, going slightly downhill, with an unlit cigarette butt in his lips, sipping a warm beer and carrying five more under his arm, he saw Dick cut around a corner two blocks away, his shaggy brown hair and navy surplus peacoat making him unmistakable to Danny - even at a distance, even with a hangover.

"Hey, Dick, I need a light!"

CHAPTER TEN

None are more hopelessly enslaved than those who falsely believe they are free.~Johann Wolfgang von Goethe

Danny secured the five-pack under his arm and ran wearily, hacking like he had tuberculosis, to reach Dick, who was leaning against the side of a building, B&L Aviator sunglasses on, even though it was a dreary day, and an unfiltered cigarette burning in his lips. Miraculously, Dick too had a six-pack with one gone.

"Got a light?"

Dick didn't answer; he just handed Danny his smoke, from which Danny could take a second-hand light. Dick asked in a hushed voice, "You hear that?"

"What?"

"Really weird music, coming from the river."

"Music?" Danny couldn't remember hearing a thing in this Sunday morning city since he'd heard the water trickling in the shower. He remembered that sound only too well.

Dick whispered excitedly, "Let's go find the music."

Danny took a quick suck on the butt and threw it down in disgust. The filter had pink lipstick on it. He wondered if the dead girl had smoked it; it looked like her shade. "Okay, but gimme a real cigarette, wouldya? And a light?"

Dick gave him a smoke.

"Aw, fuck, you and your fuckin' Lucky Strikes ..." but he took the unfiltered cigarette anyway. The idea that his lips had made second-hand contact with the dead girl's lips made Danny shiver.

From where they were standing, the boys could see a sliver of silver river in the distance. They walked toward the river, smoking and drinking but not talking. Dick heard the music now, and it *did* seem to be coming from the river. After walking two more blocks and turning a corner, they saw the source of the strange music. Big as life, tied to the dock, was a beautiful white sternwheel steamboat. Her name was printed on her pilothouse in big scrolled gold letters: *Delta Queen* - Natchez, Tennessee.

Danny and Dick approached her. They sat on the steep bank directly above her, on some broken concrete, and just stared at her. She was big and real, but to Danny, she might have just been part of the weird dream he had been living in for months now. Danny's depression, and the things he had been using to combat it, had removed most of the firmness he'd once had in his belief about the reality of reality. Danny was about to tell Dick about the girl he thought he saw in the shower, with the one lavander eye and the one blue eye, when he heard voices coming from the foredeck - the deep, rolling, melodic voices of Southern Negroes. Danny and Dick moved to get a view of the foredeck. Sure enough, there was a gathering of black deckhands, stooped down and crouching around a pile of paper money. They were "rolling the bones" - shooting craps. They were passing around a short dog of fortified wine.

One of the deckhands saw the boys, and eyeing their beer cartons, called out, "Sirs, would you young gentlemen care to partake of a game of chance? You can come aboard if you bring those beverages with you. It gets mighty dry out here on the river this time of the mornin'."

The boys scrambled down the steep bank to a rickety dock, upon which rested the gangplank. They went aboard. The boat had a smell to her that could only have been the smell of a riverboat - part lubricating oil, part cheap cigar, part swamp rot, mixed with the exciting stale smell of sweat found on carnival rides and on the last row of seats at the movies. The deckhands smelled like zoo animals that had bathed in buck-a-bottle port wine. Both sets of smells were intoxicating to Danny, rather than off-putting. Danny locked eyes with Dick and, without asking, knew that Dick wanted to go wherever this boat would take them. Danny could read Dick's mind. He had never dared ask if Dick could read his. That didn't matter anyway, because whatever Dick was thinking, Danny was thinking, too.

Danny answered the deckhand who had invited them on board. Danny's voice was full of existentialist bravado. "We don't gamble, because life itself is a gamble, but you can have some of our beer." Danny felt it was a privilege to be accepted by racial minority members of the working class. He did not begrudge them a few beers, and offered up his whole former six-pack, now numbering but four. Dick did not offer up his beer. Dick was too sophisticated to be impressed by Negroes, having talked to Negroes on more than one occasion back in his Big Eastern City. Danny had never talked to one before, and felt a need to present himself as an exemplary example of the white race. Danny even wished fervently that they would offer him a pull on their short dog of wine without wiping the top first, but they, apparently, felt no corresponding need to impress this junior member of the white race.

"Where're you taking the boat next?" Danny asked.

One of the gamblers replied, "Dis da end of the season, we goin' t' Natchez fo' a refit. We juss a skeleton crew, mosts a da crew is laid off an' took the train sout' this mornin'. You boys lookin' t' take a ride?"

78

"Maybe."

"An' what kinda cash money y'all be carryin'?"

"Nothing ... Maybe we could work?"

The big man just looked at the two scrawny college boys and laughed. His friends laughed along with him.

Danny's answer about the lack of cash money caused another of the gamblin' men to reconsider the offer of a ride. "Oh, on consideration, the owners would be mighty inflamed if they thought that we let stowaways aboard. On reconsideration, we'd best not take you gentlemen; it could mean our jobs. You gentlemen should go ashore now. We ready to cast off."

Danny and Dick left, deeply regretting not being allowed to work their way to Natchez on the steamboat. They went back up the bank and watched the crew cast off her lines. The boys passed their last remaining beer back and forth. The *Queen* was making a whole lot of stream now, and with creaking and groaning and thumping and pumping, her big sternwheel began moving, and she headed out toward the main shipping channel to her refit in Natchez.

The boys watched in silence as she entered the main channel about a third of a mile out, or so. Danny saw all of his Tom Sawyer fantasies, and maybe all of his boyhood fantasies, sail away with this pretty old boat, leaving him behind on the bank with no hope of escape from his own personal hell - which this morning, with his discovery of the dead girl, had just become more unpleasant. Danny was seeing the boat, but at the same time could feel one cold blue eye and one cold lavander eye staring at him from behind his head.

As the *Queen* straightened herself from sideslipping and got into the current for the fast downstream run home, Danny saw tiny separate puffs of pure white rise above her superstructure, and then a second or so later, he heard these white puffs as music. The boys' eyes saw the notes her steam calliope was playing before their ears could hear them. This seemed magical - seeing music.

"In the good old summertime, in the good old summertime.
Strolling through the shady lanes with your baby mine.
You hold her hand, and she holds yours,
And that's a very good sign.
That she's your tootsie-wootsie,
In the good old summertime."
George Evans - music; Ren Shields – lyrics

Danny said quietly, "I remember now. I remember her going on and on last night about skydiving. She said her fiancé was a paratrooper and got killed over there."

"Who?"

"The dead girl in the shower. I held her hand."

"Someday, Danny, they're just gonna lock you up and throw away the key, you talk such shit. You wanna smoke a joint?"

Dick fired one up and passed it over.

As the *Delta Queen* floated out of sight and the boys shared the reefer, Dick asked in a completely normal conversational tone, "Do you want to head upriver to Minneapolis and catch a plane to Samoa?"

CHAPTER ELEVEN

Look back over the past, with its changing empires that rose and fell, and you can foresee the future, too.~Marcus Aurelius

The *Delta Queen* rounded a bend and was gone, her calliope silent. The leaden skies darkened, and a wind came up off the river. It began to rain. The boys trudged along the riverbank toward the bridge they saw in the distance to begin hitchhiking to Minneapolis. The bridge was U.S. Highway 61 and, at optimal speed, it is three hours north on 61 to get to downtown Minneapolis. If you take 61 in the other direction, south out of La Crosse, it is, at best, a 29-hour drive to New Orleans, where Highway 61 ends and becomes Tulane Avenue in the downtown and runs parallel to Canal Street, until both streets terminate at the Gulf of Mexico.

Fortunately, there were a lot of cars headed north out of town with a lot of sick, half-sick and getting-drunk-again Oktoberfesters heading up Highway 61 toward the Twin Cities. The first ride took them as far as Winona. The van was full of drunken teenagers who were still drinking. It smelled of dope and sex and beer and farts, a combination of smells familiar to Danny from the back of the Muffers' hearse. The smell made Danny feel at home, even though these kids were just high schoolers. The kids gave Dick and Danny one beer that they had to split, but it was better than no beer.

Dick and Danny were soaked to the skin. The van was overheated. The damp heat and the motion of the van combined with his hangover to make Danny feel nauseous. Danny was able to get to the side window of the van and stick his head out before he puked. His puke put a swoopy pink-and-red design on the side of the moving van. Danny was sure there was blood in the vomit. All the passengers cheered as he puked, but the cheering did not cheer Danny. He wanted a bath, a light bland meal, a clean bed and a long sleep. He felt the one cold lavender eye and the one cold blue eye still staring at him, asking him a question that he could not understand, much less answer.

Danny dared not share any of his fear and misery with Dick. He felt embarrassingly weak in comparison to Dick, who seemed to Danny to be incapable of dismay. Dick was smiling and chuckling at the high-schoolers' hijinks. Dick had that visionary look he carried off with such aplomb. With his sights set on Samoa, Dick seemed completely content and at ease. Dick radiated the impression that he always knew what he was doing, and Danny was content to go along with him. Going to Samoa with Dick seemed as reasonable a thing to do as any other, given Danny's inability to form a committed relationship with reality.

The second ride, from Winona to Red Wing, was a little slower in coming. The farther away from La Crosse, the thinner the traffic. There was only some Sunday-driver local traffic - people going to dinner or leaving a late-morning church service. The rain continued, and the wind had picked up. The hitchhiking boys looked like drowned rats, perhaps even dangerous drowned rats, and no neatly dressed Christians picked them up.

The person who did pick them up was a criminal. He was driving an immaculate late-model beige Buick. He was wearing worn black shoes, a dirty gray work shirt and dirty gray work pants. He had a five o'clock shadow, close-set beady eyes and yellow teeth. Danny was pleased to let Dick sit in the front seat. Danny sat in the back. The criminal did not speak except to ask, "Where youse goin'? Ya got any money?"

Dick answered, "The Cities … Five bucks …"

The criminal answered in a surly tone, "Keep yer fuckin' fin."

That was all the conversation for the whole trip, until the criminal said, "Get out" when they hit downtown St. Paul.

The boys got out. The rain was mixed with a few snowflakes and ice pellets, and it was almost dark. The wind was still whipping at a good clip from the northwest.

Danny didn't mean to whine, but it came out sounding like a whine, anyway. "I'm hungry."

Dick said, "We should find an all-night movie. They have them in Boston, and they probably have them here."

So, off they went to find an all-night movie. And find one they did, right on the same block where they were standing. It was playing *The Russians Are Coming, the Russians Are Coming*. Dick handed the box-office lady the fin, and got two tickets for the outrageous big-city sum of 75¢ each. Danny was shocked. In his town, he could still get into a movie for 25¢.

The first time the movie played from beginning to end, it was a rollicking good laugh - a look at Cold War America's paranoia from the odd perspective of a Russian submarine running aground off a small New England fishing village. It proved to have even more depth upon second viewing. Danny slept through the third and fourth showings but woke up to see the fifth, which he found annoying, maybe because his back hurt and he was about to faint from hunger. The sixth viewing was beyond annoying; it was agony. Danny thought he would die from hunger. Throughout the night, Dick remained cheerful, and Danny thought he could hear Dick chuckling when

Danny's sleep lightened up to near-wakefulness. After the sixth showing, they left the theater and hit the pre-dawn streets of downtown St. Paul.

"Let's eat breakfast."

That was the best thing Danny had heard Dick say for a day and a half. They found a small downtown diner and feasted away the whole $3.50 Dick had left after breaking his five to get into the movie. They had nothing left for a tip for the waitress.

Danny asked, "Won't she get mad if we don't leave her a tip?"

Dick just looked at Danny as though he were crazy. "It's not like we're ever going to eat here again. We're going to Samoa."

Danny thought for a second. "Don't we need passports or something?"

"We're going to American Samoa," Dick corrected.

The day had cleared of rain, wind and snow, but it was still cold. The boys loitered in the red vinyl-covered booth at the diner, drinking coffee and waiting for the banks to open to cash a big check to get plane fare to Samoa.

Danny and Dick walked into the first bank they saw on the street. It was a big, old, marble-pillared downtown bank. Danny and Dick must have looked like orphan street children and smelled like them, too, but the prim, smiling, gray-haired teller greeted them with a smile as if they were eccentric millionaires.

"May I help you gentlemen?"

Dick whipped out his checkbook and said, "I'd like to cash a check."

"Certainly, sir. Do you have an account with us?"

"No."

"Would you care to open an account with us? We could accept your check to open an account."

"You mean you won't just cash my check, unless I open an account?"

"That's correct, sir."

"Alright, then, I'd like to open an account."

"Checking or savings?"

"Savings; I already have a checking account." Dick held up his checkbook for the nice lady to see.

"Fine. How much would you like to deposit?"

"Well, I'd like to deposit $601. See, I want to take $600 out today and keep a dollar on deposit."

"Very well, sir, but I'm afraid we can't let you withdraw any funds until the check clears. Is your account with a bank here in the Cities?"

"Boston."

"Well, it'll be sometime next week before an out-of-state check clears and you can access your account."

"Next week?"

"At the earliest, sir."

"Do all the banks around here not cash checks except their own?"

"All that I know of, sir. I'm sorry."

Dick had been defeated by his own ignorance of how the world worked, but he refused to show defeat. Danny felt so bad for him that he did not comment. The boys walked out of the bank with no money, no place to stay, and no trip to Samoa.

Dick said, "We'll cash the check back in Dekorum and go to Samoa next week. Let's hitch back."

The boys wandered around in the cold downtown of St. Paul asking how to get to U.S. Highway 52 south, the road that led back to Dekorum and Zwingli College and warm beds, dry clothes and free food. Some kind and knowledgeable soul finally told them Highway 52 was only two blocks away from where they stood.

They walked two blocks, stuck out their thumbs, and were ignored by the big-city rush-hour downtown drivers. It was well past noon before they finally got a ride. A big step-up panel van pulled over. The van had a big happy face painted on the side. The driver asked, "Where're you headed?"

"Dekorum."

"You from Zwingli?"

"Yeah, how did you know?"

"I'm headed right to the Zwingli food service to do a delivery. You look like college boys. At first I thought you were from the U and just going to the south end of town or something."

The boys hopped in the Happy Potato Chip truck.

"Go to the back and stay out of sight until I get out of town." The driver pointed to a big yellow sign in the corner of the windshield that read "!srediR oN." "Help yourself to some chips. That big open box in the front is full of crushed and unsealed bags we're just gonna throw away. I keep 'em for friends. I'm not supposed to, but I don't give a shit. I got drafted, and I gotta go for training in three weeks. One a youse can come up and sit here, if you want. I guess I don't give a shit if they catch me with riders, either. What're they gonna do, send me to Vietnam?" He laughed, and Danny laughed with him, and Dick just smiled one of his secret smiles. Dick hopped into the single passenger seat up front with a few bags of chips in his hand.

Dick asked, "You got any beer? I can give you a check."

"Nah, but there's Coke behind the seat. Help yourself. Stores I deliver to sometimes give me a six-pack or two, if I do a good job on the display."

Danny and Dick gorged on chips and Coke and the driver chattered away about getting kicked out of the U, his girl leaving him for some ice-hockey star at the U, and getting drunk with his old high-school buddies up in Hibbing and stealing cars and smashing rural mailboxes with baseball bats while speeding by them in the stolen cars - the usual topics of male bonding conversation.

"Did you know Bob Dylan up there in Hibbing?" Dick asked.

"Fuckin' Zimmerman? He was in my older brother's class. I never knew him."

"Oh. Just thought you mighta run into him ..."

"Nah ..."

Danny, fed and warm, found a spot between the boxes near the rear doors. There was a quilted moving pad on the floor that he could lay down on and was big enough to double over himself as a cover. He slept all the way to the Zwingli food service delivery dock.

Danny and Dick offered to help unload the truck.

The driver laughed. "These boxes only weigh 5 lb. They're full of potato chips, not coal."

"Hey, thanks for the ride."

"Hey, you guys'd better stay in school or all three of us'll end up humpin' 60-lb. rucksacks in the jungle. Stay cool."

"Yeah, we're cool."

Neither Danny nor Dick ever told anyone what they did after Oktoberfest. And neither one ever mentioned Samoa again, even to each other. Danny never got around to telling Dick about the girl in the shower, even though her one cold blue eye and the one cold lavender eye continued to watch Danny for years to come.

ttt
Kurt NMI Olsen; age 20; 1 May 1966; other explosive device; Vietnam; Lutheran; unmarried; Hibbing, MN; draftee

CHAPTER TWELVE

Any excuse will serve a tyrant.~Aesop

There were a lot of things that Dick and Danny did not discuss besides Samoa. Dick did not discuss things because he was too cool to say much, and when he did, the things he said were often cryptic. A lot of it went over Danny's head.

Danny did not need words to discern Dick's wishes. He knew what Dick was thinking by just observing the cock of his hip, or the glint in his eye, or that little mischievous smile he was sure Dick reserved just for him. Dick was wise in ways Danny never dreamed he would ever be wise. Dick had been on a jet plane and sailed a sailboat. Dick hinted he knew the Kennedy family but was too modest to come right out and say it. Dick could play the harmonica, which he did not call a harmonica but a "blues harp." Just listening to Dick blow his blues harp was enough to convince Danny he was not in the presence of an ordinary human.

"Did you really play blues harp in Harvard Square with Bob Dylan and Joan Baez?"

"Yeah, I played there some," Dick said in his usual casually modest fashion.

Danny did not need girls. He had Dick, and Dick was all he needed. Dick and Danny did not "do it" with each other. Danny did not think of himself as queer; after all, he had fathered a child. Danny was certainly uncertain what it would be like to even *be* a queer. Danny had never met one, and had never even come across one in his reading. Danny knew he didn't want to touch any cock but his own. To be more precise, the thought of touching another cock but his own had never even occurred to him as a possibility, until he thought of it with Dick, and then dismissed it as disgusting. Danny was not confused about his sexual identity.

Danny lusted after a lot of girls at Zwingli, but they seemed as stuck up as the girls in his high school. Danny had no problem avoiding them, because they were even better at avoiding him. No items in his wardrobe had been cleaned since his mother washed them in late August. Washing his clothes, or even himself, seemed like a waste of time, since girls did not like him, anyway. Dick never complained.

Danny saw the Zwingli girls as immature. Danny had been with Amy, who was a real grown-up woman. These giggling twits would never measure up to Amy in Danny's estimation. So Danny stuck with Dick and masturbated as often as required. The beer and dope were Danny's special friends in his struggle to avoid the lure of the lost Amy or the lure of any girl. Taken in sufficient quantities, these substances numbed more than Danny's mind - they numbed his dick.

A few weeks after Oktoberfest, Danny and Dick were driving around gravel roads, at night, in the old Henney-Packard hearse. They were sipping warm 3.2% Grain Belt beer from half-gallon bottles and listening to the big tube-type Motorola radio set in the purple glowing dash of the big green hearse. The Motorola was picking up "race music" from some big ol' 50,000-watt AM station in the Mississippi Delta. The signal was skipping into Iowa off an accommodating ionosphere this magical November night. Muddy Waters was just finishing his rendition of *Honey Bee* when Dick inadvertently steered the big Packard off the right side of the road. The hearse skidded to a stop on its undercarriage with two wheels hanging over the ditch. They were only going about 7 mph, so it was a slow-motion accident that harmed neither the boys nor the hearse. The hearse weighed over 7,000 lb. unloaded, and couldn't be budged with two wheels in the air and the undercarriage on the ground. The boys had no idea where they were as it hadn't seemed important to remember where they were, since they had a full tank and would eventually end up back in Dekorum if they drove around long enough. Being lost, they decided to wait for someone to drive by and help them.

They only had to wait a few minutes. A county sheriff cruiser pulled up, and the deputy was kind enough to offer some assistance.

"Are you boys okay?"

"Yes, sir."

"Is this your car?"

"No, it belongs to a friend."

"I see this vehicle around town all the time. So, who *does* own it?"

"Well, we all sort of own it, but the legal ownership gets passed around. We don't really know who owns it right now."

Ignoring the ownership issue, the deputy asked, "Do you guys need a ride back to town?"

"Sure. We don't really know where we are."

The deputy opened the back door of the cruiser and the boys hopped in.

"Hey, there are no door handles in here. Neat!"

Back in town, the deputy asked the boys to come into the station with him and help him with some paperwork about the incident. The boys walked into the station as innocently as lambs to the slaughter. Their rescuer introduced the boys to a couple of other deputies who were lounging around the office. They smiled amiably at the two boys and seemed very friendly.

One of them asked, "Have you two been drinking?"

"Yeah, we had a beer after the hearse got stuck." Dick and Danny were smart enough not to admit to drinking while driving.

"Well, why don't you two come back through here with me?" The first deputy pointed to a door with his thumb.

"Where?"

"We have to take you to the cells. There's a law in Iowa that says it's illegal for anyone under 21 to possess alcohol."

Danny said in protest, "We didn't possess any alcohol." Danny knew they threw the full beers into the weeds when they saw the cruiser driving up.

The deputy just said, "You aren't allowed to possess it internally, either. You two smell like a brewery, and you just admitted to drinking. That means you're guilty of internal possession. We'll have to keep you here for the night, until the judge comes in tomorrow."

With that, the deputy escorted the boys back to the drunk tank. Danny noted it was an ultra-traditional drunk tank, built of limestone blocks with room for a small crowd. It had steel bars, and one light bulb in the ceiling protected by a steel cage. It had cots with solid steel bottoms bolted to the walls. The cots had no mattresses or blankets on them. There was a little steel toilet, with no lid, sitting out in the open. The cell smelled like Pine-Sol with some puke mixed in. Oddly, the cell door was open even though the cell was inhabited.

"Who's that? And how come the door isn't locked?" Danny asked.

The deputy said, "That's Olee. He sleeps here a few nights a week, since we took his car away last year. We drive him home in the morning. He runs that junk shop out on the highway. We'll keep the door open, if you guys promise not to leave. Steve and me'll be just outside in the office all night, and if you disturb our sleep trying to do a runner, we might have to shoot you. Understood?" He winked and patted his holstered revolver to emphasize the point.

Danny protested to Dick as soon as the deputy left, "The bastards! Arresting college men for having a little beer on our breath, and not even telling us we were arrested until they had us in the clink! I thought we were living in a democracy. Apparently not!"

Dick just shrugged and lay back on a cot. Dick offered after a few beats, "I wish I had my blues harp."

"I wish you did, too."

In the morning, the boys were brought in front of a judge, who asked them if they wanted a lawyer. They didn't. He asked them how they wished to plead to the charge, and advised them to plead guilty. They did. He fined them $80 each plus $9 in costs. Dick whipped out his checkbook and paid both fines.

Danny wondered why a court in Iowa would take a check from Massachusetts but a bank in Minnesota would not. Danny also wondered about the concept of an "internal possession" law regarding alcohol. Danny came from what he thought of as a mature and sophisticated jurisdiction regarding alcohol. Everyone he knew in Illinois drank whatever they wanted, when they wanted, where they wanted, in whatever quantity they wanted. Iowa, in contrast, had a system of state-run liquor stores that did not display bottles but only offered names and number codes to choose from, in an atmosphere colder and less inviting than a post office. Iowa also apparently had an "internal possession" law, although the formal charge, as Danny remembered its being read in court, merely mentioned "possession and control of an alcoholic beverage by a minor, to wit: any person less than the age of 21 years."

After being released from custody and walking back to campus, Danny made it his first priority to search the Zwingli library for a recent copy of the Iowa State Statutes. He searched every section pertaining to the control of alcoholic beverages. Nowhere did he find the words "internal possession." The cops had lied. They hadn't looked for or produced any containers of alcohol - the very thing necessary to prove possession. Boozy breath proved nothing. He and Dick had been tricked into pleading guilty to a charge they could have beaten. The cops had lied and the judge had advised them to plead guilty, knowing full well that they were not guilty under the law because there was no physical evidence to support the charge.

Danny saw Dick coming out of his 11:30 class, ran to him and exclaimed breathlessly, "They fucked us, you know. They lied. I looked it up. 'Internal possession' doesn't exist. They can't do that!"

Dick looked up at the sky for a moment, as though asking the heavens for help with this idiot standing in front of him.

"Yeah, they can do it. They did just do it. Lying is what they do best."

Danny looked at the ground.

CHAPTER THIRTEEN

The evil that is in the world almost always comes of ignorance, and good intentions may do as much harm as malevolence if they lack understanding. ~*Albert Camus*

Compared to the lushness of Samoa in November, Northeast Iowa stripped itself of leaf and color and exposed its barrenness to the world. Iowa remained that way until the snows of Christmastide came to rescue it from its embarrassment, covering its nakedness with a blanket of white. After the gay abandon of Oktoberfest, the denizens of this lonely corner of the Midwest became, if not sullen, at least sober. So it was with the vast majority of Zwingli students, scions of the solid Scandinavian farmers and co-operative insurance representatives who stocked this self-proclaimed "Little Switzerland of Iowa," so called because it was just barely possible to make a full 15-sec. downhill ski run on perhaps 15% of the best hills in the county. Even Danny and Dick, from faraway Illinois and Massachusetts, were reduced to applying their attention to dull schoolwork by the depressing weather. Even though the boys' drinking and drug use did not slacken off much after their humiliating arrest, their substance abuse became morose and medicinal, in contrast to celebratory - as it was in better, brighter weather.

Danny was getting good grades, but was not a diligent student. He carried on the style of learning he had perfected in 13 years of prior school training, or 12 if you didn't include kindergarten (which was, in all fairness, only a half day). His style consisted of attending all classes, all the time, even - and sometimes, especially - classes in which he was not enrolled. He sat in the front row, he made eye contact, he asked questions, and he participated actively in the discussion. He occasionally read the assigned books, if they were good. What he did not do was take notes - not one, not ever. He did not make a single highlight mark in his textbooks, the ones he bothered to read, and he never studied for tests. He was a well-loved solid B-minus student, well-loved because he was the most animated student in class and set a benchmark for attendance, participation and interest. His teachers loved him. Being loved by one's teachers often means that a teacher will bump the student up a grade or two on an essay question. Danny had known about the subjective "bumping up" from about the fifth grade on, and was pleased to note that it still worked well in college.

Dick, by contrast, studied and took notes and underlined his texts. Danny found all of this odd, as Dick was obviously much smarter than Danny or anyone Danny had ever met. Dick was a straight B student. He wondered if Dick did it just to be a conformist, but soon dismissed that thought as ridiculous. Dick could not possibly be a conformist. And since Danny knew that it was inappropriate to ask Dick stupid questions, the reasons for Dick's odd study behavior remained a mystery.

Danny excelled in religion classes. He found them fascinating, no matter what religion or branch of religion was on the curriculum. They were like philosophy classes, except they did not require you to think in a linear fashion. Religion was like philosophy for woolly thinkers, as it were. And Danny was one of the Zwingli student body's best woolly thinkers.

Danny raised his hand boldly, put on a serious face, and asked, "Dr. Robins, I believe that Calvin's doctrine of pre-destination was presaged by some passages I read recently in some of the Gnostic texts you assigned, if I'm not mistaken."

Dr. Robins smiled warmly and answered, "Indeed, Mr. Harper, you aren't mistaken, and that is, in fact, the next point I wish to make in my lecture today. Good work, Harper."

Danny also found delight in drama classes because the Drama Department offerings were, in much the same way as the classes offered by the Religion Department, dependent on the mastery of woolly thinking and make-believe. Danny's drama professors, however, were not equally delighted with Danny. His drama professors correctly suspected that his ingratiating classroom behavior was just cheap acting, whereas Danny's religion professors were more predisposed to believe in Danny's sincerity. Belief was the *lingua franca* of their study area, after all.

Danny raised his hand boldly, put on a serious face, and asked, "Dr. Svanoe, do you think that if someone just pretended to be using the Stanislavsky method, anyone in the audience could tell the difference?"

Dr. Svanoe, keeping his face neutral, his tone level and his eyes fixed on a spot 35 degrees to Danny's starboard side to indicate he did not even hear Danny, said, "Next question ... Yes, Miss Dewdney, you have a question?"

Danny's "real" major, at least in his mind, was sociology: the study of group behavior. Danny's study of the college calendar led him to believe that the faculty of the Sociology Department was, as a group, probably similarly inclined to substance abuse. Danny noticed gleefully that every class, seminar and lecture held by this department, for all four years of study, was scheduled after 1:20 p.m. Danny was not the darling of this department, either. Not because the professors were skeptical of his sincerity like the drama profs, nor because Danny behaved with any less enthusiasm in their classes, but because even at 1:20 in the afternoon and later, the professors of sociology, as a group, were still suffering the ill effects of overindulging in liquid substances the night before. They could not fully appreciate Danny's brown-nosing.

Danny raised his hand boldly, put on a serious face, and asked, "Dr. Nordstromm, in the experiment with the wallet, do you think that adding that last variable could have invalidated the whole study? And further, do you believe that perhaps the very premise of the entire study could therefore be questioned on the basis of observer bias?"

Dr. Nordstromm replied, "Would you care to repeat that in English, whatever your name is in the front row? Ah, forget it, class is almost over. We'll discuss it next week, okay?"

Danny saw Nordstromm leaving the classroom and stopping at the water fountain to throw back three white pills and suck back about 45 long seconds of cold water to wash them down. Nordstromm stood up from the drinking fountain, lit a cigarette, wandered on down the hall to his office and slammed the door behind him. Danny took Nordstromm's place at the water fountain and fired three aspirins into his own mouth, stood up, lit a cigarette and wandered off to his dorm room for a nap.

CHAPTER FOURTEEN

The welfare of the people in particular has always been the alibi of tyrants. ~Albert Camus

"To every thing there is a season, and a time to every purpose under the heaven." And so it came to pass that the first semester at Zwingli ended and Christmastide began. Danny hitched a ride to La Crosse, Wisconsin, and took the Milwaukee Road to Dixon, Illinois, where his father picked him up at the ancient passenger depot. Danny had celebrated his liberation from the rigors of academe by drinking whiskey sours in the bar car of the train, until he passed out and had to be shaken awake by the conductor to get off at his stop in Dixon. Danny's father said nothing, and drove Danny home in silence.

Upon his arrival at home, Danny's mother *did* take offense at both his condition and demeanor, and had no compunction about sharing her extreme disappointment. "Your father and I work ourselves to the bone to pay the tuition to send you to that college you wanted to go to so much, and you send me letters scoffing at my religion and telling me how stupid I am, and then you show up drunk your first day at home in filthy clothes with greasy hair and the same bad attitude you've had since that sexpot English teacher of yours started to fill your head full of shit about how you're some kind of artist or genius or something. You should get down on your knees and thank the Good Lord that you have parents who love you even though you treat them like dirt. What do you have to say for yourself?"

"I don't write anymore."

"What in hell does that have to do with the price of eggs in China?"

"You accused me of being a writer. I don't write anymore."

"I saw your grades, too. Apparently you don't study anymore, either. You got A's in high school and now you barely get B's. Are you taking that marijuana or just drinking yourself stupid? Don't think I don't know about you and that 'Nick' person ..."

"His name is Dick, not Nick," Danny interjected.

"... that Nick person getting arrested for drinking

"That was an illegal arrest and an illegal conviction. I could get it overturned on appeal."

"Bullshit. If the cops arrest you, you're guilty. Don't lie to me and tell me you weren't drunk. And you'd better not get one of those college girls pregnant. I won't be supporting some little bastard you leave lying around in Iowa. There's a hell of a lot of work to do around here that your father can't do because of his hernia, and I expect you up and at 'em every day. You can start by cleaning the basement. There's still a mess down there that you and your friends made in the summer. I'm not going to clean it up, and your father is in no condition to do it."

Danny needed a nap and another drink, and he wanted to take some of that marijuana stuff, too. "I need a nap. I was up late last night studying."

"They must teach you to lie to your mother at that 'Christian' school. Huh? Some Christians! Some school! I think they're a bunch of heathen devil worshippers and drug pushers out there. Go and look at yourself in the mirror. That's not the boy I sent off to college. Your clothes are as filthy as your mind always is. You need a bath, and you're going to get your hair cut first thing tomorrow."

"Okay. Can I have a nap now?"

"Get out of my sight until you sober up and clean up and get a haircut."

Danny slumped out of the kitchen like a dog that had been kicked. He muttered to himself as he left the kitchen, answering again the only charge he could think of answering, "I really don't write anymore, so what's the big deal?"

Danny had a nap.

At 5:30 p.m. sharp, he ate a silent supper with his parents. Dinnertime was truce time. Danny and his father commented favorably on the meal and smiled. The woman of the house did not smile.

After supper, Danny retreated to the basement with his father. He sat and watched in silence as his father sat in silence at his workbench and used his handmade carving tools to hand-carve some bird decoys out of white pine. These silent times with his father had a soothing effect on Danny. His father spoke to him with his silences, and with the work that came from his hands. His birds were works of quiet grace and elegance, with not a hint of crudeness or haste in their design or execution. Once in a while, his father would tap out Bull Durham tobacco from a white cotton pouch into an un-gummed Bull Durham cigarette paper, lick it shut and light it up. He did all this with one hand.

"Danny, you know why cowboys learned to roll a smoke with one hand?"

Danny had known the answer to this question since he was five years old. This was not the first time he had seen his father roll a one-handed smoke and then ask the same question, but he dutifully asked his father, "Why's that?"

"So they could hold the reins with the other hand and keep riding."

Danny loved his father. Danny loved cowboys.

As soon as it was late enough to politely ask his father for the car to head out to the bars, Danny did so.

CHAPTER FIFTEEN

War is mainly a catalogue of blunders. ~ Winston Churchil

Danny entered Mickey's Front Street Bar, filled with a real sense of the joy of the season. His father had silently touched a tender cord in him, and the tacky Christmas decorations in the bar brought home all the nostalgia of his little-boy Christmases, with the electric train under the tree and all the magical and mysterious presents inside the rail yard. Danny was home. And this night he felt "Home" with a capital "H" because he was known here. In high school, he had been temporarily slightly famous for his starring roles in school plays and summer stock theater. All his kin, living and dead, was here in this town. All of his personal history was here. Danny's grandfather used to own a working-man's bar on this same block 50 years ago. Danny felt more secure than he had for a long time.

He had come to this riverfront street, the most historic street in town, hoping to see someone he knew in here and perhaps even someone he liked, or perhaps even a girl who would like him. Danny had bathed and shaved and was wearing a tie and a new sweater. He was a handsome young man but had no awareness of just how handsome he was. Danny had even shined his shoes. To complete the look, he was wearing a pair of plano lens glasses from the Drama Department to make himself seem more the intellectual college type.

Danny saw a boy named Willie. Willie got better grades than Danny in high school but chose not to accept the scholarships he was offered to some dumpy state schools. He had chosen instead to help run his dad's scrapyard. Danny admired him for his brave working-class anti-intellectual stance, but he didn't really have all that much in common with him, so he avoided making eye contact.

Danny saw another former classmate named Gerry, who was now married and the manager of the same tire store where he had worked part time in high school. His acne had cleared up nicely, but Danny avoided speaking to him as well.

Danny sat down at the bar and ordered a Michelob. "In a glass, please." The guy next to Danny turned at the sound of his voice and said "Hey, Danny!"

It was Tommy, the best friend of one of Danny's high-school friends. He was a year ahead of Danny.

"Hi, Tommy!" Danny thrust out his hand to give Tommy's a shake. Tommy offered up an empty sleeve for Danny to shake with an expert flip of his shoulder - and a big laugh.

"Fuck, man, what happened to you? Is this a joke? Where's your arm?" Danny was confused.

"I left it back in Nam. I got sick of college and never made first string on the basketball team, so I quit. I joined the Army. I made 2nd lieutenant and lived through two weeks 'in country' until some kind of bomb came through the door of my hooch and kind of evaporated my arm."

"Commie fuckers …" Danny said, not knowing what else to say to a one-armed veteran.

"Nah, not commies. It was one of the pissed-off brothas in my platoon who threw it in, but who knows? The Army calls it an 'unexplained wounding.'"

Tommy said all this without any anger that Danny could detect. Danny thought Tommy probably had the story memorized because he'd told it so many times, in so many bars.

Tommy went on to explain, "It seemed obvious to me who did it since they threw in a flashbang grenade the night before and a smoke grenade three days before that. I guess when I didn't choke from the first grenade they threw in, or go deaf from the flashbang grenade, the spooks thought it was time for more serious measures, so they threw in a frag grenade. Just another 'unexplained' or 'accidental' wounding to the Army ..."

"Fuck, Tommy, your own guys did it, huh?"

"Hey, it's not the end of the world. I got a bunch of money from the Army, probably to shut me up, and I'm going back to school. Life is good. I'm still alive, and I'm back in the world for good. I just can't get used to jerkin' off with my left hand. It still feels like a stranger is choking the ol' bishop, and I can't roll a joint for shit."

Danny thought he should introduce Tommy to his father, who could teach him to roll with only one hand.

Tommy continued, "If you roll one for me, we could go outside and fire it up."

"Roll it here, right on the bar? This is the Bible Belt, remember, not San Francisco. Don't they lock you up for seven years around here for one stupid joint?"

"Fuck, no. Nobody cares anymore, not even here. You haven't been around for awhile, I guess. Go roll it in the john, if you're chicken. Just bring back my bag and papers, and don't run out the back. I can still pound the piss out of you one-handed." Tommy shook his remaining fist in the air.

Danny rolled a joint with Tommy's fixins on the toilet tank in one of the stalls. They retired to the privacy of Danny's dad's car to smoke it. Danny just couldn't believe this guy. No hate, no resentment, just an all-encompassing gratitude to be "back in the world" and not in Nam. Danny thought it was unbelievable and said so.

"Yer fuckin' unbelievable."

Danny pushed Tommy a little.

"C'mon Tommy, what was it really like over there?"

"Well, imagine hell. Add some heat and humidity and bugs, and that's about it."

"Fuck off, you rehearsed that. What was it really like?"

"Okay. But the arm I don't have starts to hurt every time somebody asks me this shit."

"The dope should be helping soothe your arm by now."

"Yeah, really. Fuck, I was scared all the time. I was as scared as I've ever been, and it never stopped for a minute. I dreamed scared shit at night, even. Everything scared me, not just the gooks. I was scared to give orders. I was scared when I got orders. I was scared when I took a shit; I thought some fuckin' spider or snake was gonna bite me in the balls when I squatted down. I was scared of the brothers with guns who just looked me right in the eye, all quiet-like, when I gave an order and then didn't do what I ordered. I never knew whether they were going to shoot me in the back or in the front, but I knew they were gonna shoot me. I never even saw the fuckin' enemy the whole two weeks I was there. We got shot at a few times, but only a few rounds, and then the slope-head fuckers just disappeared. Nothing made any sense. I saw some bodies being hauled back to camp from some other outfit, and they were all blown to hell with guts hanging out and shit like that. One of 'em didn't have a head. I never saw anyone get killed in my platoon; I wasn't there long enough, I guess. Fuck, two weeks in country and the fuckers just blew me up with a frag grenade. I'm no philosopher, but I might take some philosophy courses when I start school again. Maybe, if I took some philosophy, I'd understand why the hell we were there, anyway. Vietnam is such a fuckin' dirt poor fucked-up place and exactly halfway around the world from us, and those fuckin' gooks were just trying to get us out of their country - same as we would if they invaded us, which they could never do, unless they taught those fuckin' water buffalos of theirs to swim across the Pacific."

Tommy stopped to take a breath and went on, "It's fucked up, Danny. Fucked up. Don't let 'em get your ass over there."

Danny couldn't handle any more and said, "Let's go across the street to the Sidecar and see if we can find some women."

The Sidecar consisted of two train cars linked together to make one bar. It was one of the many new trendy bars and eateries that had sprung up on this historic riverfront street, where his grandfather once served up shots and beers to roughly dressed men who worked in the zinc plants and on the towboats.

As the three-armed twosome entered the Sidecar, Tommy immediately saw a woman he recognized. He hustled over to her. He merrily flapped his sleeve in a farewell salute to Danny and said, "See you later, Danny boy. I have business to attend to." Danny saw him kiss the woman, hard too, right there in the bar. Danny knew he was not going to see any more of Tommy that night.

So he sat down and looked around, but saw no one he knew. He ordered a whiskey sour because that seemed more elegantly mature than a beer. He was nursing the drink, still feeling warm and good about being home, when he heard a voice behind him.

"Are you still as stuck up as ever?" Danny turned to see Marion Torrison. Danny and his friends used to call her M.T., as in "empty," back in the township high school.

"I saw you come in with that warmonger prick Tommy and almost decided not to say hello."

"Warmonger prick? He's just the same old Tommy, minus an arm. Have you talked to him? He hates the war more than you do, I'll bet."

"No, and I'm not going to talk to him, either. And I might not talk to you, if you have the same know-it-all attitude you always had."

Marion T. was not the most beautiful girl in school or the best built or the smartest, and she hated everyone who was even slightly better in any of those departments. She was a doctor's daughter and had an attitude problem. Her attitude apparently didn't improve with drinking. But a little while at a good Eastern college and some broader experience in the world had brought out a certain slutty magnetism in her, coupled with her apparent discovery of the magic of the push-up brassiere. Danny always had a hard time resisting the slutty magnetism of a woman in a good foundation garment, so he tolerated her intolerance of poor Tommy with the hope, not too far in the back of his mind, of seducing her before he got too drunk to get it up.

Danny quickly switched identities using the Stanislavsky method, removed his plano glasses slowly, and smiled. He stared into her eyes for just a second too long and said, "Darling, could I buy you dinner? We've never really had a chance to be alone and get to know each other." Cary Grant. Danny was Cary Grant.

As Cary Grant, Danny began an evening filled with intense listening, sincere looks, and a hefty bill for booze.

At dinner, Danny whispered softly, "We're so much alike, I wonder why we never really encountered each other before." Danny's college acting courses were really paying off.

At that, Marion T. touched Danny's hand, and Danny swore he saw her eyes mist up. She confessed, "My father wants me to go to med school, but I want to be a dentist. He won't listen to me at all. I'm just a wreck from arguing with him. Why can't all men be good listeners like you?"

Danny replied, "I just try to really *be* with people when I'm with them. That's the way I live my life and the way I always intend to live it. I'm so glad that we're now a part of each other's lives." Danny had watched a lot of romance movies, in addition to his usual fare of cowboy films, and he knew this is how Cary Grant talked to women when he wanted to get in their good graces or their panties. It seemed to be working.

"Do you want to come to my house tonight? Doctor and the Mrs. are in Florida, and my sisters are never there most of the time. It's kind of creepy being alone in that big barn."

"I understand fully. I feel alone a lot of the time, too." Danny caressed her cheek with his fingertips. He'd seen the fingertip thing in a movie with Clark Gable.

Danny went to her place. They parked their cars in the circular drive and went to the door together. She unlocked the door and let Danny in after her. Then, she stopped a few feet from the door, turned, and gave Danny a look.

Danny approached her and with a deft left hand, reached under her blouse and unfastened her bra. Using his radio announcer voice, he spoke softly and tenderly to her already erect left nipple. "I think dentists are *so* much sexier than doctors."

Marion T. and Danny found they had a lot more in common than they had imagined earlier. They had mutually unbridled lust. When they parted at dawn, they vowed to see each other again - soon and very often - during the college holiday.

Danny truly wanted to see her again. He felt guilty, however, about wanting her, because all the time he had been with Marion T., he had pretended she was Amy.

Danny called her, his guilt overshadowed by desire, the following day. Her little sister answered and said that Marion had flown to

Florida to be with Dr. and the Mrs. Danny was relieved that she was gone. He felt guilty about that, too. There was not much in his limited relationship history with women he did not feel guilty about.

Danny often thought the torch he carried for Amy was the only thing that kept his heart from freezing, and he did not want to lose even the miniscule heat it provided.

CHAPTER SIXTEEN

*So long as the deceit ran along quiet and monotonous, all of us let ourselves be
deceived, abetting it unawares or maybe through cowardice... ~William Faulkner*

T he college gave Danny a surprise on the second day after
he returned to Zwingli, following the Christmas holiday.
The surprise was not a good surprise. The surprise was a
summons from the Dean of Men.

The Dean of Men was ramrod straight, fine-boned and balding.
He decorated his colorless eyes with round, steel-rimmed glasses. He
would have looked superb in an SS uniform. Looking at him, he gave
most people the impression that he knew how good he would look in
something tailored, Nazi and black. His name was Wharton
Dipswitch. Although such a silly name would normally evoke a
chuckle at the very least, it never even evoked a snigger. His name
evoked fear. Zwingli students who dared flaunt the tenants of the
"Christian Code of Conduct," a pledge every student was required to
sign upon entry into the college, feared him the most. Danny was a
flagrant flaunter.

Dean Dipswitch was the first person to whom Danny had ever
applied one of the newer words in his vocabulary, "sardonic" - a word
that could have been invented solely to describe this man's smile,
which was "disdainfully or skeptically humorous: derisively mocking."
Dipswitch's smile could make a cobra cower.

Danny was unceremoniously marched to Dean Dipswitch's austere office after having been plucked from a history class. The plucker was a guy named Quigley, a sad-sack, part-time, janitorially uniformed and un-sworn peace officer, who desultorily patrolled the campus when he was not hiding in the arts building boiler room napping off strong drink.

Quigley escorted Danny into the Dean's office. Quigley scurried out immediately after, shooting Danny a wide-eyed look of fear on his way past. The Dean frightened staff as well as students. He had something on everyone. In that way, he was a democratic frightener.

After a deliberate dramatic pause that seemed to last about an hour, the Dean finally looked up at Danny's slouching form and said with a sardonic smile, "You're skating on thin ice, young man - you and that Dick Webster, from whom you seem to be inseparable. This is a small community and I know everything that goes on here, whether you care to believe that or not. I know about the drugs and the booze and radical ideas and all your other hijinks. They're not funny, so you can wipe that grin off your face."

Danny was not, in fact, physically grinning. Danny was exhibiting an attitudinal grin behind a blank face, a grin which the Dean, in his omniscience, easily recognized and disliked. Danny had been expecting a question before his conviction, but had underestimated the Dean's desire to play cat to Danny's mouse.

"I know about your little arrest out in the county last week for having beer on your breath, and that alone is enough of an excuse for me to kick you out of this institution, right now and on the spot. It's a breach of the Christian Code of Conduct, a signed copy of which I have here in your file." He pointed to a folder about an inch thick, upside down on his otherwise bare desktop. Danny had not, in fact, signed the Code. Well, he had signed it, but not with his own name. He had signed "Jefferson Davis." The Dean missed this little joke. He continued his inquisition, jamming his index finger into the file every so often for emphasis.

The Dean leaned back in his desk chair, widened his already wide sardonic smile, and said with real relish in his voice, "When I throw you out, and report this interruption in the normal progress of your undergraduate academic career to your draft board, your government will put you on a plane to sunny Southeast Asia. Now, we don't want that to happen, do we?" Finally, Danny heard a question, albeit a rhetorical one.

"Uh, no."

"Uh, no, Dean Dipswitch, you mean."

"Uh no, Dean Mean, I mean Dean Dipswitch. No."

The Dean passed over this lapse and said, "You know, Mr. Harper, you don't mean much to us here. You're nothing. You're a nobody from a poor nothing town in Illinois - a town from which we draw no other students, in an area where we have no alumni population. Kicking you out, while it's the right thing to do, wouldn't send a real message to the other students who are on the same path you're on and would save us no great embarrassment later on, when you get arrested for something really bad like selling drugs or burning down a draft induction center. And make no mistake, Mr. Harper; this is the path down which I know you're headed. You're headed for disaster."

Danny sat up straighter in his chair and nodded his head in agreement, thinking the Dean might throw him a life preserver if he looked properly penitent. And the Dean did just that.

"Now, wait, Mr. Harper, before you despair, the person we really want out of here isn't you but your beloved roommate, Dick Webster. We want it to happen sooner rather than later, and we want an airtight case. You're familiar with the fact that his grandfather and his great-grandfather, whose proud surname he bears, were presidents of this institution. His parents graduated from here and his uncle Richard, for whom he was named, is a bishop of our church and is headed for higher office still. Dick Webster has a name, you see, and kicking him out *would* send a loud and clear message to your fellow flagrant flaunters of the Christian Code of Conduct. We want Dick Webster out before he upsets any big apple carts. We need a lot of first-hand evidence to do this quietly, with no protestations from his family. Unlike you, Mr. Harper, Dickie is one of us, and Dickie is a rotten apple.

"Mr. Harper - may I call you Danny? - they say you're smart, and although I have seen no first-hand evidence of it myself, and your grades don't reflect it, I wonder if you see what I'm getting at ... or do I have to spell it out?"

"Uh, maybe you have to spell it out."

"Uh, maybe you have to spell it out, Dean Dipswitch."

"Uh, yeah, that's what I meant to say, Dean Dipswitch."

"See? I knew they were wrong when they told me you were smart. I want you to continue being joined at the hip with Dick, and I want you to discreetly jot down a few contemporaneous notes about the interesting things you two do together. Doesn't that sound like fun?"

After a long pause, the Dean said, "I mean 'fun' compared to a free flight on Air America to sunny Southeast Asia. Think about this, Danny, and come back to see me tomorrow at 9 a.m. sharp. And bring whatever notes about Dick you might've scribbled down. You may go back to class now."

Danny headed straight outside but not to his class. He lit up a joint right under the Dean's second-floor window.

When the 2:10 classes got out, Danny caught sight of Dick in the stream of students pouring out of the main doors of the building. He hurried to join Dick. They walked back to their room and exchanged observations on this and that - things of no real consequence. Danny was wracked with guilt about what he was about to do to Dick. Danny's voice sounded strangely false to his own ear as he chattered away with Dick. Danny kept looking at Dick for some sign that Dick could hear the betrayal in his voice.

In Danny's imagination, he saw himself in Biblical dress, taking thirty pieces of silver from shadowy men in some shadowy place. Danny saw Dick on a cross.

When they got back to the room, the boys fired up another joint and popped open some tall boys of Bud. Dick began to practice his blues harp. This mournful repetitive sound always had a soporific effect on Danny, and Danny fell asleep within minutes of the beginning of the performance.

When Danny woke up, he found Dick asleep on the bottom bunk with his blues harp in his hand. Danny also happened to see a little red notebook on the floor by the bed, where it must have fallen from Dick's shirt pocket. It had fallen open to a page with a date and a name - Danny's name. Craning his neck and not daring to breathe, Danny hung his body over the side of the bunk bed enough to read the rest of the words on the page. What he read was an account of a little misadventure of Danny's two days earlier, whereby Danny had secretly planted two joints on a professor's office desk along with an anonymous cryptic note and a pair of used white cotton panties, in size extra-large.

Danny was shocked and enraged. He fell off the bed as the sheet under him came untucked. Danny yelled as his head hit the floor. Dick jumped up, startled by the crash and yell, and hit his head on the top rail of the bed. Dick yelled in pain. From his contorted position on the floor, Danny shouted, "You were in his office!" Thinking quickly, he added, in a softer tone, as it was a lie to entrap Dick, "Carl said he saw you there, but you didn't tell me." Danny lied to elicit a confession from Dick, a trick Danny's mother often used on him and that every cop uses almost every day.

"You were in Dean Dipswitch's office and didn't tell me and now you're ratting me out in this notebook." Danny grabbed the notebook and shook it in Dick's face.

Dick said rather too calmly, while rubbing his injured noggin, "Hey, calm down. Yeah, I was there, and, yeah, I wrote that one thing down, but I never showed it to Dipswitch. I was supposed to go there this morning and show it to him, but I slept in. I can't really do it now that you know, can I? I wasn't really gonna, anyway."

"What did he say to you, Dick?"

"A lot of shit. He said I was skating on thin ice and so were you, but that I was 'one of them,' whoever 'they' are, and that you were that new kind of student who would bring this college down. He said that you were a nobody and that somebody would have to help him kick you out. He threatened to tell my parents about Corrine. How he found out about that little townie tart, I'll never know. It probably wasn't even my kid, but she just liked me best and said it was mine. Shit."

"Dick, he got me too, just today. I was supposed to rat you out."

"Fuck. Really? You know what that means, don't you?"

Danny didn't know.

Dick went on to explain what it meant. "That means Dipswitch doesn't really have shit on either one of us, unless we write it all down for him. Fuck."

The light came on in Danny's head and he blurted out, "Nice try, huh? I wonder how many other guys he's squeezing. Did you hear what Carl was saying the other night at the bar? His brother-in-law is a part-time cop over in Walkon, and he said that once a month, these two FBI guys drop in for a chat with the chief over there. And do you know where they come from before they go to Walkon? Here. They see the chief in town here. And do you know where they come from before they see the chief here in town? Huh? They come from Dipswitch's office."

"No shit."

"All that shit we're supposed to write for Dipswitch was going to go right to J. Edgar Hoover in Washington."

"Fuck. That's some fucked-up shit. We're supposed to be in a free country, right? We'd better tell those SDS guys about this and the Panthers, and all the other guys we sell dope to. This could get us killed."

"No, Dick, this couldn't get *us* killed. You're medically unfit to serve. It could get *me* killed. Do we still have a good stock of used panties from the last raid?"

"Yeah."

"In size extra-large?"

"I dunno. Maybe."

"I wonder if the Dean locks his car. I wonder if he locks his glove box."

The boys laughed like dirty little hyenas at the dirty little trick they had in mind. Dick and Danny were okay with each other again, but would keep one eye open from now on, for betrayal was in the air. In 1918, U.S. Senator Hiram Warren Johnson purportedly said: "The first casualty when war comes is truth." The lies were filtering down from the top, even into this isolated corner of Iowa, even into the friendship between roommates.

CHAPTER SEVENTEEN

The cry has been that when war is declared, all opposition should be hushed.
A sentiment more unworthy of a free country could hardly be propagated.~William
Ellery Channing

It was the beginning of Danny's second year at Zwingli. So far, Danny was somehow still afloat, treading water in the academic well he had fallen into the year before. He had, thus far, avoided any "interruption in his normal progress toward an undergraduate degree" that would have sent him into the arms of his draft board and, in short order after that, into a rotting jungle full of bugs and bullets. Danny much preferred the climate in Iowa. Danny was pleased that he had an arrest record now. He hoped that might keep him out of the Army, but he wasn't certain.

Danny was standing and looking at the list of returning students at the Year Two registration table. Thor Wilson, Danny's freshman roommate, was not on the list. Danny and Thor had switched rooms after two weeks, anyway, and never hung around with each other. It was no loss. Thor snored at night and farted all day. Danny hated him after two days.

What was of greater note to Danny was that all the hot girls had returned. Danny never actually spoke to any hot girls, nor they to him, but Danny liked to look. Danny was constantly aflame with unrequited lust; the flames constantly having to be manually doused.

These Iowa co-eds were not magnetically drawn to this handsome but unshaven, unshorn, stoned and usually unwashed former poet, who was lost in a miasma of self-indulgent depression. It seemed unfair to Danny that they were unable to see beneath his loser surface to the lovable loser who lay underneath all the dirt.

Danny didn't find celibacy a huge price to pay when balanced against the joys he found in life, which an impartial outside observer would have described as that of a monkish thespian doper and weekend radical, whose best friend was the Buddha. Danny had started hanging out with the political radicals since they shared many of his proclivities, like not washing regularly and swearing a lot in public. Danny didn't share their politics so much as their lifestyle. He went to a few little protests with them, but mostly just for the parties afterwards.

Danny's new role as "monkish thespian doper and weekend radical" didn't require a female lead. It only required the mystical, Zen-like companionship of the all-knowing Dick. Dick hung around with the political types, too, but Danny suspected to his dismay that Dick was actually interested in the politics. Danny wondered if there was something to the political stuff, since Dick was never far wrong about anything. Dick had been to a private school in Vermont and had worn a school uniform and played lacrosse. How could a person with that background be wrong about anything? Danny didn't even know what lacrosse was until he looked it up in a book.

Lost in thought about Dick and lacrosse, Danny was shocked to see a girl he recognized march right up to him in the registration line, bold as brass, and say, "Hi, Danny. I'm glad to see you're back."

She stared right at Danny. Her eyes were owl-like behind very thick glasses. She touched his arm as she said this. She may have been pretty behind the glasses … or not. But she could not, and did not, try to hide her other physical assets. She was majestically endowed.

Danny stared at her chest and spoke rather loudly and slowly, because he couldn't be sure her breasts could hear him through the snowflake and reindeer-patterned Norwegian sweater, white cotton blouse, and industrial-strength foundation garment it must have taken to hold those things up.

"I'm glad you're back, too." Danny couldn't remember her name.

"Are you still as stuck up as ever, Danny? And are you still joined at the hip with that Dick character?"

Girls always accused Danny of being "stuck up" when they bothered to accuse him of anything at all, which was seldom.

"Uh, I'm not stuck up, and he's my roommate - at least, this year he is."

"If you can ever get rid of that dopey Dick Webster for long enough, I brought a tent with me to school this year and a double sleeping bag."

Danny was speechless. Danny mostly didn't go out on dates or hang around with girls because he couldn't understand all the social niceties involved in the process of getting them to go out on a date, much less the even more laborious process of getting them to do the only thing they were good for. College girls frightened him but also offended him slightly. They seemed so vapid after Amy.

His experience with Amy had given him no clue about the rituals of dating before mating. And here was this girl, pretty or not, making a bold invitation to him in broad daylight. Danny was pretty sure this was not one of those dating rituals of which he knew nothing. She was making an end run around dating and getting right to business, just like a guy.

Danny got an erection.

She asked, "Well?" and her eyes grew even bigger behind her owl glasses.

"Uh, yeah, we could go on a woodsie sometime in your tent." Just then remembering her name, he added, with an audible pause for a comma, "Julie." Julie S.

Julie plowed straight ahead with her pitch. "What're you doing tonight, Danny? There aren't any classes tomorrow."

"I gotta find Dick and find out what he's doing."

"Can't you do anything on your own, Danny Harper, or do you intend to bring him along?"

She even knew his last name. What planet did this woman come from? Women didn't act as forward as this in Iowa, even if they did originate in Illinois. Julie was from a Chicago suburb. Danny remembered that his high school had played her high school in some sporting tournament sometime or other, or so she had said in their one and only previous conversation almost a year before.

"Okay, but I still have to find Dick and tell him where I'm going. Do you want me to bring some wine or something?"

"Got it in my backpack, Danny. See you in front of my dorm after supper - 6 sharp."

Danny's erection was holding up well, but he was glad to see her go. A registration line is an uncomfortable place to be standing for a long period bent backwards at the pelvis to hide the old power tool.

He met Julie at 6, 6 sharp, in front of her dorm. Danny hadn't bought any rubbers, because they didn't sell them to minors in Iowa, and the one that had been in Danny's wallet for the past year was probably no good. Danny left it there anyway to produce that cool embossed ring in the leather that said you were a "man of the world" as you whipped out your wallet to pay for a girl's drink. Knowing

Julie's level of preparedness from her pitch in the registration line, Danny figured she would have rubbers in her backpack, too.

Julie looked radiant in her blue jeans, sneakers and another Norwegian sweater, this one with a traditional codfish motif, accented by what appeared to be figures of anxiety-ridden Norwegian Lutheran barley farmers. The backpack straps pushed her bodacious boobs together and up - up, up, up to the farthest heights of that sexual paradise that all bottle-fed boy babies dream about at night when their hands are busy, busy, busy under the covers.

Danny offered to carry her tent and the double sleeping bag, but he didn't offer to carry the backpack. The backpack strap configuration was just too good at emphasizing Julie's appeal. Danny's erection returned in short order. This annoyed Danny, as having a third leg made it a hard walk to Melody Springs Park where they planned to pitch their little canvas love nest.

The campers reached Melody Springs. Danny's erection wore away from banging against his leg. After some initial greedy kissing, his stiffy quickly returned to stay. They got down to work pitching the tent and making their little camp. Pitching the tent took longer than either one of them wanted; they both wanted more greedy kissing.

Danny opened the wine. Danny was impressed to see the wine bottle had a cork. Classy. And Julie had a corkscrew too, in her magical backpack. They drank from real glass-stemmed wine glasses that she had brought as well. In her backpack ... She had some definite ideas about how Danny should seduce her, and, apparently, had all the goods and equipment for him to accomplish this feat.

Danny decided to slow down the determined march to intromission. Danny noticed Julie seemed to react better to a routine that had a certain rhythm: a little talk and a little more wine, and a little more talk and little more wine, with the random kiss thrown in, followed by more talk and more wine. Danny was remembering some of the lessons Amy had taught him about taking it slow and teasing a little.

As Danny followed Amy's rules of engagement with Julie, his mind inevitably turned to Amy herself. Thoughts of Amy were troubling, so troubling that Danny, even though he was at his teenage sexual peak, had been deprived of sex for over a year. Danny conveniently forgot his midnight madness with Marion T. at Christmas. Thoughts of Amy tended to push a lot of other thoughts aside. Booze and dope didn't help Danny's memory, either.

Danny knew success with Julie this evening would be an important milestone on the road to forgetting Amy, and he really wanted to do it right. He wanted to do it right, even more than he just wanted to do it.

Julie talked and talked about her feelings, and talked about her feelings some more, and talked about her feelings until she landed on the topic of her brother, who was flying a B-52 bomber on raids over Cambodia. She said she prayed for her brother every night. Danny had a few drinks and felt he needed to share some of his own feelings. In the course of sharing his feelings, Danny made some clever remark or other, paraphrasing an article he had read in a copy of *The New Republic* he had glanced at in the faculty lounge, about an illegal and immoral air war over Cambodia bombing helpless peasants and water buffalos.

Julie struck at Danny like a maddened mongoose when he recited his newly borrowed political opinions. If Julie was a hot-to-trot co-ed, she was an even hotter-tempered co-ed. "Whose side are you on? I'll bet you want the commies taking over the whole world. You want the commies to shoot down my brother?"

Danny said what all guys say when they stick their feet in their mouths with women. "Aw, hey, come on Julie, I was just kidding."

With tears of rage in her eyes, she said, in a tone borrowed word for word from Danny's mother's phrase book, "You'd better be kidding!"

Danny was quiet for awhile, while his humiliation drained off and his mother's voice faded from his inner ear. Julie let her anger cool, too. Danny kissed Julie lightly. Then they began a session of passionate kissing. Julie said, "I'm getting cold; let's get into the sleeping bag and warm up."

Danny went into the tent and took off all his clothes, except his underwear, and crawled into the sleeping bag.

Julie said, "I'm coming into the tent to get ready for bed. Turn your head and don't watch."

When she came into the sleeping bag, Danny felt that Julie had stripped down to her knickers and a firm pointy bra. Julie's feet were cold - just like Amy's feet. Amy's feet always used to be cold. As if the Amy thoughts weren't bad enough, Danny couldn't help replaying the "mother" tone of voice Julie used to shut him up about the war. "I don't hate her brother," he thought defensively. Danny just heard that the war was bad for a couple of pretty good reasons, and he had begun to believe those reasons. Why couldn't she understand his logic instead of using *that* voice to reprimand him like a little child and make him back down from his principles like a scared dog? Danny felt he had a right to his beliefs, after all, and some woman was not going to muzzle him. Dick said the air war and the whole war, in fact, were wrong, and the fact that her brother was in it didn't automatically make it right. His erection melted, and Danny started to panic. He wanted Dick. He wanted help. He wanted Amy.

"What's wrong, Danny? Don't you like girls, or is it just me you don't like? Huh? Everyone in my dorm says you and Dick are too friendly to just be 'friends.' I stuck up for you because I thought you were cute. You can just get out of my tent right now. Go find your little Dickie because I can't seem to find yours." She took her hand away from the front of his underpants.

"Hey, it's just … I dunno, let me stay a while."

"Nope, you had your chance, and you blew it."

Danny put his clothes on in the dark of the tent. Outside the tent, Danny lit that all-important after-impotence cigarette, and walked back to campus with no interference from an erection. He needed to find Dick before Dick left for downtown to do some serious drinking. He wanted to ask Dick some more about the war, because he was starting to think Dick and Dick's new political friends might be right, especially since some dumb girl like Julie was in favor of it.

Danny still hoped Julie's brother was going to be okay.

CHAPTER EIGHTEEN

In peace, sons bury their fathers; in war, fathers bury their sons. ~Herodotus

D anny missed his father. Danny missed their fall hunting ritual. He and his father had shared this ritual since Danny was nine years old, the year his dad gave him his first rifle. Danny's father taught him how to hunt with that rifle. His father thought the best way to teach him to hunt was to break him in by hunting the wary fox squirrel. Rabbits and pheasants were moving targets and best hunted with a shotgun, but squirrels were stationary targets, hunted most effectively by shooting them in the head with a rifle.

Danny picked up the phone and dialed home. "Hi, Dad. It's me."

"I know my own son's voice. What do you want? You run out of money already?"

"No, I have some left; it's only the beginning of October. I don't usually run out until the end of January."

"They kick you out of school?"

"Nope, not yet ..."

"Your mother tells me you're going to be a preacher? The last I heard, you were an atheist and you wanted to be a cowboy."

"Come on, Dad, I'm not going to be a preacher. I just like studying religion. But anyway, I really, really called because Barry has to drive to Kewanee for some relative's funeral tomorrow, and he can give me a ride almost all the way home. I don't have any do-or-die classes tomorrow and none at all on Friday. If you could pick me up, over in Kewanee, that would be nice. And do you know what else?"

"What?"

"Maybe we could do some hunting. We haven't missed a squirrel season since I was nine and you gave me that single-shot Remington. I can't hunt here. All they have here in Iowa are those stupid tiny gray squirrels - hardly worth cleaning. I wanna hunt some nice fat red squirrels down at the lake place, and maybe you want to hunt, too."

"Nah, I don't hunt much anymore, and your mother probably wants me to put up storm windows this weekend. I don't know. I could pick you up in Kewanee, but I don't know about this hunting."

"Oh, come on. Maybe we could just hunt on Friday morning, and then Friday evening we could come home, and I could help you with the storm windows on Saturday."

"I don't really need any help with the storms, but you come home and we'll see about hunting."

Danny knew what "we'll see" meant when his father said it. It meant "No, but I just don't have the heart to disappoint you right now."

"Actually, Dad, I won't come home unless you hunt with me. I'm not coming home just to put up storm windows. How about that? And I'll tell Mother why I'm not coming home, and you'll be in trouble."

"Yeah, I guess. Your mother misses you, stinky. Call me from Kewanee tomorrow, and we'll go straight down to the lake from there. Which gun do you want?"

"I don't want to use that piece of crap you keep down at the lake. Bring my Anschütz. And bring the Remington 38-grain Yellow Jacket hollow points it likes to shoot."

Ah, the Anschütz. It was Danny's boyhood dream gun that he bought with money from driving a bicycle ice cream wagon for two summers. It had a fancy-grade French walnut stock with a rosewood fore tip, with ivory spacers and similar spacers on the pistol grip cap and the butt plate. It was adorned with basket-weave hand checkering on the grip and fore end, and a special deep-gloss finish. The bluing on the barrel was so deep you could see your reflection. Danny could hit a quarter at 50 yards, four out of five shots. It had a German Zeiss 4-power scope on it that cost as much as the gun itself.

Danny's father thought this overly pretty Teutonic gun was pretentious. He owned solid basic American firearms in working-man's grade. He always gloated that "It isn't the gun that makes the shot, it's the man behind the gun."

Danny met his father in Kewanee the next day and they headed "down to the lake." As requested, his father had Danny's Anschütz rifle in the trunk, along with his own basic pre-WW II Remington Matchmaster with Redfield peep sights. They rode in silence, but then, they always rode in silence. Danny's father's keen and enquiring mind never stopped, but his mouth very seldom gave voice to these musings. Danny knew it was not his place to harass his father into speech, nor did it ever do much good when he tried. Danny's dad was like Dick that way.

Upon arrival at the humble little cabin on the lake, deep in the fall woods of Illinois, the two males carried out their tasks in silence: unloading the car, turning on the propane refrigerator and stove, and checking the beds for mouse nests. Danny's dad snapped open a beer and threw one to Danny.

"Don't tell your mother I corrupted you with a can of beer."

"Shit, I drink more than both of you." Danny knew even as he said it, how wrong it was to say it.

Danny got "that look" from his father that said it was time for him to shut up and stay shut up. They ate a "guy supper" of beans and toast and drank another beer in silence. They turned in early, as the key to squirrel hunting is to get into the nut grove while it's still dark, before the squirrels get out of bed. Then you sit in silence, without moving, until dawn and shoot the squirrels when they become active. The best nut groves were maybe 20 minutes of easy walking from the cabin, so Danny wound and set the alarm on the Westclox Big Ben beside his bed for 5:45 a.m. He fell into a dreamless sleep in the blackness and silence of the woods, the only the sounds being his father's rhythmic breathing in the next room and the mechanical ticking of the alarm clock. Danny was aware that his father's spirit was alive in the clock, because his father worked in the staff and pinion department of the factory that made the clock back in the 1940s. The clock next to Danny's bed probably had staves and pinions from the Brown and Sharpe automatic screw machine his father operated back then.

Morning arrived what seemed like a minute later. The Big Ben chattered insistently but the sound was muffled, as Danny had chosen the "soft" setting on the Westclox alarm. Danny's dad had an instant coffee and a smoke for breakfast, and Danny had a Coke. Thus fueled, they set off for the big hardwood stands, armed and ready to harvest the wily red rodents. Danny let his father pick his ambush spot first. Danny then hurried to a more-difficult-to-get-to spot about 15 minutes away. Danny knew that no one else hunted his area.

About 10 minutes before dawn, Danny heard the first scrambling noises in the crispy leaves. Danny saw movement near a tree, and then another movement in the tree. The target tree was about 25 yards away. Danny remained motionless in his camo while the squirrel disappeared around the backside of the big oak. When the squirrel was out of sight, Danny moved the rifle into a shooting position, using his left knee for a rest. He put the crosshairs of the German scope on a spot on the oak tree just above where the squirrel had disappeared. The squirrel came into view again and froze in place, only a few inches away from the crosshairs. Danny took him cleanly in the head. The squirrel fell to the golden leaf-covered earth with a little thump, dead before he hit the ground.

The supersonic crack from the high-speed, .22-caliber, 38-grain, long-rifle hollow point and the thump of the carcass were enough to silence the woods for five minutes or so, but squirrels, though wary, are attention deficit by nature. They soon began to scramble around again, harvesting and burying acorns for the long winter ahead.

Danny took two more reds, one with a headshot and one a little too far back in the shoulder area. The first of these two, the headshot, was at 30 yards, and the shoulder hit was out at 75 yards. Both were "clean" kills.

Danny sat and waited for a long while and smoked one of the Herbert Tareyton cork-tipped cigarettes he had stolen from his father. What a glorious day it was. It was a pure and crystal-clean October day in Illinois. The sky was clear; there had been a frost in the morning but the sun was heating up the day very quickly. Danny felt he was the king of this perfect old-growth oak grove hidden from the world. There were no bugs. Danny hated bugs. Danny never wanted to leave this little corner of heaven. The feeling of peace that overtook him out here told Danny that he didn't belong in the world of cities and concrete. He belonged, out here instead, where things were simple and primal. All the complicated crap at school and all the ugly political crap infecting his America just seemed so unnecessary when viewed from this hallowed grove.

Danny's pastoral reverie was interrupted by the sound of a small-caliber rifle shot. It was from the right direction and distance to have come from his father. Danny sat some more, because he didn't want to ruin his father's hunt by tromping through the grove scaring game. Danny waited almost an hour; waiting was not a sacrifice, not in this paradisiacal grove. He finally collected his three squirrels and put them in the game pouch of his camo jacket. He walked back toward his father, whistling loudly and tunelessly, to alert his father that he was coming through. Danny was safety conscious with guns. His dad had drilled that into him.

Danny saw his father sitting where he had left him. He was asleep with his rifle across his lap. Danny walked up to him quietly and shook him gently. His father opened his eyes and stated the obvious. "Oh, I must have dozed off."

"Dad, get your squirrel and let's go."

"I missed it."

They walked back in silence.

When they got back, his father said, "You'd better go gut those things right now. It's getting warm."

When dealing with the chronically silent, it's important to understand the messages in the silence. His father never asked how many squirrels he had killed or asked to see them. He never asked where Danny had hit them or at what range. He just went inside the cabin after giving Danny a look that said, "You've disappointed me, again."

Danny knew from "that look" that he had disappointed his father but did not understand how he had done so.

Back home on Saturday, in the late morning, Danny was awakened by the clatter of a ladder outside his bedroom window. His father had started putting up the storm windows. Danny crawled out of bed and rapped on the window to get his attention and shouted, "Wait a minute, I'll help you with those."

His father shouted back, "No, you just sleep. I've been putting up these goddamned things every fall since 1939, and I don't need your help now."

That night, Danny took off after supper to visit all the bars where he thought he was likely to see someone he knew from high school. He didn't see anyone he knew well enough to sit with, so he drank alone. The booze didn't seem to be having much effect on him. The kids in the bars all looked like kids - kids having a good time. They seemed too young, even though they were all Danny's age and older. It made Danny uncomfortable to be a stranger in his own town.

Danny headed home before the bars closed. He crept in the back door and saw a light on in the kitchen. Danny straightened himself up, put on a smile, and prepared for a confrontation, or at least, a lecture about drinking. He saw his father sitting at the kitchen table. The only light was just the dim little one over the sink. His father was sitting there immobile, just staring straight ahead. He didn't register Danny's presence for a long time. Danny saw a mostly empty bottle of Old Thompson blended whiskey by his elbow.

The old man was drunk. It looked to Danny as though his father was drunker than he was. He proved to be far drunker, however, than Danny could imagine. Suddenly, his father lurched, and his arm struck the bottle, and the bottle fell to the floor. The bottle must have been as strong as the stuff inside; it didn't break. His father mumbled, "Fuck."

The old man was a good solid beer drinker on weekends during the day, but he never hit the hard stuff, and he never drank at night. He'd never seemed particularly drunk on his weekend beer. And he'd never said the word "Fuck" before in Danny's hearing. Danny didn't recognize this wreck of a thing at the table. His father couldn't even focus his eyes.

He looked in Danny's general direction and said, "Gotta walk."

Danny, feeling slight contempt, said, "Good luck."

At that remark, his father looked at Danny for a second with murderous eyes. Danny had never seen murder before in his father's normally mild and pleasant eyes.

"Do you want me to walk with you?" Danny said, backing off from his high horse.

"Fuck," the old man said with an inflection that indicated "yes" to Danny.

And so they walked, or Danny walked him, half carrying him like a gut-shot comrade-in-arms. He kept pushing Danny away, but he really couldn't walk upright unassisted. Danny chattered away as they walked, in that singsongy way you use with a dog or a baby or your old senile grandma. Danny didn't know what else to do, so he tried to keep the one-sided conversation light.

"Shut the fuck up. I gotta puke."

With that said, the old man puked. He lifted his head, his task finished, and looked at Danny with one eye open and one closed and said, "You shit." With that, he collapsed on their neighbor Ira Brown's front lawn.

Danny sat down by this comatose figure and was quiet for a long time. He began to stroke his father's thinning hair. He was surprised at how silky soft it was. Danny began to hum a little tune that was no tune. Humming seemed stupid after awhile, so he quit humming and was quiet for a time, looking into the night sky for answers to questions he could not articulate. Danny decided to tell his father everything he felt.

"Do you remember when I was 10 and that carnival came to town, and I was riding my bike around the park and saw it pull in, and hung around long enough for one of the roustabouts to call me over and ask if I wanted a job? And I worked all day helping set up? And they said they'd pay me a quarter an hour? Then when I went back at night to collect my pay, they told me they'd pay me the next morning, and I came home early from the carnival because I didn't really have enough money to go on any good rides, 'cause I never got paid. And you saw me looking all depressed, and asked me what was wrong, and I told you, and you said we'd both go there in the morning and collect.

"And when we got there, no one was awake but this one old guy drinking a grape pop. Do you remember how you made me stay in the car while you asked him for my pay? And this one old guy held up his finger to tell you to wait a minute, and then came back a few minutes later with three more guys who appeared from all different directions, all walking kinda slow with their hands in their pockets and their eyes locked on you. And then I saw you pull your shirt up in the front, real slow-like, and they all stopped like their brakes had seized. And then the one old guy with the grape pop smiles his semi-toothless smile and reaches into his pocket, really carefully, and pulls out some bills and walks over and gives them to you, still smiling, but only with his mouth.

"And then you got back in the car and pulled the big black Colt automatic out of the waistband of your work pants and put it gently under your seat and handed me my $2 pay and said, 'God made men, but Colt made them equal. Never threaten anyone with a gun unless you're willing to kill them, or they'll see the weakness in your eyes ...'"

Danny stopped stroking his father's hair. He looked at the pathetic, balding, puke-stained figure crumpled like a discarded candy wrapper on the neighbor's lawn. "Dad, sometimes I think all I have is weakness in my eyes."

CHAPTER NINETEEN

In modern war there is no such thing as victor and vanquished...There is only
a loser, and the loser is mankind.~U Thant , Burmese UN Secretary General

D anny was barely passing French. Zwingli College
required taking, and passing, two years of a foreign
language to graduate. Danny was too lazy to memorize
grammar and spelling, although his acting skills ensured that every
badly constructed sentence and out-of-place word he recited in class
was perfectly accented. His French teacher, Mademoiselle Odeail
Glasson, was a strikingly beautiful young woman, with a comely form
and an outlandishly large nose that looked as if it had been stolen
from de Gaulle himself. She reminded the class constantly that
although she was a French citizen, she came from Alsace-Lorraine, as
though that would mean anything significant to a kid from Blue Earth,
Minnesota, or Alice, Iowa.

She called Danny aside one day after class. Her purpose was to
warn Danny that he was in danger of failing French. Her eyes were
fixed on Danny's. She smiled warmly after she gave this warning and
seemed to be inviting a comment. Danny misinterpreted the warmth
and hoped she was going to invite him to dinner.

"Well, Monsieur Harper, what do you have to say?"

"*Oui.*"

"Yes to what, M. Harper?"

"Yes to whatever you have in mind," Danny said, with an expression close to a leer.

"M. Harper, what I have in mind is that you spend more time on your lessons, so you don't fail my course. I can be available to help you occasionally after class, if you are truly needing it."

"Oh, okay, I truly need it." Danny grinned a little wider.

"I don't mean I'll help you today. I mean, after you have shown me that you are making an effort by passing the next several pop quizzes."

"Okay, I'll do my best." Danny resolved to pass a few little tests in order to get some alone time with Mlle. Glasson. Danny was still leering, so she gave him a dismissive Gallic shrug and told him he had better get to his next class.

After barely passing the next few French quizzes, Danny stayed after class again the next week to ask for the help Mlle. Glasson had promised him. He began with a plea to her humanity. "Mlle. Glasson, I do need help passing this course. I dropped one course this semester, and if I fail this one, I won't be considered a full-time student who is making progress toward a degree, and I'll get drafted and have to leave school and probably get killed."

Mlle. Glasson looked at Danny with a neutral smile that said she would help Danny, but really didn't want to. She didn't trust Danny.

Mlle. Glasson said in a flat voice, "I'll help you because I don't want you to be killed in a stupid war, but I do not believe that you really need help. I think you are a *renard*. That is a fox, yes?"

She found Danny easy to read. Danny was interested in seducing her, and not very good at hiding it. She was four or so years older than Danny, and French, so not much got past her in the lust department. Danny knew he was going to fail with her and probably fail the course too, but she was so sexy that he stuck to his plan, and pleaded that they should meet a lot, because he needed a lot of help. Danny wanted another Amy in his life, but this one did not seem to understand.

She shrugged and said, "I'll meet you on every Tuesday and every second Thursday after class starting next week."

"Oh, thank you. You saved my life." Then Danny said, slightly out of maliciousness, sensing he had failed in his bid to seduce her, "Hey, you said it was a 'stupid war.' Is that because you French got beat and had to get us Americans to go in to whip the commies for you?"

At that remark, she turned toward Danny and there was real anger in her eyes, but she controlled her voice. She used her "teacher voice" and used it softly. "Sit down, please, M. Harper. I will give you your first lesson." And she did.

"M. Harper, I am not French; it is only because France now claims my village that I am French. I am from Lorraine. My village has changed nationality four times since 1871. I have no love for the nation of France or for the nation of Germany. I love my village and my family. I do not speak to you as a 'French' person when I say your war is stupid. I speak to you as one who hates all war. My village has been much hurt by soldiers marching in and out of it for centuries, killing my people every time they come through.

"No, I say your war is stupid because it *is* stupid. My mother's older brother was a *général de brigade* in Vietnam and was wounded there. He's told us about the war. He says that you can't defeat people who are fighting for their own land when they are on their own land."

Danny felt testy and retorted, "Yeah, but we're Americans, and we have the best army stuff, and we're the strongest country in the world. There's no way they can beat us."

She said, now blazing with Latin pique, "You and all of you Americans, no matter how old you are, are just children with a lot of toys. You, Danny, are a child, if you think you know more than my uncle - a general - who has been there."

Danny couldn't let this go. "But we have to be there or the communists will take over that whole part of Asia. We have to beat them."

"M. Harper, everyone in my family, including my uncle *le général*, is a communist. What is your point in talking like this?"

Danny was nearly speechless. "You're a communist?" Danny was from Illinois and had never met a real communist before. And just minutes before he had wanted to fuck her ...

All Danny could say was, "Wow!"

"Yes. I mean, I am telling you we sometimes vote for the communists when they promise to let our region be more independent, and promise to pay us more for the things we grow on our farm. Voting for the communist party is a way to make the French mad at us."

"But the communists over there in Vietnam are bad communists who are going to enslave the whole country. Americans are good guys who are going to give the country freedom." Danny knew all the anti-war arguments, but had not quite taken them to heart. After all, he had won an American Legion prize for patriotic writing in high school.

"*Ferme ta gueule, monsieur.* I'm sorry; you are talking like such a child that I get angry. The communists 'over there,' as you call it, are just trying to help the farmers in their country, too, and to make the French mad, and now to make you Americans mad. What is so bad about communism? What if you Americans give them their 'freedom,' as you call it, and they have an election, and they elect the communist people? Then what are you Americans going to do - go back and kill them all because they don't want your 'freedom?'"

Danny was not used to getting out-argued, but he had no reply for this, maybe because he was still smarting from being called a child. He couldn't think straight when he was mad. Danny could only manage to say, "I don't think I really need any help after school." Danny could not bear the humiliation of being in her presence after she had seen through him and out-argued him. Danny had been caught being a fox, and he hastily recited, his mind somewhere else now entirely, "I'm sorry I bothered you, Mlle. Glasson. I think I'll be alright if I just study more by myself."

She briskly agreed. "Je pense que *oui* aussi, M. Harper. *Au revoir.*"

Danny felt trapped in this classroom, and close to panic. Danny saw the walls caving in to crush him. He had underestimated how close and how powerful Amy still was. Danny saw Amy appear like a Japanese movie monster from beneath the sticky callow film of lust he had projected onto Mlle. Glasson. He knew the Amy monster was about to destroy the building. Danny ran from the monster and out of the building and across the lawn of the common, and just kept running. He forgot to take the books he had rested on Mlle. Glasson's desk.

CHAPTER TWENTY

All war represents a failure of diplomacy. ~ Tony Benn

A t the end of Year Two, Danny secured one of the coveted announcer spots on the campus radio station. He took, and passed, his Federal Communications Commission Third Class Radiotelegraph Operators License exam and also passed the station's own announcer course, run by Straight Stan, the chief announcer. Danny loved the radio world. Talking on the radio was, to Danny's imagination, a performance, performed one-on-one with the listener. Doing radio was somehow also an intimate act. Danny was hungry for intimacy. Danny's only intimate act was being with Dick, doing whatever Dick wanted to do, but Dick, sadly, was not aware of Danny's need for intimacy. Danny didn't expect him to be. Dick was above having petty personal needs. The Buddha ...

Danny loved doing every kind of radio show, and he did them all. He did jazz shows in a low, smoky, mumbling voice. He did request shows in an upbeat, higher pitched, "I'm-your-best-buddy" voice. He did classical shows with a mid-Atlantic accent - that indefinable accent that is not quite British Royal Family but still has enough plummy tones and perfect diction to differentiate it from anything remotely American. He did rock shows and went wild in a cracky-whacky voice, like his favorite DJ, Dick Biondi, from WLS in Chicago.

Danny's radio station was full of "characters," as was any venue anywhere full of performers. Danny was not considered particularly odd, which illustrated on which part of the oddity curve the staff rested. While oddity was tolerated within the station, the listening community outside was soon tested for its tolerance of what this band of media mutts broadcast over the public airwaves.

The pounding on Danny's door didn't stop until Danny extricated himself from the tangle of covers on his bunk and opened the door. Danny was napping, having ingested a goodly amount of booze and dope the night before. The pounding people were Straight Stan and Billie O, of the *Billie O Show*, the jumpiest rock jock from the station. Although the pair were using their radio voices, which they always did to let everyone know they were local celebrities, Danny - still in his naptime fog - could only decipher the word "emergency" in their jumbled yelling outside his door. They were both shouting at the same time and talking very quickly.

After Danny unlocked his door, his two stationmates rushed in, ignoring Danny. They switched on Danny's RCA RFG320 transistor radio and turned it up LOUD, making the little speaker buzz excitedly. During the day, Danny tuned his radio to the station that he worked for. As well as being his favorite station, it was the only station that anyone could receive here in the wilds of Northeast Iowa during the daytime. In the middle of the night, however, a listener could tune in such great 50,000-watt clear channel AM stations as WLS in Chicago, KAAY in Little Rock, Arkansas, CKLW in Windsor, Canada and WWVA in Wheeling, West Virginia.

Hearing the word "emergency" cued Danny into thinking that, surely, this was the day all emergency responders had trained for and feared: the day the Emergency Broadcast System, in which his station was a key link, announced that the Soviets had finally gotten tired of the Cold War and were opting to start a hot one. Danny had been practicing "duck and cover" since he was five. The grammar schools taught Danny and his peers to hide under their desks in case of nuclear attack. Later, in high school, they taught students to run to the inner hallway, sit down, and bend over with their heads between their knees - presumably to kiss their asses goodbye.

What Danny heard on the little overloaded RCA speaker, instead of the dreaded emergency announcement about the end of the world, was a semi-coherent but nicely modulated female voice ranting and railing about this and that: how the curfew in the girls' dorm was a product of the same system that was sending poor black boys to Vietnam as cannon fodder, and why couldn't attractive clothing be produced in larger sizes, and why did candy bars go up a nickel in price when workers' wages in cocoa-producing countries were being cut by greedy landowners … There were a lot of pauses and groans and false starts to the rants, and some raves were gibberish, making no sense at all. The rants and raves and gibberish were being broadcast at top volume into the Northeast Iowan ether with 5,000 watts of pure AM power.

Danny recognized that voice immediately. It was the senior announcer, Bobbi - "his Bobbi." Bobbi and Danny were in love, well, not in *that* way, since she was well over 300 lb. and homely as sin and bad-tempered. Danny liked 'em pretty and somewhat smaller, but he loved her nonetheless, after a fashion. Somehow they knew their souls were one, or possibly one and a half since Bobbi was so big.

Billie O, of the *Billie O Show*, piped up and said, "She just got done playing that filthy *Howl* poem - Allen Ginsberg's seminal but highly obscene masterwork."

Straight Stan said, "We're going to get our license lifted by the FCC when they get complaints." He didn't say "if" they got complaints. The station executives would also be hung without a trial, if the town had its way.

Danny ventured to comment, "What do you want me to do about it? Why don't you two just go in and haul her out?" Danny quickly realized his folly in telling these two radio wimps to haul a 300-plus-lb., obviously drug crazed, bad-tempered Bobbi out of anywhere. Bobbi had a habit of getting physical when she lost an argument. People had learned the hard way to let her win. It was clearly a job for Daniel No-Middle-Initial Harper, Bobbi's closest and only friend, or for Superman.

Danny looked at them, and they read his thoughts about what wimps they were, and Straight Stan said, "No, it's not that we're afraid of her. It's that she has the blast doors jammed and is on standby generator, and we can't find the keys to the transmitter house to shut her off down there, either. We're screwed. We have to negotiate. We've picked you to do it."

"Doesn't Uncle B. have the keys to the transmitter shack? He's the chief engineer and must have the keys to everything on that 3-lb. steel ring of his," Danny offered.

"Yeah, but he's a hundred miles up in Minnesota helping a PBS station with some transmitter problems," said Billie O, of the *Billie O Show*.

The station was screwed. The federal government had contributed an obscene amount of money to the building of this new radio station, having determined that this part of Iowa and its critical cow and corn production was a priority Soviet nuclear target and needed a blast-hardened Emergency Broadcast Station. The station was dug into a hillside and had three solid steel, scientifically staggered blast doors in its hardened reinforced concrete walls. It had a diesel generator with three weeks of fuel, a secure filtered air system, and a month's supply of food and water that had to be rotated on a strict schedule and the rotation logged in the big Emergency Broadcast System logbook.

Bobbi was high on something, or probably several drugs at once. She was babbling the station's broadcast license away. She could hold out for a month, at least, or until Uncle B. got back with the keys to the big steel door on the transmitter shack and could shut her voice down from there. Billie O, of the *Billie O Show*, suggested they might be able to call in an air strike of F-105D Thunderchiefs from the Air National Guard base in Rochester to take down the transmitter tower, "if we could convince them Bobbi was a Soviet agent." Five minutes of listening to her leftist ravings would certainly convince anyone in the Air National Guard that she was a commie agent, but calling in the jets would take too long to save the license.

Straight Stan asked, "Why don't you talk to her, Danny? She listens to you."

"Since when?"

Billie O, of the *Billie O Show*, pleaded, "Call her on the station's private line, and get her to let you in. Tell her you'll bring her a pizza and some beer."

Danny could see the wisdom of the pizza, but not the beer. This woman couldn't get drunk on beer, so Danny suggested a few jugs of wine, at least, or preferably vodka.

Straight Stan said in his voice of command, "Done. We'll have the pizza delivered, and I know someone who'll buy us the vodka. How much do you want?"

"Three quarts should do."

Straight Stan said, "Good. Her methods are unsound, Harper. I want you to go in there and terminate her show."

Danny asked, "Sir?"

Billie O, of the *Billie O Show*, added gravely, after having made eye contact with and received a nod of approval from Straight Stan, "Terminate her broadcast with extreme prejudice."

Danny was not happy with this assignment, but felt relieved. Finally, he had a mission. Danny knew he needed to get her down off the acid or mescaline or psilocybin or speed or whatever shit was fueling her rampage. Three quarts of vodka would be a good start. Danny also had three tabs of Phenobarbital he had stolen from his mother, who got them from her stupid doctor, who told her they would cure her menopause. Danny had been saving them for an emergency, and this certainly qualified as one.

Danny phoned the station's private number. "Bobbi, honey, I love your new show. If you let me in, I could help with the engineering, and maybe bring some pizza and drinkee-poos with me, too."

"Fuck you, you worthless sack of shit. I might die in here, but I'm going to tell it like it is first."

"Great, Bobbi. I'd be willing to die with you. We belong together - even in death. You know that, don't you, Bobbi honey?"

This shut her up. In fact, she hung up. She started playing some Motown tracks that sounded pretty good to Danny's discerning ear for soul. Maybe she was coming down all by herself.

After Smokey Robinson's *Tracks of My Tears* had finished playing, Bobbi proved Danny's guess wrong about her coming down. She was still highly out of control. She put on more Ginsberg poetry, *Kaddish* this time - an epic poem "written in one one-stop 40-hour marathon session fueled by Dexedrine, LSD and coffee." Danny knew this was a recording of Ginsberg's reading at Brandeis University, and that this recording of the poem was 63 minutes and 49 seconds long, and not terribly, terribly obscene, but still too obscene for Iowa. Danny knew he had some time to talk his way in and wrest control of the station from his sweet Bobbi.

On the phone again, Danny asked, "Bobbi, what do you want on your pizza?"

Danny knew he had her attention, at least for now, when she said, "Pepperoni, extra cheese, black olives, green olives, Italian sausage, bacon, ham, pineapple, green peppers, hot peppers, pickled peppers, mushrooms, ground beef, and did I already say extra cheese?"

She let Danny in half an hour later, when he kicked at the outer blast door and screamed "Pizza!" She let him in quickly and then jammed all three doors shut behind them with steel rods. Danny was trapped inside with a very big, very crazy woman.

Kaddish had run its course, so she let Danny put on the Geno Washington & The Ram Jam Band's album, *Hand Clappin' Foot Stompin' Funky-Butt ... Live!* - one of Danny's personal favorites, actually, but one which brought angry calls from the townies about that "jigaboo noise" every time Danny played it. Rowdy black British funk bands didn't have a large following in this part of Iowa. Danny didn't care; he was going to let Bobbi take the blame for playing this one, too.

"Hey, Bobbi, you want to put some spin on that high of yours before we eat? I have some far-out pills here - two for you and one for me. I know how to treat a lady. And I have some vodka to wash 'em down." Danny put a pill in his mouth but held it in his cheek and made a gulping sound, and Bobbi made the same sound, but for sure her pills got down her pipe, because she chased them with a quarter quart of vodka, all in one go. Danny grabbed the bottle and faked a big swig, sticking his tongue in the hole to stop most of the flow. Bobbi never noticed, because her eyes were rolling around, following the motion of things that were not moving, and possibly not even there.

They ate the pizza, and slugged back vodka, and put on another soul album and then another one, and even danced a little. Well, they both danced and were in the same room, but didn't touch. They were not in *that* kind of love.

Bobbi's dancing slowed a little as she and Danny were on their third soul album. She quit dancing and walked toward Danny quietly and even got one of her eyes to focus, just on him. "I knew you would sell me out to the pigs. All I wanted to do was dance with you." And she slapped Danny so hard he saw stars. He closed his eyes to protect himself, so he didn't see the fist coming right behind the slap. Danny fell down hard, flat on his back, on the floor of Control Room #2. Danny saw Bobbi as a large shadow looming over him, teetering slowly back and forth like a big tree about to fall to the woodsman's axe. And she did fall, shaking the bombproof walls in the process and making the record skip. Her shadow fell across Danny, but her body missed his by inches.

Uncrushed, Danny ran to the turntable and quickly put on Wayne Newton's 1966, very locally popular, smash-hit album *Red Roses for a Blue Lady*, thinking that it might begin the healing process with the community and the Federal Communications Commission. He opened the blast doors after some time spent figuring out how Bobbi had jammed them. Danny let in Straight Stan and Billie O, of the *Billie O Show*, and half a dozen other radio staffers who had gathered outside the bunker to see who would come out alive.

Danny was the one who walked out. He had a pair of fat lips that were bleeding down his chin and a bruise beginning to show on his cheek. Danny stank of anchovies, booze and betrayal.

As Wayne Newton sang *Laughing on the Outside (Crying on the Inside)* in the background, Billie O, of the *Billie O Show* said, apparently without a trace of irony, "I'm glad we didn't have to call in an air strike. There would've been a lot of collateral damage and many needless deaths."

Billie O, of the *Billie O Show*, couldn't know that Danny's sanity had suffered collateral damage. Danny had died a little that day too, but not in any air strike. Danny had sold out a woman he loved, and with her, whatever small sense of self-worth he had amassed since Amy had disappeared.

†††
William Wilson Owens; age 24; 12 December 1972; air loss, hostile; Cambodia; Methodist; married; Dayton, OH; Air Force

CHAPTER TWENTY-ONE

Patriotism lies not in blind obedience to authority, but in the desire to search for the truth.~Ramman Kenoun

"Some guy on the phone for you ... Danny, you in?" somebody yelled, while pounding on Danny's dormitory door.

"Keep your shorts on, while I put on mine, okay? Tell him I'll be there in a sec."

Danny ambled into the hall and picked up the poor old battered hall phone. It was Danny's father. Danny was surprised. "Yeah, what? You're in town? Really? What the hell are you doing here? Yes, I know it's a free country, or was. No, tell me you're not at the Shit Pit; how'd you know about that place? I know it doesn't say that on the sign, that's just our name for it. Yeah, I cash a lotta checks there. Oh, right, you get my bank statements. No, I wasn't planning on going there right now. It's only noon. I don't usually get up this early."

Danny looked heavenward for help. Talking to his father – master of the laconic - was weird enough in itself, but talking on the phone was even odder. "Okay, I can meet you there in a few hours. There's a class at 1 that needs me to be there to provide some laughs. I can meet you at the Shit Pit at 2:30."

Danny's father said, "That's okay, I met some guys who know you, and we're having a few drinks. Nice guys ..."

"Yeah, okay, just don't let them borrow any money from you. I have a feeling I know which characters are there at this time of day, and they're all deadbeats. They talk about politics all the time, but all they actually do is drink. And don't leave your smokes on the table when you go to take a piss. They believe in the politics of sharing."

Danny's father replied in a voice tinged with drink, "You just worry about yourself. You go on to class and get here when you can. We're doing fine without you."

"We?" Danny thought. "We're doing fine?"

Danny wandered into Bella's Basement Bar, familiarly known as the Shit Pit, at the approximate time he promised his father, and found him entertaining three of Danny's cronies. Said cronies were raptly lapping up his father's every word, seemingly transfixed by what Danny would discover to be his father's "working-class hero act." Danny had only heard this "act" once before, and then only a small part, and it had also been when his father was drinking. His normally silent father was spinning yarns Danny had never heard before about the Dirty Thirties, and his father's dream of a Great Proletarian Agrarian/Industrial Revolution. He orated on the theme of his union organizing work, busting the heads of scabs in the Great Uprising of '34. He segued from that to detailing the physical hardships of working in Roosevelt's Civilian Conservation Corps in Southern Illinois and Northern Kentucky, building roads and timber bridges and lodges for state parks while faced with sweltering heat, rattlesnakes, bad food, leaky tents and sadistic old WW I drill sergeants for supervisors. He told the boys in the bar how he and his mates plotted the great proletarian democratic revolution every night in those leaky CCC tents by the light of oil lamps, playing cards and sharing a jug of moonshine they had chipped in to buy from the locals. All the while singing Wobbly songs written by Joe Hill ...

Danny was speechless, observing his father's newfound talent as a raconteur.

Danny observed sourly that his father had so impressed Danny's mates they had been buying *him* beer all afternoon, probably with money they had borrowed from Danny the day before. They never bought Danny beer, not even with Danny's own money.

Sensing he had a hot audience, and fueled by his drugs of choice - draft beer and Herbert Tareyton cork-tipped cigarettes - Danny's father further certified his revolutionary credentials by telling tales of *his* father's labor-organizing adventures. He boasted that Danny's grandfather went from being a soft-coal miner to a United Mine Workers organizer, then a blackballed worker who had to travel across the continent by rail to escape the "black ball" he had been given for trying to organize the mines in Illinois. Grandfather landed a job in New Mexico's fledgling frontier silver mines, and sent his pay back home by mail to support his growing family. His letters were filled with the rousing language of solidarity, and he asked his wife to share them with his former co-workers in Illinois - now underground but still trying vainly to organize against the bosses.

This heretofore never-witnessed chatterbox of a father bragged on into the late afternoon, broadening his topics to include his three-month stay, alone, on an island in the Illinois River before he was 15, and riding the boxcars through the hobo jungles of Depression America when he was 16, and his intimate but platonic affair at 17 with his proper Victorian-holdover spinster English teacher, who thought of Danny's father as a latter-day Natty Bumppo, who had grown up with Indians and was therefore knowledgeable about all manner of forest lore. "One shot, one kill" was his motto.

"Natty Bumppo indeed!" thought Danny. "Poet, dreamer, hermit, warrior and man of socialist principles!" Danny's head reeled at these thoughts.

Danny's beer-swilling compatriots didn't know by late afternoon where James Fenimore Cooper and Leon Trotsky began, and Danny's father left off. Danny was embarrassed at his father's seemingly naked pandering to every romantic notion a politically awakening white middle-class Midwestern college kid could have in the late 1960s. Danny tried in vain to shut him up by asking distracting questions about mundane things, like car repairs or the merits of air conditioning. Danny could not distract him for more than a few beats. His father just ignored Danny's attempts to divert him from his oratorical course and plowed on.

Father and son left the bar near dark to get something to eat, and Danny's compatriots hurried off to the school cafeteria before it closed. Once they were alone, Danny's father shut up and became his normal laconic self.

Danny asked him, "Are you becoming a communist now or something? You sure had those guys back in the bar fooled. I always thought you were a Democrat."

When his father finally answered, he did not answer the question Danny had asked. This was more like the father Danny knew. Danny's father just said, "Oh, I had a little disagreement with your mother and thought I'd drive up here to see you. Let her cool off ..."

They ate in near silence until Danny's father said, "I'd better get some sleep. I'm driving back home in the morning." He dropped Danny off at his dorm, and did not go in with Danny. He drove back to his motel. He left the next morning without saying goodbye. Of course, Danny slept until noon and had no phone in the room, so it was not any big deal that his father didn't say goodbye.

Danny had to put up with his political friends worshiping his father for the next week or so, exaggerating his father's beer ramblings into the stuff of myth in the retelling. They began to idolize the "working-class hero" who had graced their table in the bar. This worshipful talk went on each day until someone shot Martin Luther King Jr. and Danny's confreres had something new to talk about. Danny was relieved.

CHAPTER TWENTY-TWO

Terrorism is the war of the poor, and war is the terrorism of the rich.~Sir Peter Ustinov

Marvin had disappeared, and Danny was frantic. Marvin was Danny's third-year roommate. Dick had deserted Danny in the first semester to study abroad in Germany, and Danny was so devastated with the loss of his Dick that he had foolishly marked the "no preference" box on the roommate preference section of his application for residence in the upper-class dorm. Danny foolishly believed he wouldn't care whom he lived with; everyone would be a disappointment after Danny had spent four semesters living with Dick. The college had jumped on Danny's lack of preference and paired Danny with the single most undesirable male student on campus, who, as it turns out, was the only other dorm applicant to mark his box "no preference." Danny was wrong not to care with whom he roomed. Danny was eccentric, but Marvin was black, crazy and, moreover, dangerous.

The liberal colleges, at that time, were all struggling to bring ethnic and geographic diversity to their student bodies. Not to be left behind, Zwingli recruited black students from the inner cities or, at least, the suburbs surrounding the inner cities, the rural South and even from Africa. The Africans Zwingli recruited seemed to major in track and cross-country and did very well, despite their difficulties with English. The college also recruited an Orthodox Jew from New York City complete with kipa, beard and a refusal to answer the hall telephone on Saturday or to eat any normal food in the cafeteria. They also snagged a poor girl in a wheelchair, who was only able to attend classes held on the first floor and was, as a consequence, going to get a very odd major.

Danny was also a product of this diversity campaign, but more subtly chosen. Danny was chosen because he scored shockingly high on the Minnesota Multiphasic Personality Inventory in three principal categories: Depressive Symptoms, Odd Thinking with Social Alienation, and Level of Excitability. The administration was conducting an experiment in social engineering and needed Danny to help balance out the mix of well-adjusted Midwestern farm kids, who had been filling the ranks at this school since the first day it opened over 100 years before. Even though Danny looked like all the other students, perhaps even blonder and more handsome than most, he had purposely been chosen because he did not fit.

Marvin, on the other hand, was from shotgun shack sharecropper Georgia, and was as black as Danny was white. He looked like he did not fit, and he did not. Marvin was perpetually angry and made no effort to conceal it. This accounted for his unpopularity. He was also short and had a bad case of short-man syndrome, in addition to being black. He was a radical, so radical that the other blacks on campus, who were from Africa or the middle-class suburbs, shunned him. Marvin made no effort to conceal his disdain for black people who hated white people one iota less than he did.

Marvin was heavily armed. He carried a gravity knife in an ankle sheath and a bottle of Louisiana Hot Sauce – another weapon of sorts - in his back pocket, and used it to douse all of his cafeteria meals, including breakfast. He kept an M2 .30-caliber folding-stock carbine in full automatic configuration under his mattress, complete with a half-dozen 30-shot clips of ammo. And now he was missing, and so was the gun.

Danny looked everywhere: the classes Marvin was supposed to be attending, the cafeteria, the Student Lounge, and finally the Black Student Union. Marvin normally avoided the BSU, as he though the beret-wearing weekend radicals who hung out there were a bunch of Oreo pansies - black on the outside and white on the inside.

Danny burst through the door of the Black Student Union, shouting, "Marvin is gone! I need some of you bad-ass African gentlemen to help me find him!"

Danny saw two "Black Panthers" lazing on the sofas looking like their killer-cat namesakes. They were watching the talking heads on TV talk their heads off about the King assassination. They looked bored or stoned or both. "Shit, it's Goldilocks. What the fuck you want? Help yourself outta the door unless you got any smokes for me."

Danny replied, "Muhammad, Muhammad, is a 'smoke' all that you think about besides white pussy? I have a real emergency. Marvin has disappeared with his .30-caliber carbine, all his ammo and his hot sauce!"

"Fuck Marvin and fuck you, too. He's not here, and he's not welcome here, and he knows that. What the fuck you want us to do about that crazy nigger? Maybe he gonna off him some crackers with that machine gun a-his. Am I my brother's keeper?"

Marvin was no one's brother, especially not to these brothas. But he was Danny's roommate, and Danny, white as he was, cared.

Danny hadn't always cared for Marvin. He and Danny started off their relationship with surly silence, interspersed with neutral avoidance, and salted with stiff politeness when encounters were unavoidable. This seemed like a fine arrangement, until the first assault on their room. The assaults brought them together in a stubborn alliance against the racist bullies who attacked both of them.

The first assault was only a few days after Marvin and Danny's "arranged marriage of inconvenience" began. The first assault was just shouting and banging on their steel dorm door once the bars had closed for the night. Drunks shouted a litany of "nigger" this and "nigger" that, with a lot of "fucks" thrown in to provide some continuity between the "nigger" parts.

The first assault was on a Friday night - a drinking night. The second assault was the next night, Saturday - a heavier drinking night. Saturday mirrored Friday in intensity, with a few thunderous boot kicks thrown in, in case Marvin and Danny couldn't hear the fist pounding and yelling.

That second night was the first time Danny saw the M2 .30-caliber folding-stock carbine with the 30-shot clip. Marvin pulled it out from under his mattress. Danny, the gun nut, thought, "Wow, I recognize that! It's the rare selective-fire version produced by Inland after 1944." Danny even knew that Inland was a division of General Motors in 1944. Marvin just sat there in bed and pointed it at the door. Danny really wanted to take a closer look at it, but Danny thought it would be more appropriate to ask at another, calmer time.

The attacks went on, not every night but enough nights to make life hell. Later attacks included shit smeared on the door. The attacks progressed to shit being squeezed under the door using plastic bags like cake-decorating accessories. Piss under the door was more frequent than shit, since most of the racist goons had been drinking. One night, one of the harassing idiots wrote the word "n I g E r" on the door with what looked like blood. They topped that the next weekend by hanging an eviscerated chicken on the doorknob.

Marvin and Danny hung together at night, mostly in silence, sitting up in bed. They didn't discuss the attacks in the daylight. Their silences with each other were becoming less surly as time passed and they survived attack after attack. They began to look at each other in a different way. Marvin respected the fact that Danny didn't desert him by asking for another room or roommate. Marvin thought maybe Danny was beginning to understand a little about what it was like to be black. Just a little ...

In Danny's mind, at least, it took one incident outside the Shit Pit at closing time to hammer into his corn-fed head what it was like to be black.

Three big guys backed Danny up against the building. Danny had drunk just enough to get his testosterone boiling. "Shit, what're the three of you gonna try an' do, beat me up? Does it take all three of you to do that, you pussies?" Danny figured that it wouldn't cost him any more pain to insult them than if he just let them beat him, anyway.

The two biggest guys grabbed Danny's arms and held him while Danny tried in vain to kick them, without much result.

The third one, the small mouthy one, approached Danny and got right in his face. "If you try to kick me, all three of us will pound your head until it breaks. So tell me, are you a nigger lover?"

"Fuck you, I just live with one."

"Well, are you a nigger lover or not?"

"Who gives a shit?"

"Just answer the question, fucknuts."

"Yeah, I'm a nigger lover. So what?"

"So this is what we think of nigger lovers." And all three spat in Danny's face. Danny could not wipe it away because his arms were pinned down.

Then they let Danny go, and walked away. To Danny, what they had done was way worse than getting pummeled. It meant they had so much contempt for him that he was not worth the time or effort it would take to beat him up. Danny was shocked and shaken and without a shred of self-respect. Danny had tried to deny being a "nigger lover" twice, but finally admitted it the third time they asked. What was so bad about being a nigger lover that Danny couldn't just admit it and take his beating? Danny thought that Marvin was just a regular guy, and a pretty brave one at that. If this was the kind of shit Marvin had to face every day in Mississippi, then Danny had to admire his restraint at holding his fire as he sat up in bed being called filthy names night after night, pointing the M2 carbine at the door.

Danny returned to his room and needed to talk to Marvin. Marvin was there but didn't even look up when Danny let himself in.

"Marvin can we talk?"

"I ain't got shit to say to you, but you kin talk all you want. What on your mind?"

"They spit on me tonight."

Marvin looked at Danny, and Danny knew Marvin knew the whole story just by looking in his eyes. Marvin said, "So?"

"So, they spit on me."

"And you think that's so bad? You think you bein' treated like a real African now, an' you want a medal for it? Sheeit, honky, you think again; you got a thousand miles to walk before you get to where I be at."

Danny just shut up and hung his head. Danny felt useless. He wasn't a racist anymore and he wasn't a nigger lover. He didn't know what he was. Danny thought, "Maybe I'm just a guy. Maybe Marvin is just a guy, too. We're just guys."

Danny was quiet for awhile. "Marvin, could I handle your carbine? I've always wanted to see it. I'm good with guns."

"You gonna be a bad nigger like me, you better be good with guns." Marvin smiled and nodded in the direction of his mattress.

Today, the second day after Martin Luther King Jr.'s murder, Danny's annoying, paranoid and well-armed roommate had disappeared. No one cared but Danny. Danny looked for him on the TV news of the riots, but the black rioters running through smoky TV nights all looked the same to Danny on the little black-and-white television in the rec lounge.

Marvin turned up a few weeks later, looking gaunter than before and without his .30-caliber carbine or his hot sauce. He now looked on the verge of tears, much more than he looked angry. He quit eating. Some kind of sadness had broken through the wall of anger he had built around himself. He carried this sadness like a millstone around his neck. He never said where he had been, and Danny never asked.

One night, in the darkness of their besieged room, Marvin said, "I can't take this shit no mo'."

"What shit?"

"Any of it, my man, any of it."

After that, he quit talking completely, even to Danny. He didn't return to school the following term. He disappeared, never to reappear anywhere that anyone ever knew.

Danny hoped he had hitched a ride on a tramp steamer to the Union of South Africa. Danny pictured him joining up with the military wing of Nelson Mandela's African National Congress, the Umkhonto we Sizwe, and becoming a deadly secret agent in Mandela's struggle against apartheid - still sad, still silent, but home with his people in Africa. Danny had learned from Marvin that all niggers were not bad. There were good niggers and bad niggers. Danny liked the bad ones.

†††

Marvin Oree Washington; age 28; 10 April 1975; accidental injury; U.S. Disciplinary Barracks, Fort Leavenworth, KS; Muslim; married; Columbus, GA; draftee

CHAPTER TWENTY-THREE

Criticism in a time of war is essential to the maintenance of any kind of democratic government.~Sen. Robert Taft, (R) Ohio

Ozzy the Oddball ran up behind Danny after history class. "There's a teach-in at the U. A lot of us are going. You wanna come?" Ozzy the Oddball was short, nearly totally bald at 20, and a good-natured but angry guy - good-natured because that was his nature, but with a load of anger he had acquired while attending Columbia and taking political science courses from bug-eyed-mad firebrand long-haired Marxist professors, and learning realpolitik on the streets of New York by demonstrating against the war and a dozen or so lesser evils at rallies led mostly by these same professors. Ozzy failed all of his required courses for graduation at NYU, while excelling in the elective political science courses. His grand failure to progress toward a degree was the direct result of his spending too much time at demonstrations, rallies and Stalinist cell meetings. In order to save him, his parents, both moderate Republicans and Zwingli grads, had, in desperation, shipped him off to Iowa to get him away from leftist politics. Instead of getting him out of politics, they had unintentionally loosed Ozzy upon the Zwingli campus like some political Typhoid Mary. Ozzy set about infecting dozens of nice farm kids from the

Midwest with the ideology of the East Coast Jewish Homosexual Trotskyite Conspiracy. "So, do you want to go to the teach-in or not?"

"Don't we get enough teaching right here without driving a hundred miles to get some more?" Danny replied distractedly.

"Oh, shit, you don't know what a teach-in is, do you?" Ozzy said with feigned sadness but sincere superiority.

"Okay, I give - what's a teach-in?"

"It's a big meeting with all kinds of professors of everything, science and philosophy and political science and stuff, talking about Vietnam."

"Like talking about how we can win it?" Danny wasn't concentrating. He was stoned on hash.

"No, asshole, like how we can lose it. We're not supposed to be there," Ozzy the Oddball said in frustration, thoroughly exhausted with the ignorance of kids from Minnesota, Wisconsin, Iowa, and in Danny's case, Illinois.

Danny shot back, annoyed at Ozzy's tone, "Well, I know *I'm* not supposed to be there. That's why I can't afford to flunk out of here and get drafted, which will happen if I don't show up at my astronomy test tomorrow."

"Danny, the teach-in starts at 6 or so and'll be over by midnight. You can sleep in the car on the way back."

"Nah, fuck it. I don't want to go to that political crap. It gives me a headache. All you commies can go to Russia for all I care."

"Listen, Danny, a lot of chicks are hot for this political stuff, and they're the ones on campus who fuck like minks. It's part of the whole political thing to fuck a lot of guys." Danny had to agree, having observed that Ozzy, although he was short and bald, was getting more than his share of pussy.

Ozzy went on, sensing an awakening of interest on Danny's part, "The girls at the U aren't like these tight-asses here at Zwingli. You can get action from almost any of those political chicks at the U and, even if you don't get laid, there are some real big names gonna be there."

"Like who?"

"That radical priest from back East, the one with the famous brother in *Time* magazine, and Joan Baez for sure and maybe even Timothy Leary. That's what I heard."

Danny relented some; he had heard of Joan Baez and Timothy Leary and that priest with the famous brother in *Time* magazine.

"Yeah, okay, I'll see if Dick wants to go. When are you leaving?" Danny couldn't conceive of going a hundred miles without Dick being in the lead.

"Around 3 from the student union parking lot."

Danny found Dick loitering in the union lounge talking to one of his girlfriends.

"Hey, Dick, do you want to go to a teach-in?" Danny was hoping Dick wouldn't know what one was so he could tell him. But Danny could immediately see in Dick's eyes that, of course, he knew. "Shit!" Danny thought. "I should've known he'd know. What doesn't he know?" Danny could also see a complete lack of interest in Dick's eyes.

Danny babbled on, "I hear Timothy Leary is going to be there, and Joan Baez." Looking for some reaction, Danny still sensed Dick didn't want to go.

Then Dick did the unexpected and asked, "Joan Baez?" Dick raised an eyebrow, and that gave Danny hope, but the eyebrow dropped just as fast, dashing his hopes.

Dick spoke again, "Where?"

Danny was again becoming hopeful, listening to Dick "ramble on" like this. When Dick spoke, Danny listened.

"Iowa City," Danny added hopefully.

Dick spoke yet again, making Danny's heart race. "How much dope do we have?"

A sentence! Danny knew that now there was a good possibility they would go to Iowa City. Dick was clearly interested. Danny started preparing for the trip in his mind. Danny thought they would need a few more people to share the gas for the hearse, because the Muffers couldn't all fit in Ozzy's car. Ozzy wouldn't let anyone smoke cigarettes, much less dope in his precious car. Some of these political types were puritanical about dope. Danny hoped, for his own sake, what Ozzy said about the political chicks at the U was true - that they weren't tight-asses like the Zwingli girls. Danny had still not had a girl since Amy. He kept forgetting about bedding Marion T. two Christmases ago. Danny was more than ready to just do it with just about anyone to break the monotony of just doing it by himself, two or three times a day. No one could replace Amy, but Danny fantasized Amy was probably doing it with some other 17-year-old in the British West Indies, now that she had had the baby. He couldn't think about her now. He had to get things going for the trip: find guys to share gas, buy beer, and roll joints.

When Danny got back to his dorm room and found their stash of dope, he knew then why Dick wanted to go to Iowa City. He and Dick were down to sticks and stems and seeds. They needed to score some weed at the U of I. Dick, in his wisdom, knew they were almost out; that's why he'd asked Danny the rhetorical question about the dope. That's why Dick was a leader - he thought ahead and Danny did not.

Danny rounded up a few guys who were always good for an adventure. Danny cashed a check at the service desk in the student union to get money for dope and beer. Danny made a beer run to the Shit Pit and got seven half-gallons of Grain Belt lager. Half-gallons stayed colder longer than cans. If you didn't have any ice, you could just wrap them up in blankets for insulation in the back of the hearse. They were in for a three-hour drive at the best speed the hearse could maintain, about 45 mph, and Danny didn't want warm beer to spoil the trip.

At 3 o'clock, three Muffers and three random guys jumped into the hearse. Dick was driving, as usual. Dick was like Neal Cassady in a book Danny had not yet read called *On the Road*. Dick often quoted the book. Like this Neal guy, Dick could drive anything, intoxicated with anything, find anywhere without a map, make good time getting there, and do it for hours on end.

Dick wheeled the big hearse around campus in a show of driving skill, his arm hanging out the window, and spun off Campus Drive toward Iowa City. All of his passengers trusted that Dick could find Iowa City blindfolded; after all, Dick was from Boston. Dick knew the Kennedys. Played lacrosse against them, too … Finding Iowa City when you were already in Iowa didn't seem like much of a trick to ask of a worldly guy like Dick.

The boys guzzled beer and burned weed; time passed in a pleasant blur. Before they knew it, it was getting dark. And before they knew it, a cop pulled the hearse over in some Podunk town. The hearse riders all knew the drill. They hid the beer and dope in the flower compartment beneath the casket roller bed in the back. They threw open all the doors and windows of the hearse, jumped out and acted casual. The boys leaned on the sides of the vehicle and crossed their arms. Some of them whistled. They believed themselves to be the picture of innocence.

The cop asked, "Which one of you was driving?" Dick flicked his chin up when the cop rested his eyes on him, signaling to the cop that he was the driver. Danny could tell the cop could tell he was dealing with a "somebody" when he was dealing with Dick.

The cop walked up to Dick and asked him, "Son, have you been drinking?" Dick just raised an eyebrow, as though offended at the thought.

"Show me your driver's license." Danny imagined the cop was more than a little humbled when he saw on the license that Dick was from Boston.

"Are you aware you have a defective tail light?"

Danny saw Dick smile, like he had heard this one before and wasn't going to be fooled.

"I want you to get that repaired at your first opportunity." Dick rolled his eyes, indicating to Danny's perceptive eye that he was telling the cop there was no question that he was going to get it repaired, and why was this cop even asking a stupid question like that.

Danny could see the cop got Dick's message loud and clear. The cop wrote something on a pad and handed a copy to Dick. Dick took the paper with what Danny thought was the most dignity he had ever seen in his life. Danny realized, in that moment, that "dignity" was what made Dick a leader.

"Drive carefully." The cop walked back to his cruiser.

All the teach-in-bound boys clambered back into the hearse. Dick fired up the big straight-eight engine and hauled the bulky machine back onto the highway, her flying swan hood ornament pointing the way to Iowa City. The cop followed the hearse for a long time.

The hearse hit the big university town at about 6:30 p.m. No one had bothered to tell Dick exactly where in Iowa City this event was to be held, and Danny had been too witlessly stoned to remember to ask Ozzy, so Dick drove around the campus looking. Danny was not dismayed; he figured the political types who were organizing the event wouldn't get it started on time, because political types couldn't organize a weenie roast without hours of discussion that led to their eventual devolution into factionalism, descending finally into total paralysis.

The guys in the back of the hearse saw some buildings that looked busy and pounded on the divider. Dick ignored their pounding. Danny was sure Dick knew something they did not. Dick pulled up outside a rundown bar. Dick shut the big hearse down and went in. His passengers followed. Since 11 quarts of beer do not satisfy seven guys for four hours of driving, the boys decided to get a drink in the bar before they went out again to look for the teach-in. There were some kids in the bar dressed like hobos, so the Muffers knew they must be pretty close to campus.

The boys all had a drink and then had another. Dick was standing away from the group talking quietly with some older guy at the bar. Soon Dick disappeared out the back door with the older guy. Danny sensed a dope deal going down. When Dick came back, he had that hint of a sly smile that only Danny could see. It told Danny that Dick had scored some weed. The curve of Dick's shoulder told Danny to follow him back out again. Dick and Danny sampled some of the weed. It was good weed, indeed.

At about 11 that night, the bar started filling up with more students, and with older guys who might have been teachers or at least grad students. The Zwingli/Muffer seven had snagged a table in the back by the restrooms. The tables there were huge, seating 10 or 12 drinkers. Danny saw a couple of old guys with a priest, or some kind of "god guy," approach the Zwinglian table. The threesome was polite and asked if they could sit in the three empty seats. The boys were mostly too drunk to care if old guys sat with them. Danny motioned them to the empty chairs.

Danny looked at Dick and knew Dick wanted to ask who the hell they were, but was too dignified, so Danny asked on Dick's behalf, "So, who the hell are you guys?" And looking at the guy in the dog collar, asked, "Are you that famous priest who has the famous brother who was in *Time* magazine who was with Joan Baez tonight at that thing?"

"Infamous is more like it," the dog-collar guy said, with a merry twinkle in his eye.

"How come you're 'infamous?'" Danny challenged.

"I speak truth to power," he replied with the same merry twinkle.

"I wasn't at that thing tonight," said Danny, as though answering a question.

"I wish I could say that, too. It was pretty dull." The twinkle turned down a notch. "Otherwise good people get all tied up in complicated talk, when all that's needed is simple action."

Danny woke up a little and thought, "Wow. He's like Dick - all action and not much talk." But he was actually talking a lot, really, compared to Dick. "So where are you from back East? Dick is from Boston." Danny nodded to Dick, as though the two might know each other.

"I'm a guest of the Maryland Correctional System, but I left their tender care temporarily to await an appeal. I'm a bad boy sometimes." The dog-collar guy knocked back his second shot of bourbon. He had six shot glasses lined up in front of him.

Danny was beginning to like this guy. "What were you in for?" Danny said, in a voice that said this was one con to another.

"I was a guest of the correctional system for destroying government property. It was my privilege and, indeed, my duty as a man of God, a fan of freedom and a believer in peace to destroy some Selective Service files."

"Aw, shit, you really think we shouldn't be helping get the commies out of Vietnam?" Danny asked, feeling more sober by the second.

The dog-collar guy threw back another bourbon like it was water and he was dying of thirst, and said in a mock Irish accent, "My son, my son, how can you possibly be so stupid?" He smiled like an angel when he said this. Danny felt a wave of love wash over him. For a second, it felt as strong as his love for Amy, but it was a much different love. This love brought peace along with it. Amy's love never did.

Danny was shaken when the man called him "son." The man did not use the term "son" to belittle him. He did not use that condescending tone some older men give to the word "son." Danny couldn't think of anything to say, so he just looked at the man.

The whiskey-drinking priest looked at Danny looking at him, and said, "You really don't know, do you? You look like you're afraid of the truth. What you *should* be afraid of is your own ignorance. I was in combat at the Battle of the Bulge in WW II; I know about fear, and I can see fear in your eyes right now. I've seen it in hundreds of eyes. I sometimes see it in my own eyes when I look in the mirror.

"The truth, and I won't preach about it, even though I'm a priest and I'm supposed to preach," he chuckled at his own little joke, "is that this war is just plain wrong. I won't try to tell you why it's wrong. You can learn that for yourself, I'm sure. It's not hard."

Danny said, "But we're Americans and we don't do bad things. We're just trying to help. Everybody knows that."

"Okay, what's your name, son?"

"Daniel No-Middle-Initial Harper."

"You Irish?"

"Half Irish."

"Catholic?"

"I'm sorta nothing now ..."

"Well, Danny, are you up for a sermon? What're you drinking? You want a shot of Wild Turkey to help wash down my preaching? Here." He pushed a shot glass across the table to Danny.

Danny looked around and saw that all the Zwingli boys were listening to the big, smiling, soft-spoken priest at their table, as were the two men he came in with. Some others from nearby tables had pulled their chairs up to listen to the conversation. In the din of the bar and in the haze of a thousand cigarettes, this man had created an oasis of calm reflection that somehow pulled in a crowd.

"Danny, do you ever do bad things?"

"Yeah, sometimes."

"Do your parents do bad things?"

"Sure."

"Do your friends do bad things?"

Danny just looked at the guys around him and heard them sniggering in their beer at that remark, and looking kinda proud of being bad.

"Danny, are they all Americans?"

Danny nodded a "yeah."

"Why's it so hard, then, to believe that a country, which is just a collection of people like you and your parents and your friends and me, can do bad things? Countries can do bad things and they *do* do bad things. What do you do when you get caught doing a bad thing, Danny?"

Before Danny could catch himself, the answer just slipped out. "I lie." It was the truth, and Danny was ashamed to say it. Danny was just starting wonder how he could backpedal from this answer when the priest spoke again.

"Countries lie too, Danny. And they back up their lies with laws and armies and secret police. See those two cool-looking guys over there, two tables away? They've been near me at every speaking engagement I've had for the past week. They're not my fans. They're not groupies. They're FBI."

At that remark, the whole group around the priest looked at the FBI guys, and some of the group unconsciously signaled with their hands which pocket had a bag of dope in it.

"Drink up, my old friend, Danny." He smiled at Danny and winked. Danny felt like a stupid kid. Danny didn't just feel like a stupid kid, he realized that he *was* a stupid kid. But he realized he was not as stupid as he had been just an hour before.

Danny threw back the shot of Wild Turkey the priest had given him. He pounded the shot glass on the table and walked to the john. Danny had a long piss. He zipped up and stepped to the sink and looked at his stupid face in the stupid mirror. He took a pen out of his pocket and plunged it like a spike into his left palm. He then took the pen in his left hand and plunged it into his right palm. He turned on the cold water and put both his hands in the sink and watched the blood and water swirl, blend and disappear down the drain. He turned away from the sink and saw the girl in the shower. She was watching Danny with one cold lavender eye and one cold blue eye. She was holding out her arms and her eyes were inviting Danny inside her skull.

†††
Oswald Randall Wisette; age 22; 4 July 1969; misadventure; Vietnam; no religious preference; unmarried; New York, NY; draftee

CHAPTER TWENTY-FOUR

Those who do not move, do not notice their chains. ~ Rosa Luxemburg

"Get me a carton of milk and a pack of Salem Lights -- not the regulars either, like you did the last time I asked you. Do it before you go to work, so you don't forget. Take this five, and bring back the change, and put some gas in the car when you get to the station. You can use your own damned money for that. You're the one who drives the hell out of that thing and brings it back empty," said Danny's mother, who had never learned to use the word "please".

Danny was home from Zwingli for his third summer holidays, and pumping gas at a Jones Oil/Gulf Oil truck stop for a fourth summer. Danny was in his Jones Oil/Gulf Oil uniform and headed to work when his mother issued her shopping command and gave him $5. Danny had on his blue uniform shirt with an asymmetrical racing stripe that carried patches for both Gulf Oil and the Jones Oil franchise. The shirt had Danny's name embroidered over the pocket ("Daniel"). The rest of the uniform consisted of navy blue wool worsted pants with an orange zigzag pinstripe, black clip-on bow tie, and navy blue Gulf Oil fore-and-aft forage cap with an asymmetrical racing stripe that complimented the shirt. Danny had on freshly shined, black leather lace-up round-toed shoes to complete the outfit. Danny had added non-regulation sunglasses to make himself seem more mysterious and theatrically aloof to his customers.

Danny was proud of his position in the company as "senior pump attendant."

The pay was good at Jones Oil but the discipline was severe and the rules many. Having spent a week at an army-run leadership camp in his junior year in high school, Danny was well prepared for the worst the Jones Oil management could throw at him from its thick book of practices and procedures. Danny had spent much time studying this book and religiously read updates to the manual that arrived regularly in the company mail.

Danny was a model pump attendant, having risen from junior attendant to senior attendant to acting temporary assistant shift leader on occasion. He volunteered for all the roughest duties and took extra shifts on short notice with no complaint. Danny felt he provided an example for the other less diligent attendants, and suggested extra service practices to his superiors which were keenly adopted by management, much to the dismay of many of his less ambitious fellow workers. Danny suggested things like offering to clean the headlamps and tail lamps in addition to the windows of customers' cars, and offering to dump the ashtrays for clients in specially designated bright red painted portable ashbins.

Danny had faithfully served Jones Oil and its motoring clients for four summers, four Christmas breaks and four spring breaks for a total of 379, eight-hour shifts without complaint and without ever being late, leaving early, taking a day off or feigning sickness. Danny worked from his first day back in town from college until the last day before returning. His attendance and attitude were so flawless that the Jones Oil owner's son, Joe Jones Jr., on an inspection visit from the head office, had hinted to Danny that he thought Danny might have a "future" with the company.

Danny stuck the keys in the ignition of the 1956 Rambler Custom station wagon and couldn't for the life of him think of one good reason to either pick up the smokes for his mother or go to work. He began to laugh, but there was no mirth in it. This was a Moses-and-the-burning-bush moment or a St. Paul-on-the-road-to-Damascus revelation; it was a moment of profound confusion and a kind of blankness of mind. It was the moment when Danny began to question why he could not answer even the simplest of questions. "Why should I go to the store? Why should I go to work? Why am I sitting here right now doing nothing?"

Sitting in the car, keys in the ignition but with the engine still off, Danny realized, without formulating it in actual words in his mind, that he had lost faith in his country, his family, his school, women, and in his own worth as a human being. More importantly, he did not want to return to Zwingli in the fall. Dick had told Danny on the last day of third-year classes that he'd been accepted at Yale in the International Studies Program and wanted to complete his undergrad work at the same school where he planned to do his graduate degree.

The sun reflected hotly off the metal dashboard of the Rambler. The glare distorted and diluted the scene through the windshield. Danny had to squint to look out the windshield. He saw a too-bright world, lacking in detail, to which he no longer felt any attachment.

Danny knew instinctively, having been given cues from every corner of American culture - movies, TV, books - that if there were to be an answer, or even a properly framed question, they would be found on the road. Dick said there was a great book about being on the road called *On the Road*, but Danny had not yet read it. He might never read it, because Danny was mad at Dick for deserting him to go to some fancy school in the East to study some shit that Danny didn't even know Dick had any interest in.

Danny gripped the black plastic steering wheel of the 1956 yellow, black and white American Motors Rambler Custom station wagon. He felt as though his hands were gripping the reins of a strong steel steed that would carry him to some marvelous frontier place, west of the Mississippi, where Danny hoped and dreamed all the answers in America were there for the taking.

Danny turned the key, and the sturdy straight-six engine turned over and purred at idle. He sat in the driveway of his boyhood home for a few seconds, made his decision, reached up to the steering column, and pulled the shift lever up and back into reverse. He drove the Rambler past the town limits and headed west on the Interstate. When the Rambler ran out of gas after an hour of hard running, he abandoned the car and hitchhiked. The car had died a few miles from the turnoff to Kewanee, Illinois, the home of Barry Hanson, one of his friends from Zwingli. They had become friends during freshman year, when they were assigned seats next to each other in mandatory first-year lectures because their surnames were next to each other in the alphabet. Barry had a lot of zits, but was otherwise a pretty good guy. Barry laughed at lot.

Danny arrived at Barry's house to find Barry alone. His parents had gone on vacation. Barry was sleeping outside in the back yard in a mildewy tent trailer that his parents no longer used. Barry was drunk when Danny arrived and laughing even more than usual. Barry's parents had made the mistake of leaving Barry alone in a house with an unlocked liquor cabinet. Danny joined in the fun and was soon laughing along with Barry. Being on the road felt right.

Sleeping that night in the tent trailer under the mildewy canvas felt right, too. Sleeping there gave Danny the feeling he was in a covered wagon in the mining and lumber camps of yore. This wagon had rubber wheels and thin foam mattresses for sleeping, instead of iron-banded wooden wheels and a saddle blanket, but it was the mildewy canvas smell that made it seem cowboy real.

On the third morning of their drunken cowboy back-yard camping trip, the boys awoke to the sound of zipping. Danny's father poked his head into the tent.

Danny mumbled through his hangover fog, "Hi … How did you know I was here?"

"The state police found the car, and I figured you would head to the closest person you knew."

"Oh." Danny uttered the word more like a groan.

There ensued a rather one-sided conversation in which Danny's father established, using unassailable logic, that Danny was an irresponsible asshole who cared only for himself, and who would waste all the opportunities he had been given and end up a total failure. Danny had all his suspicions about his own worth confirmed by his father. This only added to the pain in Danny's head. Danny's father informed him that everything bad Danny had feared about himself was true. The truth that he was worthless somehow freed Danny, and gave him the license to disentangle himself from his father's excoriation.

Danny said not a word in his own defense. He loved his father deeply and knew how much it must have cost him to use so many words in such a short period of time. Danny often joked that the word "laconic" had been invented expressly to describe his father. Danny knew the words he was hearing were not his father's words, but were words his father had memorized from one of his mother's harangues. Danny knew his father had been ordered by his mother to repeat the harangue, and that his father had to be able to truthfully report that he had repeated it. Danny put on his Gulf Oil pants and his once-shiny black leather lace-up shoes. He slipped a partly full short dog of port into his back pocket and stood in front of his father. Danny cast his eyes on the ground between them.

When his father ran out of words, Danny said, "Thanks for coming, Dad. I gotta go now." Danny felt like crying because he felt his father's pain. He saw the humiliation in his father's eyes at not being able to influence his 20-year-old son. Danny walked down the driveway and took a left on the street that would take him back out to Interstate 80. His father did not call out or try to stop him as he walked away. He got into his 1962 Rambler Custom station wagon; he caught up to Danny after half a block.

"Get in."

"I'm not going home."

"I know."

"I'm going back out to the Interstate."

"I'll take you. Don't you ever tell your mother."

"I won't tell her."

"Which way are you headed?"

"West."

"That's the way I'd go, too."

Danny got on the west on-ramp and stuck out his thumb, knowing that in America, the future always lay in that direction. That's where the cowboys lived.

Danny got a ride almost immediately. The driver was a nice man, dressed in a nice new suit in a nice car. He smelled of aftershave. The car smelled of "new." The nice man said he sold men's clothing to men's clothing stores. After awhile, he asked Danny in a conversational tone, "You got a girlfriend?"

"No one in particular ..."

"You like girls?"

"Sure."

After a few minutes of silence, he asked Danny, "Do you liked naked girls?"

Danny chuckled a nervous chuckle. "Yep, the best kind ..."

"Reach under the seat."

Danny reached under his seat. He pulled out a pile of magazines with naked girls on the covers. These girls were more naked than the girls in *Playboy*. They were showing their pussies.

"Go ahead, look at them - they won't bite you." The man must have noticed the look of shock on Danny's face.

After Danny had looked at one for awhile, the man asked, "Are you getting hard?"

"Well, sorta ..."

"You can jack off if you want to. Just don't get any on the seat." And he handed Danny a car-sized box of Kleenex.

"I don't think I want to."

The man asked, "Have you ever had someone else jack you off? I mean, not like a queer or anything, but just a friend. You know, it feels better than when you do it yourself. I'd do it for you, if you wanted. I'm not a queer or anything, but sometimes when I'm out on the road and can't find a broad, well, we men have to help each other when we get so horny we just can't wait for a broad."

"Well, I'm not really horny now. I think I should get out pretty soon. My cousin lives on a farm around here and I can call him from the next gas station and he'll pick me up."

The nice man said, "Sure, sure, I'll let you out at the next gas station. I have to fill up, anyway."

He did let Danny out at the next gas station, and gave him $10 for something to eat. Danny was hungry and bought some chips and a Coke. The man beeped his horn three times when he pulled out. Danny decided to avoid the Interstate and cross the Mississippi further north on a two-lane road.

✝✝✝

Robert Barry Hanson; age 25; 22 August 1971; multiple fragmentation wounds; Vietnam; Church of Christ; married; Standard, IL; enlistee

CHAPTER TWENTY-FIVE

If you sacrifice liberty for security, you will lose both. ~*Ron Paul*

D anny left the gas station and headed out to the exit road that led north. It seemed pretty busy, and Danny had good luck in getting a ride. It did not hurt that the gas station he had just left was a Gulf Oil station, and Danny was wearing a Gulf Oil uniform complete with hat.

Danny, by accident or unconscious design, was heading toward Northeast Iowa and Zwingli College. His first ride took him almost two hours north, nearly to the Wisconsin border. Danny's ride ended in some little river town that had a bridge over the Mississippi into Iowa. Danny walked to the bridge and stuck his thumb out.

Hours went by, and no one would give him a ride. Danny's hitchhiking luck had run out. It was summer, and the days were long, but the day finally ran out. Danny gave up. Hitchhiking at night was an iffy proposition at best, so Danny had to weigh his options.

He had money: most of the ten from the salesman, the five his mother had given him, and $8 in coins from Barry, who had not only stolen most of his parents' booze, but had rifled their drawers and pockets for change. Danny did not believe in stealing, but Danny had not exactly stolen anything - Barry had. Danny thought it wasn't really a serious crime to steal from your parents, because kids get all of their parents' money anyway when their folks get old and die.

Danny had to find a place to sleep but didn't want to spend money on a motel. Because he was raised by parents who had gone through the Great Depression, Danny had unconsciously learned how to squeeze a dime. He sought alternative bedding arrangements.

In the failing light, Danny saw a small wooden sailboat under the bridge, moored to a rickety dock along with some open aluminum fishing boats. It looked like the tiny craft had a cabin of some sort. Danny scrambled down the bank to the dock, and upon examination, saw it did have a small sheltered sleeping area. Danny checked around the dock to see if anyone was watching him, and stepped aboard the little craft to examine the cabin. It had two narrow built-in bunks angled into the bow. One of the bunks had a thin foam pad on it. The boat smelled entirely different from the mildewy tent trailer he had been sleeping in at Barry's, but the foam pad looked the same, although narrower.

Danny popped his head out of the cabin, looked around and saw no one. Danny walked to the rail and pissed into the big river. He wondered how long it would take his piss to get all the way down the big river to New Orleans. Danny thought about the *Delta Queen* and wondered if she might pass by so he could see her and wave. Danny thought about Amy. Danny went back into the cabin, took out the half-full short dog of port wine he had grabbed before he exited Barry's tent trailer, and finished it in a few gulps. He curled up on the foam waiting to feel the alcohol hit. He hoped it would put him to sleep. He rolled his hat into a small pillow and stuffed it under his ear.

The boat did not rock; the river was dead still. Even in its stillness, this watery bed felt different than any land-bound one. Danny fell asleep quickly, but as deep and restful as his sleep would be in this cozy boat, his sleep was not dreamless.

Danny had the dream he had dubbed "The Dream" with capital letters - a puzzling recurring dream that had been haunting him for a year or so. "The Dream" starred Danny and a perfectly beautiful young woman dressed in white, with white-blonde hair and one cold blue eye and one cold lavender eye. Danny did not need a fancy dream analyst to tell him from which corner of his psyche these eyes had sprung. They were the eyes of the dead girl in the shower from Oktoberfest weekend in La Crosse. The dream started, as it always started, in Dekorum, Iowa, and always ended in the stars.

In the dream, there are thousands of silver ships patrolling the skies. They have been there for several days. They're not of human origin and Danny is afraid. Danny realizes all of humanity is similarly afraid.

Danny sees himself walking through a deserted town. He sees no humans anywhere, dead or alive. After some time spent wandering the deserted streets, he sees a female student he knows from Zwingli named Diana; she is walking away from Danny at some distance. Danny hurries to catch up to her. Danny knows she is The One. Danny feels he has known her forever, although back in the real daytime world, they have only spoken on one occasion. Danny walked with her once to a public park and pushed her on a swing. She cried as he pushed her and she wet her pants. Danny does not remember what it was that made her cry. Danny *does* remember her saying that she always wet herself when she cried. These daytime memories have no impact on Danny's dream feelings for her. He knows she is The One. She is The One in a way that Danny once thought Amy was The One - only this feeling about Diana feels stronger and more dangerous.

It takes a long time and a lot of effort to catch up to Diana. He is slowed in his pursuit by the thing that always slows a dreamer who is trying to escape or is in pursuit - leaden legs that only move in slow motion. When Danny does catch her, she turns and asks Danny, "What took you so long to find me?" Danny says, "I'm sorry, I didn't even know I was looking for you. I was just looking for someone, anyone." Danny and Diana's eyes become united. They are no longer separate entities, as proven by the fact that they can see through each other's eyes. They embrace, and in that embrace, achieve a complete unity with each other that is both timeless and transcendent.

She says, "We must go to the collection point and find the others who were made not to exist by our friends in the ships." Danny does not feel the beings from the ships are "friends." He is still frightened. The beings from the ships are landing everywhere, but they are invisible. They are pointing shimmering pen-like devices at all the people in the world. The humans don't die from being targeted by these devices, and people are not "evaporated" by the pen-like space weapons, either; they are simply made never to have existed.

Diana and Danny do not react in any way to the effects of the pen-like devices wielded by the invisible invaders. The aliens tell them telepathically to go to the "collection point" Diana spoke of earlier in the dream. The creatures tell the two- who-have-become-one to join with the others who still exist. Diana/Danny are aware that they are among only a handful of existing earthlings.

Diana/Danny walk hand in hand to the collection point. The two have merged into a new type of being - a perfect creature, the first of its kind. Diana/Danny feel at once more peaceful and also more excited than they have ever felt.

Diana/Danny are transported in one of the silver ships to what may have been another planet or dimension. Once there, Diana/Danny join hands with a score or so of others. They all face outwards in a circle. They are like batteries being hooked up in series, and become more and more powerful until they feel as if they will explode. They lose the power to move, and turn into alabaster statues in a human Stonehenge. They don't need flesh-and-blood bodies any longer. In this circle, they create one energetic creature of immovable, immortal, universal mind.

CHAPTER TWENTY-SIX

One more such victory and we are undone. ~*Pyrrhus of Epirus*

After a rough sleep in his increasingly ripe-smelling clothes, Danny picked up his journey the next morning at the place where he left off. By noon, still no one wanted to take him across the bridge to Iowa. Danny took the hint that fate did not want him to cross the big river just yet, so Danny stuck his thumb out in an easier direction: not backtracking east, not west over the bridge and not south - which Danny perceived as a threatening direction - but north along the river, where Danny noted most of the traffic was actually heading. Danny liked north almost as much as west as a good direction for his escape. The North was as good a place to find escape into "the frontier of freedom" as the West, although most Americans did not traditionally think of the North in those terms. Danny knew Wisconsin was upriver, and Danny had always had a good time in Wisconsin. It was the land of all his boyhood family vacations (except for one miserable car trip to Key West during which he got attacked by fire ants) and also the home to Oktoberfest and a 19-year-old age of majority. Rides north came easily, heading upriver - long rides with almost no waiting in between. Danny was across the Wisconsin border within hours, and once in Wisconsin, headed north again but this time started to hook around east, away from the Big Muddy River, in the direction of Madison, Wisconsin.

Danny knew Madison's reputation as being the Midwest's version of Haight-Ashbury. Danny had taken the bus there once from Zwingli to buy dope in bulk, but he had not explored much beyond the bus station where he had arranged to meet the dealer. Danny heard that U of W students in Madison had thrown bombs at a recruiting centre, put blood on Selective Service files and generally raised the kind of hell normally only seen in California or New York. Danny imagined, as his rides took him toward Madison, that the smell of burning dope and burning draft cards was wafting toward him on an offshore breeze from scenic Lake Monroe. Danny had heard of a street called Mifflin Street, a whole street of hippie crash-pad co-operative houses near the university. He was planning to go there when he got to town. He bet that Mifflin Street would welcome this rank-smelling refugee from a Gulf Oil truck stop. Danny bet he would find a temporary home there. Danny bet he wouldn't have much trouble scoring some reefer and speed.

What Danny did find on this street was a bunch of tedious political nuts who ran the whole gamut from left to lefter - large "D" Democrats through social democrats through Trotskyites and other middle-of-the-road communists to Maoists and a scattering of true-believer Stalinists. Danny had been unaware that the big universities were busy turning gentle hippies into not-so-gentle politicos. All the disparate factions were against the war, but this was their only uniting creed. They spent more time arguing with each other than arguing against the war. They were all stoned or drunk most of the time. This degraded the quality of the argumentation, but it was the only trait Danny found endearing in these otherwise boring zealots.

Danny was still the proud son of capitalism, although lately he tended to feel guilty about this belief as a result of the religious indoctrination at Zwingli that included a fair-sized helping of Social Gospel. Danny's capitalist plan was to find a good source for good dope, buy low in bulk, and sell high in smaller units. Capitalism at its most basic ... Danny knew that the road to ruin he was on would need some cash to grease the skids.

It took Danny nearly an hour on Mifflin Street to find a mid-level dealer. He sensed that the more doctrinaire and puritanical political types were multiplying like rats and somehow driving out street-level free enterprise. That political type could become dangerous.

Danny approached the dealer and the dealer asked Danny earnestly, "Are you a narc?"

Danny was incredulous that anyone would ask him that. After all, he had long hair and smelled bad. "When was the last time you saw a narc in a gas station uniform?"

The dealer saw the logic in that. "Well, you have a point there."

Danny began the deal by asking, "Oh, yeah, I only have $16 in cash. Will you take a check for the rest?"

The dealer only hesitated a half-second and said, "Why not, if it's good?"

Danny wrote him a check. And it was good. With the stroke of a pen, Danny had a pound of good-quality weed and twenty tabs of Dexedrine that the dealer threw in as a gesture of goodwill. Danny was not the only one who knew about the value of goodwill in the capitalist world. Such was the easygoing nature of the times, and such was the trusting nature of many drug entrepreneurs in 1968.

Danny rested the night at a Trotskyite house which seemed like the calmest place on the street. Danny felt safe among these gentle orthodox Marxist/Leninists who advocated a truly universal revolution of the proletariat based on democratic principles. Danny took a shower in the morning in a stained and rusted stall, scrubbing his body with a dab of Prell Shampoo in the absence of soap. Danny borrowed some semi-clean but shabby proletarian-friendly clothes from the bathroom hamper and replaced them with his Gulf Oil uniform. It was his offering to the gas-pumping workers of the world, who would one day unite to crush their imperialist lackey running-dog capitalist oppressors in a universal democratic revolution. Danny had been obliged to listen to a lot of Trotskyite cant the previous night to earn his place on the sofa.

Danny lit a big joint for breakfast and grabbed a stale organic spelt muffin from the beer bottle and cigarette butt-littered kitchen table. Thus fueled, Danny headed back out on the road.

The shabby clothes from the bathroom hamper turned out to be a real hit with the people Danny was beseeching for transportation with his thumb. Danny got ride after swift ride. He was headed back west to try to cross the Mississippi again.

Danny crossed the Big Muddy on the bridge from La Crosse, Wisconsin to La Crescent, Minnesota. Danny's wheeled benefactors took him on a mild left turn and dipped him into the upper-right end of Iowa. Danny landed on familiar ground in Northeast Iowa. Danny's last ride took him into downtown Dekorum, Iowa, "Home of Zwingli College - One of the Top 100 Small Colleges in America."

Danny called Greg, a townie student, who lived in Dekorum all year. They met at the Dairy Queen. After they smoked a joint and each ate a Dairy Queen sundae - courtesy of some cash Danny had made selling three of his 16 oz. of weed to some high-school kids from Spring Grove, Minnesota - Danny allowed that he needed a place to crash. Danny thought that Greg might be able to put him up. Greg's dad taught pottery making in the Art Department at the college, and his dad had a beard. Greg's parents might even be pleased to have him stay. As it turned out, they were pleased to house Danny on a sofa in the basement. They even fed him dinner. For all his long hair and dope smoking, Danny still remembered his table manners.

The next morning, drawn by thoughts of Diana, the girl in his recurring dream, and not wanting to push his luck with Greg's parents by staying a second night, Danny set off again hitchhiking west. Danny felt that he had a mission. Diana, the girl in his dream, lived not too far away to the west. Danny had to see her again. He didn't exactly know what the question was, but he was pretty certain she had the answer.

The reason Danny now felt he had a mission was because when he walked halfway over the bridge across the Mississippi several days before, he had suddenly remembered what it was that had made her cry in the park on the swing and pee her pants. He had told her about "The Dream" as she drifted back and forth in the evening light. She listened and made no comment, but Danny knew intuitively she cried because she had had the same dream. Danny reasoned that if she'd been having the same dream, then they were meant to be together forever and live the dream. He'd made no attempt to touch her that evening in the park. He remembered fearing her slightly. She seemed perfect. That's what made her frightening. That's what made her irresistible.

Physically, in the light of day, outside the dream, she was no fragile flower. She was tall and big-boned like a fashion model, and also like a model, without an ounce of fat. She had waist-length, ruler-straight natural blonde hair. She had brown eyes that were blank, flat and emotionless. She never showed emotion in any of her other features, either, even when she was crying. The tears just rolled down her blank face.

Her breasts were large and high and sharply pointed, like the ones Danny once saw on a coal-black Ethiopian princess in a 1957 *National Geographic*. Diana's skin was a clear white, unmarked and blemish free, except for a birthmark on her left calf in the shape of 7th century White Serbia or, for those not familiar with maps of Central Europe in the 7th century, whimsically reminiscent of modern-day Albania.

If there were degrees of uniqueness - as, of course, there are not - she would appear unique to the nth degree.

She not only betrayed little or no emotion, she rarely spoke. She kept her own counsel, and in this way, made more of a statement than she could have by babbling and spewing. Danny was free to fill in the blanks. And, to Danny's rich imagination, she spoke volumes of whatever Danny most wanted to hear. With her silences, she told Danny things he believed that Amy should have told him, but never did. All Danny had to do was listen to his inner ear to hear her inner voice.

Danny had to see her again and hear her voice again in her rich silences. Danny was more than in love, he was "in" something else and he meant to find out what.

CHAPTER TWENTY-SEVEN

A thing is not necessarily true because a man dies for it. ~*Oscar Wilde*

D anny had no trouble getting to Diana's town. Fate, in the form of quick direct rides, seemed to be pushing him in a fateful direction. The last ride dropped him off in the middle of the little city where she lived. Danny had copied her number down from the student directory. Danny phoned her from a phone booth, and she answered on the first ring. She told him she would pick him up directly. Fate was being very kind.

Danny sat down to wait on the curb outside the phone booth. He spied a miniature naked Barbie doll in the gutter, her brassy blonde hair snarled and pulled outward into a grotesque explosion, arms and legs akimbo. He wanted to photograph the doll for some reason, but he had no camera, so he burned it in his memory instead. Diana told Danny on the phone that she had to deliver lunches to her father's men in the field before she could drive into town to get him. She said that she would bring a lunch for him. That was good. Danny was hungry.

She showed up within a half-hour, driving a big new white Cadillac convertible, sparklingly clean, with the top down. The car impressed Danny. She impressed him even more. Her silky natural platinum blonde hair was mostly hidden under a big straw fashion hat, but the hair that snuck out from under it was fashionably tousled by the wind.

Diana wore cut-off jeans and sported big sunglasses. She had on a loose white top that was nearly transparent. It was obvious to Danny she was not wearing a bra. Danny thought she looked like a movie star in a car like that, in a get-up like that, in a farm town like this. He could not remember the name of the film she was in, but it was clear to Danny he had seen the film or maybe dreamed the dream. Films ... dreams ... visions ... They were all sort of the same to Danny's brain, poisoned as it was by depression, harmful substances and love songs.

She smiled a brief wan smile. She drove Danny in silence to her family's farm, which was at the very edge of town. She pulled the shiny new Caddy behind a chicken coop at the farthest end of the property, where the cleared homestead ran out and endless fields of corn began.

"This is where I live in the summer."

"You live in a chicken coop?"

"Yes."

When she led him into the little structure, Danny saw that the chicken coop had been cleverly converted into a summer house. It was furnished with antiques. It had a big oak bed, oriental rugs and pictures on the wall. There was no furnace or water supply that Danny could see, but there was electricity. A radio was playing softly, and there was a light on in a little ceramic lamp, whose base was the figure of ballerina on point. The ballerina was missing a head. All in all, the converted coop was an attractive space and smelled not a bit like chicken shit. It smelled like marijuana, ineffectively camouflaged by incense.

Diana locked the door and pulled down the shades. She lit more incense to cover the smell of the additional dope fumes the two immediately introduced into this rather confined space.

Danny and Diana finished the weed and put on some music. There was always music in the background in this little building, the whole seven days they stayed together. Danny played Simon and Garfunkel's *Bookends* album over and over; it said something special to him, but he could not define what. It was totemic. Whenever he felt lost, and he felt lost most of the time, he felt less lost by playing *Bookends*. Danny also played Bob Dylan and the Grateful Dead and Santana between his attempts to wear out *Bookends*. Once, Danny and Diana took Dexedrine together, and Danny talked all night. He poured out, if not his feelings, at least what seemed like every thought he had ever had, along with most of his notions. Danny was not comfortable with his feelings. His feelings were seldom pleasant. The one cold lavender eye and one cold blue eye set in the dead gray face of a nameless dead girl in a blood-spattered shower still stared at him from behind his back, Amy mocked him from some Caribbean paradise where Danny imagined she lived with a very widely read and very handsome writer who looked a lot like Errol Flynn or maybe Clark Gable, and his recurring dream - the one starring Diana and the space invaders - called him like a siren's song, even in the daytime, seducing him to leave this world for the dubious joys of another dimension.

Treading water in his stew of nameless fears, Danny clung to this perfect rural beauty who never smiled, seldom spoke and had a huge appetite for speed, wine and weed. Danny clung to her like a drowning man clings to flotsam, even though he wondered if she were really and truly there.

Once in a while, she would talk, and when she did, Danny took no comfort in what she said.

"What's your mother like?"

"Nice."

"Do you think she cares we're living out here in this chicken coop?"

"She's frightened of me."

"Frightened?"

"Yes."

"What about your dad?"

"He's in treatment a lot, but he's back now. He's crazy."

"Shit." Danny had one more thing to worry about - a crazy father.

"How crazy is he?" Danny envisioned a blood-soaked farmer with a skinning knife in his hand, his eyes rolling randomly in their sockets, reminding him of Big Bobbi's eyes, his radio announcer pal, when she was going to bad places on bad drugs.

"He's not as bad as my uncle who lives in the trailer behind the house, but he's worse than my brother. They threw Deek out of the Marines on a Section 8, and now he rides his motorcycle all night because he can't sleep anymore."

That explained the beautifully restored pre-WW II Indian motorcycle in the yard, and probably also the presence of the 1966 Shelby Mustang GT350 parked in the drive shed. For all their madness, these were not poor farmers.

Diana walked to the heavy oak sideboard and picked up a small black lacquered box. She opened the box. It had a red velvet lining. She showed him a shriveled thing that looked like a gray corn curl. "Do you think he was crazy?"

Danny was puzzled by this question and by the object in the box.

"Who?"

"The boy who sent me this."

"What boy?"

"The one I did it with last summer."

"What is that thing?" Danny felt mounting dread that it was a penis and mounting hope, also, that anyone who defiled this perfect creature had his dick cut off. The image of Diana's father with the skinning knife returned.

"It's his little finger. He cut it off with his pocketknife in a phone booth when he was talking to me. He wanted me to marry him."

She didn't marry that boy, but she'd kept the finger that he'd mailed her the following day. Danny felt annoyed. He felt that keeping it meant she must have had some feelings left for him. Danny was jealous.

The finger was the beginning of the end of their week together. Danny had run out of the Dexedrine the Miflin Street dealer had given him. Diana loved dexies and became visibly irritable when he told her he didn't have any more.

"Do you want me to leave?" Danny asked.

She replied with a thousand-yard stare. Danny could read the answer in the stare. Danny wanted to cut off his head to trump the boy with the finger. He wanted Diana to put his head in a big black box on the sideboard and think of him even more fondly than she thought of the boy who had defiled her the summer before.

Danny did not cut off his head. Danny picked up what few things he had and stuffed them in his army surplus gas mask bag, which he had been using to carry his personal items on the road. He walked to the highway and stuck out his thumb.

When he returned to Dekorum, he called Greg. Greg asked where he had been. Danny said that he had visited a friend on a farm.

Danny and Greg drove to the Dairy Queen in his sister's new Triumph TR3 British Racing Green roadster. They smoked a joint in the back lot of the Dairy Queen as they ate their treats.

On the way back to Greg's house from DQ, as they were sedately driving down a peaceful, shady, small-town residential street in the little roadster, suddenly and without a warning there was a huge crash, the world spun and everything seemed to come to an end.

Danny woke up staring at the sky. Someone was up there, asking him if he was alright. As Danny couldn't move his limbs or feel his body, he replied, "Whadda *you* think? Am I alive?"

"Yeah, you're alive. Does anything hurt?"

"Nope."

"Well, you got a lot of blood on you. Maybe you should stay there until the ambulance comes."

"Where's Greg?"

"The guy over there? He lost an ear. I have it here." The person standing above him dangled the ear in front of Danny's face. Danny fainted.

When Danny woke up, he was in an ancient hospital surrounded by nurses, who assured him that they had sent somebody out to the golf course to find one of the doctors. It was Wednesday and all three docs in town took Wednesday off to play golf with each other.

Danny passed out again.

Danny woke up when a doctor in a golf shirt started prodding him and asking questions. When Danny had apparently passed all of his tests, the doc told the nurses to clean up his cuts and abrasions and send him home. Danny had no home. They told Danny that his one-eared friend would be in all night for observation. That ruled out staying with Greg.

The nurse gave Danny a bottle of pain medication and a bill he couldn't pay. Danny looked at the label on the tablets and smiled. He knew if he took a handful of 10-mg Morphine Sulfate Oral tablets, he would be able to sleep on a picket fence if he had to. Thus assured, Danny ceased to worry about accommodations. Danny took a handful of morphine tablets, stopped to wash them down at a drinking fountain, and went across the street from the hospital to a little park.

Danny sat at a picnic table and rolled a joint. This was the same park where he had pushed Diana on a swing last spring and told her about his recurring dream. Danny looked at the swing and wondered if the seat was still stained from her piss. He lay down on a picnic table and smoked some weed. Gazing up at the sky, he saw Diana's face in the clouds. He closed his eyes and saw her inside his eyelids. He smelled her strawberry shampoo smell and felt her being enter his body through his nose, his mouth, his ears, every pore in his skin and even his asshole. Danny got a throbbing erection. Danny felt his whole awareness shift to his erection. He knew this picnic table was the sacred altar upon which he would be willing to sacrifice everything, including his very life, in order to be joined with her forever. She had become "The One Woman." She no longer had a face and no longer had eyes. She had become Danny's face and Danny's eyes. If Danny died on this table, Diana and Danny would be one with each other forever.

The cops found Danny the next morning asleep on his picnic-table bed in the park across from the hospital. When the cop pushed his side, Danny cried out in pain and woke up to a strange darkness. Danny jabbed at his eyes with his fingers and felt that they had crusted shut in his morphine sleep. He was relieved that he had not gone blind. As he moved his arms to get his fingers to his eyes to pry them open manually, the arms screamed in pain. His back screamed in chorus. Danny's mouth screamed.

The cop asked flatly, "Are you okay?"

"No, I was in a traffic accident and landed 100 ft. from the car."

"Actually, it was 42 ft. I measured it."

The hospital had ratted Danny out to his parents and the cops had come looking for him at his parents' request. Since Danny was not guilty of any crime the cops could think of on the spot, they merely asked him if he needed a ride somewhere. He told them to take him to Greg's house, hoping Greg would be home from the hospital.

When the cops dropped Danny off at Greg's, they ordered Danny to stay there until his parents came to pick him up. Since the bolus dose of morphine Danny had given himself the night before had worn off, Danny found he couldn't walk or even stand with all the stiffness and pain. The cops had to help Danny from the picnic table into the patrol car and then again into Greg's house. Greg's bearded potter-professor father was home when the cops rang the bell, and he told them Danny could stay there until his parents picked him up. He helped Danny hobble downstairs to the basement sofa.

Danny had no alternative but to wait for his parents, since he had so many muscle tears and bruises that he couldn't physically escape the ignoble fate of being dragged home by his parents like some small child lost at the supermarket. Danny was humiliated, and his depression grew even darker and deeper.

"Professor Rankin, could you get me some water so I can take my pills?" Danny intended to take them all.

Danny was not able to distinguish day from night or hallucinations from dreams for some time, until he woke up in his own narrow bed in his own house in his hometown. He was flat on his back and so weak he could not speak. His mother was standing over him. Danny saw darkness and anger in the blue eyes that had terrified him as a child in this bed. He closed his eyes and waited for a blow that never came this time, yet he felt as if it had.

CHAPTER TWENTY-EIGHT

Preventive war is like committing suicide out of fear of death.. ~Otto von Bismarck

D anny somehow survived the summer. The truck stop took him back, but gave him a letter of reprimand that would forever remain a dark blot in his personnel file. His future as something other than a pump attendant with Jones Oil was no longer a certainty. There would be no more hints from district supervisors about assistant managerial positions for Danny in exotic locations like Ohio or Kentucky - the kinds of incentives they once dangled just over the horizon of Danny's employment future. Danny's parents became mercifully silent after a few days of not being mercifully silent following his "accident" with the pain medication, coupled with the discovery of a moderately large quantity of weed in the WW II surplus gas mask bag.

Danny, for his part, went on emotional autopilot. He did his job, brushed his teeth, and returned to Zwingli in the fall like a good boy. Danny attempted to telephone Diana several times, but her family members who answered the phone always told Danny politely that she was "unavailable." Diana did not return to Zwingli in the fall. Just like Dick - another deserter ...

Several weeks into the fall term, Danny got a phone call from Diana. His heart leaped in his chest. He instantly felt everything for her that he had not allowed himself to feel for almost two months. Danny was mad with joy as soon as he heard her voice.

"Hi, Danny."

"Diana?" He couldn't believe his luck at her return.

"I'm pregnant."

Danny couldn't believe his luck at hearing *this* news, but it was a different kind of luck. "Where are you?"

"Home."

"I'll borrow a car and be there this afternoon."

"My dad will kill you. He's crazy."

Danny remembered his visions of the bloodstained, rolly-eyed farmer with the skinning knife. "He knows?"

"I told my mom and told her not to tell my dad, but she told my little brother, who should know better, who told my big brother who was drunk, as usual, and he told my dad."

Danny thought "Oh, great!"

Then she added, as if Danny had forgotten, "My dad is mentally ill."

"Then you should come here."

Diana did show up at Zwingli later that day, driving the white Caddy convertible. The Caddy looked like it had just left the showroom. Diana looked like hell. Her eyes were swollen and red. Her hair was tangled and greasy. Her clothes looked and smelled like she had been sleeping in them for a week. Her breath stank of gin and cigarettes. She had been drinking from a half-gallon jug in the car. She carried the jug with her into Danny's dorm room, dangling it from the little glass loop on the neck.

Danny thought she looked sexy. He thought the right thing to do to make everything better was to have sex. He was wrong. She cried the whole time Danny molested her. Down below, she was dry as a bone. Danny gave up on that idea pretty quickly.

Danny had no other ideas for making it all better beyond the usual solution in 1968 when you get a girl pregnant: you marry her. However, Diana's presence in his dorm room presented Danny with more immediate problems than dealing with her pregnancy, and he had to handle those first.

Having a girl overnight in the dorm could be cause for suspension or expulsion, especially if you were caught in *flagrante delicto*. Expulsion for Danny meant ceasing to make "uninterrupted progress toward an undergraduate degree" and, therefore, cancellation of his student deferment from the draft. There was little doubt someone would see Diana sooner rather than later. Between her drinking and her pregnancy and her congenitally weak urinary sphincters, she had to pee more than once an hour and throw up occasionally, too. The communal bathroom was 60 ft. down the hall. Her trips to the john could mean a trip to Vietnam for Danny. There was no ladies room on the third floor of the senior men's dorm, because no ladies were allowed up there. Danny could think of no way of disguising her.

Danny summoned up all the courage he didn't have and finally suggested the two of them go back to her farm and face whatever music there was to face. They would be strong together. It wasn't much of a plan, but Danny had always been told that only good things happen when you do the right thing. Facing her parents seemed like the right thing.

She said, again, "My dad will kill you."

Danny hoped she was wrong, and that all the adult wisdom he had heard over the years about "doing the right thing" was right.

To reassure her, Danny said in a cowboy-sure voice, "I can deal with him." Danny even half-believed himself; after all, he was a father now and a soon-to-be husband. He felt he had to start acting like an adult, but he still wished he had Dick around to give him advice.

His first act in acting as an adult was to tell Diana to run down the back stairs and wait for him in the car. His second adult act was to take over the driving. Diana was still swigging gin and had produced some pills of an unknown type and popped them. She was in no state to drive. Diana fell asleep a few miles out of town and slept most of the way to her farm. She woke up once, and seemed surprised to be in a car and to see Danny at the wheel. Her eyes fell shut again pretty quickly. Before she fell asleep again, she slurred, "My dad will kill you."

When they arrived at the farm, Danny parked near the back door of the main house. He did not shut the engine off because he intended to put the power top up before they went inside. It looked like rain. Diana was still passed out. Danny shook her a few times, but she did not come around. Danny saw Diana's father open the back door and walk in the direction of the car. He held a vintage Winchester Model 12 Field Grade pump shotgun with the traditional corn-shucker fore end. From the look of the muzzle, it was either a 12 or a 16-gauge, but probably a 12. Danny would have liked a closer look. He got it.

The armed man raised the muzzle that had been pointing at the ground so that it was now aimed at the driver's seat of the Caddy. He growled, "I'm gonna kill you." So much for doing the right thing ...

Danny dropped the Caddy into drive and floored it, cramping the wheel to make an exit from the farmyard. Danny heard a boom and kept his foot to the floor. As the Caddy screeched onto the highway in front of the farm, Danny heard another boom and heard shot striking the passenger side of the car. He couldn't look to see if Diana had been hit as he had to get the car out of range. There was another boom, but no shot reached the car. Danny slowed and took a look at Diana. She appeared unbloodied. Danny took the first side road he saw, raced down it until he saw another side road, and took that one. He took gravel roads all the way back to Zwingli, just in case the old man came after them in his pickup. Diana must have taken some super-duty pills; she did not wake up during the bombardment and escape. He was glad, for her sake, that she was into downers now and not speed.

Once back in Dekorum, Danny hid the car in an old falling-down garage in the back of Dick's granny's house, and persuaded friends of friends who lived off campus to hide Diana. One look at the bedraggled beauty was all it took to persuade them to hide her. Danny could see it in their eyes. They thought they might get lucky letting her sleep on the sofa. The friends of friends had no idea how crazy and dangerous this alabaster stunner could be.

Danny saw Diana every day and most of every night for a week. They did not have sex although Danny longed to comfort her that way. She cried at his slightest advance. She preferred to take her comfort in booze and drugs. During her few lucid moments, Danny tried to have conversations with her about exploring options. The conversations were mostly just Danny doing the talking and Diana staring into space.

One day, in the middle of one of their talks, Diana handed Danny a scrap of paper. She had written a phone number on it and a Chicago address. She said they needed $500 for the abortion.

CHAPTER TWENTY-NINE

Have you ever thought that war is a madhouse and that everyone in the war is a patient?~Oriana Fallac

D anny and Diana drove all night to Chicago in the white Caddy with the shotgun rash on the passenger door. Far from the Gold Coast, and way west of the Loop, Danny found the address of the "doctor." The address was in the baddest and blackest part of the West Side ghetto. The effects of the riots in April were evident all along West Madison, in the corridor from Roosevelt Road to Chicago Avenue. No one wanted to rebuild or even clean up, apparently, because no one knew when the next riot would erupt. Danny wondered if his crazy roommate Marvin had rioted in these streets in April, sniping at the Chicago Metropolitan Police with his M2 carbine.

Danny was frightened to be in this part of town. He kept the windows rolled up. He kept the top up. Danny had $500 in cash in his back pocket and his father's Colt M1911A1 automatic pistol stuffed in his waistband. He had purloined the Colt from his father's sock drawer before he left for Zwingli in the fall, just in case. That "just in case" was now. Danny checked and double-checked the street address he had on the scrap of paper Deek had given to Diana. The address had originated with Diana's older brother. Since Deek was batshit crazy and drunk all the time, Danny didn't trust this address at all.

They stopped in front of the building at the address Deek had given them. Danny did not kill the engine. The building didn't look like a medical clinic. The building didn't even look habitable.

Danny reached out to Diana, who was crying softly. He held her gently. That caused Diana to cry harder. Over Diana's shoulder, Danny noticed that some black people, who were on the street when they pulled up, had started to saunter closer to the big white car. They came in ones and twos and threes - not coming too close yet, and not yet threatening, but definitely interested in the big white Caddy idling on the street. They likely had never seen a brand new drop-top Caddy in this neighborhood before, unless it was being driven by some dark-skinned pimp. A boy-girl team of young platinum blonds in such a car did not fit with their world view.

The crowd drifted closer, an inch at a time. Their numbers slowly grew and grew. Danny and Diana were exhausted and hungry. They had driven all night from Iowa. Danny was crashing off speed and had the creepy crawlies. Danny had now gone nearly 36 hours without sleep. This crowd just added a new dimension of fear to his already wrecked emotions.

Danny smelled something. He looked over and saw Diana had pissed herself. He saw the dark stain spreading on the white leather seat. Danny and Diana heard voices in the crowd saying things to them, but couldn't understand the individual words. The tone of the voices was clear, even if the words were not. Danny wanted to tell these deprived victims of white capitalist oppression that he was a nigger lover now. Not in those words, of course ... Danny couldn't think of a convincing way to convince this crowd of his political solidarity with their just cause in time to save him from their wrath.

So, in lieu of conveying his racial solidarity, Danny pulled out the big black Colt automatic and slapped it on the dashboard, as soon as the first black hand touched the hood and the first black face bent into the windshield for a look. The man with the hand froze and a slow smile spread over his face. He did not remove his hand, and just stared harder into the windshield. Danny now heard the words this man said very clearly and saw his mouth shape the syllables, "Dis heah honkey gots himself a great big gun, an' he be cryin' an' she be pissin'. Whoa, we gots us a pussyboy wit' a piece, in a shaggin' waggin with a piece a-pissy pussy!" He removed his hand from the hood and turned to the crowd, bowing to receive kudos from his peers for his poetic observations.

Just then, Danny heard and saw a long knife blade pierce the canvas top on Diana's side of the car. He saw the knife begin to cut a line.

Danny slammed the Caddy in gear and mashed the accelerator. There were no big thumps under the tires for the first few seconds as he laid a big strip of rubber down the street, so Danny was sure he hadn't hit anyone. He heard something bounce off the trunk, maybe a rock or bottle, but didn't turn his head to look. He drove hard until he hit the Eisenhower Expressway and took it out of town. Danny was glad to be out of danger and also glad there was not going to be any abortion. He didn't feel right about abortion, but had never told Diana that, and he had never discussed the matter with anyone else, either. Danny had never known or even heard of anyone who had had one.

The knife blade was still stuck in the top, inches above Diana's head.

Seven hours later, with the assistance of some more Dexedrine, Danny pulled the Caddy with the shotgun rash and the ripped ragtop safely into Dekorum and into the old garage behind Dick's granny's house.

"Give me the keys, Danny."

"Why?"

"I'm going home."

"Aren't we getting married?"

"No."

"Why not?"

Diana did not answer.

Danny handed her the keys. She put the top down, even though it was September and getting cooler, especially at night.

Danny watched the Caddy move west on Campus Drive, Diana's platinum hair whipped into a golden pinwheel by the wind as she drove straight into a September sun that was going down behind the old clock tower on the admin building. Danny knew he would never see her again. Danny knew he would never stop trying.

Later that night, Danny called the farm. Diana's mother answered. Danny had met her once during his week at the chicken coop, and she seemed a gentle, decent sort.

"May I speak to Diana, please, Mrs. Holloway?"

"Danny, she doesn't want to speak to you, and if she did, I wouldn't allow it. Please don't call again."

Danny didn't call again for half an hour. It was one of the worst half-hours of a life that had been full of some pretty bad ones. This time, Diana's little brother, a ten-year-old also named Danny, answered the phone.

"Is Diana there, Danny?"

"She locked herself in her room, and she's crying. My mom says I can't let you talk to her. Sorry." And 10-year-old Danny hung up on 20-year-old Danny.

The older Danny waited until the next morning to phone again. He had not slept much more than an hour all night. This time, Deek answered.

"Is Diana th-"

Deek cut him off. "Look asshole, quit phoning. If you come around here again, it won't be Dad who's handling the gun. The Marine Corps taught me how to shoot and not to miss. Besides, Dad is taking her to Omaha or Oklahoma to one of those 'homes' tomorrow, so you can quit bothering us."

Danny didn't think this was the right time to remind Deek that the Marine Corps had also kicked him out for being crazy, so he just hung up and decided to try a different strategy.

Danny called on the campus youth pastor, who probably hated him since Danny laughed rather pointedly whenever he saw the man. The pastor had grown long sideburns, and wore granny glasses and tie-dyed shirts to show how hip he was. Danny had asked him to share a joint at a party to which some of the younger faculty members had invited their favorite students. Danny was a favorite student of many young faculty members because he sold them weed. The plastic hippy pastor had actually blushed and warned Danny that drugs were illegal, as he vigorously declined to partake of the devil weed.

The youth pastor seemed glad to hear that Danny was in trouble and asking for help. It gave him a chance to one-up Danny by helping him. This would be partial compensation for Danny's public disdain.

The pastor drove to see Diana's parents, deliberately without calling them first. He felt if he wore his collar and most sober suit and expression, he would be better received than if he were a faceless voice on the phone. Danny would later hear the pastor give an accurate description of the vintage Model 12 pump shotgun that had plastered the Caddy a few weeks earlier.

Danny briefly considered going to Oklahoma or Omaha to look for Diana, but with his recent luck at hitchhiking, didn't think he could complete the task before winter.

Danny settled into a slough of despond that was somehow below his usual sea of despond. Danny was now traversing the circles of hell looking for the bull's-eye.

CHAPTER THIRTY

I hate those men who would send into war youth to fight and die for them; the pride and cowardice of those old men, making their wars that boys must die.~Mary Roberts Rinehar

The Reverend Doctor Oliver ("Call Me Ollie") Wendell Woodman was waiting to ambush Danny outside his modern English theater class. The Reverend Doctor was the reason the Religion Department had lost its reason. He was a one-man Red Guard unit, doing to Zwingli what Mao had done to China during the Great Proletarian Cultural Revolution. One of the older members of the Religion Department had been overheard at a faculty party, at which he had imbibed too deeply, referring to Woodman as "that sanctimonious phony prick." This drunken theologian was perhaps more flattering in his appraisal of Woodman than most of Ollie's students.

Poor Danny was shuffling, shoulders up, head down, out the door of a lecture on method acting, trying to look like Marlon Brando's kid brother, and greatly anticipating his between-class cigarette, when he felt a hand on his shoulder and heard the august Reverend Doctor ask, "Danny, could I have some private words with you?"

Danny knew the voice instantly without turning to look, because Woodman had a lisp that made him sound like Elmer Fudd. The good Doctor of Divinity also had a habit of speaking in a broad oratorical manner that could easily be heard in the back pews of a cathedral. Unfortunately for his listeners, his volume remained the same in a room the size of a broom closet.

Danny sensed this booming invitation to be more of a command than a request, but Danny charitably chose to answer as though it were a friendly request. Danny answered, "Sure, let's go in the green room, Dr. Woodman. I need a smoke and a Coke."

"Great, I'll buy the Cokes. You can call me Ollie, you know." He offered this familiarity to everyone he talked to, no matter how many times he had talked to that person. Danny thought the habit came from over-reading *How to Win Friends and Influence People*. Danny thought Woodman probably used the same phrase with his wife.

The professor slipped some quarters into the green room Coke machine, handed a bottle to Danny and kept one for himself.

"Thanks, Ollie!" Danny saw Woodman's expression curdle, as though he'd been sucking a lemon. No one dared call Dr. Woodman "Ollie" despite his invitation to do so. "Oh, boy!" Danny thought, "this is going to be a wonderful scene to watch." Danny knew the guy was a prick by reputation, even though he had never suffered through any of Ollie's classes. Woodman was an Old Testament scholar, and Danny avoided his classes because they had a reputation for being as dull as dirt. Plus, Woodman was a known low grader. But Danny was also aware Woodman was the very active acting chair of the Religion Department, and was very ambitious to secure that position full-time. The rumor mill had it that Woodman had graduated second in his class at Harvard Divinity; Woodman himself started the rumor, in a moment when pride momentarily ripped through his usual hair shirt of somber humility. What Woodman didn't ever let slip is that the theologian who had graduated first in Woodman's class year was still at Harvard, and this valedictorian, who outranked Ollie by a mere

3/100ths of a grade point, had been granted tenure at Harvard before he was 30 years old. Why Ollie had come to this respectable, but small, Iowa institution could only be guessed. Whatever was responsible for his fall from Harvard to Zwingli was perhaps responsible for his lack of mirth. Here he was, a Harvard magna cum laude, adrift in the Bible Belt with a bunch of overly sincere blond farm kids full of Sunday School religion. Danny knew anything this god guy said to him would be grist for the method actor's mill. The lecture Danny had heard on the Stanislavsky method, only minutes before, was percolating in his mind.

Danny lit his smoke and accepted the Coke from Woodman and settled into one of the sad, broken-down, overstuffed sofas that littered the Theater Department lounge. Danny thought there must be one store that sells all of the used sofas found in all of the theater green rooms on earth. The sofas in all green rooms are identical to all the other sofas in all the other green rooms.

Woodman settled down on a sagging sofa facing Danny. Woodman first checked it for any artistic fallout that might cling to his expensive suit that screamed "I want to be head of the department!" Ordinary Zwingli profs wore suits that looked like they came from the same used-goods store that supplied the green-room sofas. Woodman tried to look like a British banker.

Woodman was about to begin booming out his prepared statement to Danny, but then stopped to comment on the smell of Danny's Marlboro. "What's that you're smoking? It smells just like licorice."

"Yeah, sometimes I dip my smokes in flavoring, you know, vanilla or strawberry. This week it's licorice." In fact, the smell was paregoric: a compound of camphor, water, alcohol, anise oil and 4% opium. Dick and Danny had found a nearly full quart-bottle of the stuff in Dick's grandmother's bathroom. From their multiple readings of Bill

Burroughs' fractured tract on hard drugs and other fine perversions, *Naked Lunch*, the two learned that paregoric made for a very good smoke indeed, when you used it to soak cigarettes. When the smokes dried, there was just the licorice left and the opium.

"Interesting smell ... Anyway, you must be wondering what I wanted to talk to you about," Woodman lisped and boomed.

Danny nodded a "yes" and smiled a paregoric smile to let Woodman know he should go on with his statement. Danny was feeling his acting chops and knew his face and posture conveyed keen interest.

"All of your religion professors are impressed with your original scholarship, curiosity and creativity. Even though your grades don't reflect it, you're the one student the scholars in our department are pinning their hopes on for someone, sometime, to put our emerging cutting-edge department on the world map, academically speaking. So, I thought I was called upon to feel out your intentions regarding how far you want to take a career in the church. Maybe I could help you sort things out regarding your vocation. First, explain to me why you selected religion as your major, in your own words."

Danny wondered how he could explain himself in any *but* his own words. Woodman was nuts. But Danny answered him, if somewhat dreamily. "Well," the paregoric mellowness talking, "I'm also triple majoring in theater and sociology."

Ollie took this to be an encouraging answer, "Good, good ... I can feel the synergy among those fields."

Not remembering what synergy was at that exact moment but feeling this was a compliment of some sort, Danny nodded a beneficent nod of agreement. Danny felt as though his face and body were now bestowing a sort of blessing upon Woodman. Danny was beginning to feel close to this man. Danny was beginning to feel close to all mankind, in fact. Danny was even beginning to feel at one with the colored lights of the Coke machine, which was creating a multicolored rainbow around Ollie's balding pate.

Woodman pressed his question. "But why religion? Do you know why?"

A cute answer just fluttered like a moth into Danny's mouth. "Because I'm an atheist and Sun Tzu said, 'Keep your friends close, and your enemies closer.' I wanted to keep a close eye on you God pushers."

Woodman laughed. "Your teachers have told me you're the class clown. That's good. That's good. You know, I've always said that humor is what a lot of otherwise good sermons are lacking. Jesus wanted us to laugh, I'm sure."

Danny thought, "Wow, this Harvard freak is seriously connected; he's been talking to Jesus."

"And that's what I want to talk to you about, Daniel. We're thinking of starting a series of Sunday Service student sermons at our main campus worship, and would like to ask you to join us in this groundbreaking endeavor. The first student Sunday Service sermon is on the upcoming Homecoming weekend. The chapel will be stacked with alumni as well as students."

Woodman continued, now in a conspiratorial stage whisper, "Furthermore, Daniel, we'd like you to be the student to kick off this innovative sermon series on Homecoming Sunday. Don't worry, Daniel, I'll work very closely with you on the actual text. With your stage and radio skills, I'm sure we'll create something with real impact for our distinguished alumni and honored guests."

Danny took a deep drag from his paregoric Marlboro, held it in a little too long to be discreet, exhaled, smiled warmly at Ollie, and agreed to do the sermon. Danny's gentle drugged eyes blessed Ollie as Ollie stood up to leave, even though there was an expression on

Ollie's face that would not have looked out of place on a well-fed lizard.

In the three weeks' lead time the two conspirators had to develop the Homecoming sermon, Ollie and Danny *did* work closely together on the text. Danny took Ollie's every suggestion to heart, no matter how tiny. The sermon they wrote was by turns challenging, but comforting; intellectual, but emotional; reasoned, yet placing a great deal of weight on pure faith. The structure was crystalline but not brittle. Its genius lay in its accessibility to the heart of the congregation, despite its obvious origins in high academe. Ollie was simply thrilled with Danny's sermon, mostly because Ollie wrote 93% of it and heavily edited the other 7%.

They made quite a team - confused, depressed, desperate, drugged-up Danny and the Lizard King of Religion.

The night before the sermon, even though it was a Saturday night, Danny took no drugs, drank no beer and got a full eight hours of sleep. Danny knew he had a job to do, and he wanted to do it straight, clean and sober.

Sunday morning, Danny took a bath and brushed his teeth, shaved and put on his least dirty shirt and his only suit - the same suit he wore on the bus to Iowa City to look respectable when going to pick up a bulk load of weed. Danny met with Ollie, as planned, an hour before the service for a final chat and, more importantly, a final prayer for success.

Danny sat on the dais at the front of the crowded field-house-turned-church for Homecoming and stared at the sea of faces, all engaged in worshiping in Danny's direction. Danny half-listened to the drone of the liturgy, but maintained an awareness of his cue to rise, which was the ending of the second hymn. The butterflies in his stomach threatened to fly Danny right up to the big wooden cross that was roped to the basketball backboard behind him.

Danny stood. He walked to the pulpit. He paused. He lifted the text of Ollie's sermon high above his head in a pose worthy of Abraham raising the knife to sacrifice his only son Isaac to God on a mountain altar in the land of Moriah. Danny ripped the typed pages of Ollie's sermon into pieces and let the pieces flutter into the first few rows of worshippers.

Danny was aware that some power had overtaken him. He thought he heard the whiskey priest say, "Do the right thing, son." Danny felt his mouth go dry. He had to pee. And vomit.

Danny began a sermon that was constructed from things he had been pondering in his heart for the last year, grown from seeds planted by the whiskey priest. Danny looked at the scars on his hands from the self-inflicted puncture wounds he had made in the bathroom of the bar on the night he had met the whiskey priest. It was the night the dead girl had summoned him to the other side.

Danny began his own sermon, not Woodman's. Danny had written down a few notes after his morning ablutions on a single little note card - the kind of card he had used in competitive debating. But the sermon did not come from the note card. It came from his heart.

Danny began to speak softly, slowly, almost robotically. "We're engaged in an illegal and immoral war halfway around the globe. Last April, Martin Luther King Jr. said, 'The pursuit of this widened war ... is making the poor white and Negro bear the heaviest burdens both at the front and at home.' Bertrand Russell, in his war-crimes trials in Stockholm, has both indicted the U.S. and convicted it. Governor Ronald Reagan of California has said that 'we should win or get out and, more importantly - we can't win.' His statement echoes the Gallup poll's measured opinion of most Americans. Even *Life* magazine has withdrawn its support for the war."

Danny was warming to his topic now and no longer speaking robotically. "Why must a 20-year-old be charged with telling you this?" Danny paused for a second to let that rhetorical question sink in.

"Over half a million young Americans my age are in a jungle somewhere - guarding what, defending what? Killing for what reason? Getting killed for what rational reason, what moral reason?"

Danny's volume increased as his passion rose. "Enough of that, you say! Okay, war is hell. So what, you ask? You've heard all this anti-war rhetoric before. *You* aren't in the jungle. *You* are safe here in Iowa because *you* are a student or *you* are a girl or because *you* are a parent or teacher and therefore too old to be drafted. Aren't you just too smug hiding here in Iowa in this great sea of corn, hogs and hypocrisy?"

Danny became dramatically quiet as he asked, "What about God? Isn't a sermon supposed to be about God?"

Danny's voice rose to a muffled shout, "Well, this one isn't. You won't be hearing about God from me."

Danny's voice began to ring with hellfire. "This God-fearing church, whose president is sitting right in front of me intently studying his fingernails, released a statement about the war that was pure liberal mealy-mouthed waffling. On the one hand 'this' and on the other hand 'that,' but essentially it was no statement at all. This church is not on the list of official pacifist churches that your local draft board consults when grilling conscientious objectors like me."

Danny paused and pleaded, "My church, my church, why have you forsaken me?"

Danny made no attempt to conceal his emotion from the congregation. He boomed, "You won't be hearing about the God of this school, either. This school's capital campaign director, who is also sitting in the front row studying his hymnal, just accepted three-quarters of a million dollars for a new science centre from the chemical company that's making napalm for the Air Force. And he accepted a smaller, but still tidy, sum from a private construction company that's maintaining air bases in Thailand, from which brave American B-52 pilots fly five miles up to bomb civilians in Cambodia, a nation that's not even *in* this war, by the way. Recruiters from every branch of the Armed Forces are welcome here on career days. The Dean of Men, who is smirking at me from second row and taking notes, meets with two FBI agents every month to rat out students opposed to the war."

Danny's voice became a whisper. "Why has this Christian school forsaken me?"

From this reasoned whisper, Danny's voice rose slowly in emotion and volume. "This crappy civil war we've stuck our noses into has been going on in one form or another since the end of World War II. God won't end this war. He's shown no interest in doing so in the last 23 years. You won't hear me praising that God either, the one whose sad-sack son you believe was hanged on that wooden cross behind me.

"No, there's no God in this sermon, because we - the rational, just, and humane citizens of the United States of America - must end this war by our own efforts. Just you and me ... God has taken a few decades off. Edmund Burke said, 'All that is necessary for the triumph of evil is that good men do nothing.'"

Danny's voice assumed a tone of reasonableness. "So, *do* something, *please*. Start by getting your fat asses out of this house of hypocrisy." Danny extended his arms to include the whole building.

"That's my plan. This place is just plum full of devils." Danny's voice hissed with anger as he said this final sentence.

With that note hanging in the air like smoke from a six-gun, Danny left the pulpit and walked down the centre aisle of the field house. As he walked, Danny shed first his tie, then his jacket, and finally his shirt. Danny strode bare-chested down the aisle, looking neither left nor right.

His footfalls were the only sound in the building. No one walked out behind Danny. As he staggered away from the chapel, he was half-naked, dazed and drained. It was a clear crisp October morning in the Midwest. Danny heard the congregation launch into the third hymn:

This is my Father's world:
He shines in all that's fair;
In the rustling grass I hear Him pass;
He speaks to me everywhere.

Danny was listening for *his* Father. Danny was always listening these days. But all he could hear was Satan.

CHAPTER THIRTY-ONE

The ultimate measure of a man is not where he stands in moments of comfort,
but where he stands at times of challenge and controversy. ~*Martin Luther King, Jr*

D anny was in bed the morning they came for him. It was the morning after he had preached his sermon. Danny was ill and shaking but not from booze or drugs. He had abused no substances for several days. He was fairly certain he had malaria, although the closest he'd ever been to a jungle was the Chicago Brookfield Zoo in the eighth grade. But he was not as sick as he would be in an hour or so, after "they" had finished with him.

"They" in this case included Dean Dipswitch backed by Quigley, the sad-sack campus cop, who looked sicker than Danny - either because he had had too many the night before, or too few this morning to straighten him out again. The third "they" was a gray man in a gray suit whom Danny had never seen before. Danny thought he looked like a lawyer. Danny's guess was correct.

Because Danny slept naked, he felt at something of a disadvantage talking to these three clothed men: two in suits and ties, and one in uniform. When Danny stood up to face his visitors, Danny was clothed only in a green, red and yellow Hudson's Bay 2-point blanket that he had wrapped fetchingly around his waist like a sarong.

"Harper, you really did it this time."

Danny smiled without knowing why. He was sweating, shivering and felt like he was going to throw up. It was not a happy smile, it was just a muscle twitch like a pickled frog's leg in high-school biology.

"Did you just smile?"

"No, Dean Dipswitch, that was the guy behind me." Danny was impatient. He wanted whatever the hell these people were bringing to his door to be unwrapped and dumped in his lap with maximum dispatch. "Cut the crap."

Ignoring Danny's remarks, the Dean went on, "This man is the college lawyer. He has some papers for you to sign."

"Papers?"

"We just want to straighten out a few things, Harper."

The Dean went on, "Apparently, Doctor Woodman told the faculty members at his weekly departmental meeting that he had written an important sermon that you were going to read for him yesterday. We, the administration, are certain that's not true. We've prepared a document stating that Doctor Woodman didn't write a single word of that vile trash you spewed yesterday. Here. Sign it."

"Nope, Ollie and I worked very closely on that sermon, and I wouldn't want to take away any glory that's his alone," Danny said through chattering teeth.

The Dean turned and asked the other two to leave and shut the door.

"Harper, I won't be blackmailed. Doctor Woodman has asked to go on medical leave. We granted it. You'll leave here, too, but not before you sign this document."

"Nope, I can't lie. It's not in my character, sir," Danny said, through teeth he was gritting to stop the chattering.

"Sign and we'll let you come back next semester."

"Okay, and refund my whole tuition and room and board, in cash, for this semester ..."

"Done. You'll be gone before sundown today, or I'll have the authorities drag you out. Are we clear? Our lawyer will prepare the paperwork to facilitate all of what we've just agreed to. Stop by my office on your way off of campus." The Dean paused. "I note that you've experienced some admirable character development since we last spoke." Danny admired how the Dean stayed in character - smirking sardonic asshole to the very end.

"Admirable isn't exactly the way I'd phrase it." And with that, Danny's life as a free man ended. Dipswitch would make sure that Danny's draft board hunted him down like a mad dog. Danny had just failed to make "uninterrupted progress toward an undergraduate degree" by being thrown out of college in his seventh semester. The fact that Dipswitch had promised to let him back in for his eighth semester was of no practical consequence in terms of the draft.

The hit squad left Danny for dead on his bed. Danny pulled the Hudson's Bay 2-point blanket up over his head and tried to stop shivering.

CHAPTER THIRTY-TWO

War will exist until that distant day when the conscientious objector enjoys the same reputation and prestige that the warrior does today. ~John F. Kennedy

The county draft board scheduled Danny's conscientious objector hearing for January. Danny was back at Zwingli by that time. Danny had taken refuge with a friend from high school who lived in Chicago, after Dipswitch kicked him out of school.

Danny used his idle time in Chicago to meticulously prepare for his Selective Service hearing. In his written submission, he quoted everyone from Bob Dylan to Jesus, Joseph Heller to Bertrand Russell, and Noam Chomsky to Dwight Eisenhower. He ended with this quote from Russell, which he thought would clinch his case to be reclassified as a conscientious objector: "Patriotism is the willingness to kill and be killed for trivial reasons."

At the hearing, after the panel had studied Danny's five-page, closely argued and properly footnoted written submission, it gave Danny 15 minutes to make an oral submission, in his own words, if he so chose.

This was the moment Danny had waited for. After six years of honing his skills as a tournament-winning debater, and eight years of stage acting to good reviews, Danny knew he could move an audience with the sheer force of his language, logic, research and personal magnetism. This was Danny's most critical audience to date, but he had every confidence. He made his presentation with grace, power, humility and precision.

The panel hung on Danny's every word. There was a long silence after he quit speaking. Danny was waiting for applause or perhaps even tears. He adopted a proud, but humble, posture in the silence.

What Danny got, instead of applause, was throat clearing from the head of the Selective Service panel, followed by, "Son, that was a powerful lot of words you gave us. You really did some deep thinking, and I believe every word you said. I think I can speak for all of us up here," he said, looking for the nodding approval of the other board members.

"Son, now, you don't belong to a church that has any problem with serving in the Army, do you? I know you're not a Quaker or one of those other religions like that.

"We know you were an active speaker in the election campaign of Congresswoman O'Brien in this district, who - by the way - appointed most of us. You know, Mrs. O'Brien strongly supports the war. She has a son in the Navy over there, proudly serving. Now that's neither here nor there regarding your case, really, but we're not philosophers in this district. We're farmers and factory workers like your daddy. We've never in all of our history as a board had a conscientious objector from this district, and I'm afraid you're not going to be our first. Your President and Commander-in-Chief, who was elected in a democratic manner, wants you to serve your country in this time of need, and that's exactly what you're going to do. We wish you the best of luck and hope you give a good account of yourself in the service.

"Your application is denied."

Danny felt frozen in place. He couldn't move or speak. He had failed.

The head of the panel looked at the frozen figure in front of him and spoke with some irritation, "Son, you can leave any time now. We have other work to do."

Danny thawed, turned and walked away.

"No," Danny thought, "for once I didn't fail. I was brilliant. I was believable. I used footnotes properly. My country has failed me. Fuck 'em. Fuck 'em all!"

Danny went back to school for the rest of semester 8, even though he had lost semester 7 and lost his draft deferment. Danny thought he was a dead man walking. He sat in hallways in academic buildings, sometimes for hours, lost and stoned. He had no idea what classes he had enrolled in and what classes he just liked, and sat in on by accident. Danny dropped into professors' offices and wanted to talk about dreams he had been having, or sometimes he just went in and ranted about what a bunch of frauds they all were. Danny's friends said the sheriff had been around the dorm a few times asking for him. Was it about dope or about a hit and run on a parked car in front of a Presbyterian church across the river in Wisconsin one Sunday morning, witnessed by dozens of parishioners streaming out of service, and Danny driving dead drunk with a half-gallon bottle of vodka between his knees, or was it about the paternity suit that awaited him in the student post office in the form of a registered letter that he refused to pick up, and a paper saying why he refused to pick it up which he also refused to sign, so he slept in a different bed every night and sometimes in an abandoned car in an old garage. Or maybe it was some drug thing the sheriff wanted him for, or maybe it was something he couldn't even remember, or maybe the hit and run at the church or maybe the paternity thing, or maybe it was the draft coming to get him early or it could have been signing a false name on the motel register and not paying or maybe, finally, they were just going to kill him and put him out of his misery if he didn't do it first, and Danny tried when he took his grandpa's Ithaca 20 Gauge Grade 2 side-by-side box lock Damascus-barreled shotgun and shoved it in his mouth, loaded on both sides, and took off the safety and pulled the front trigger and nothing happened but a click, and ever since that day Danny was sure he was dead, so no one could see him and no one could hurt him and they would all be sorry they took Diana away from him to Oklahoma or Omaha and wouldn't let him see the baby. Danny had lost his dreams. The nightmares remained. Danny had run into the outstretched arms of the girl with one cold lavender eye and one cold blue eye.

CHAPTER THIRTY-THREE

The shepherd always tries to persuade the sheep that their interests and his own are the same.~Marie Beyle

Danny finished page 11, the final page of the Peace Corps application form. It had been a struggle; not because he couldn't write well, but because he had no idea how to couch the answers to the rather fuzzy essay questions they asked. Danny tried to figure out who they were really looking for, and how to be that person in the answers. Danny hoped they were looking for him, because he was certainly looking for them. Getting into the Peace Corps was his last real hope of avoiding the draft.

His conscientious objector application had been chewed up and spit back in his face by the Selective Service board in Lamoille County. They had also voided his student deferment, because Danny missed most of semester 7 due to Diana's pregnancy and disappearance, which led to his temporary insanity, that led to his preaching the Homecoming sermon and getting kicked out of school, thus creating an interruption in his "progress toward an undergraduate degree at an accredited institution of higher learning."

Danny had passed the Selective Service pre-induction physical, despite his obvious mental instability, drug use, optical nerve blindness and propensity to faint at the thought of his own death.

Danny had only two days to meet the deadline for mailing this 11-page masterwork, and he had yet to solicit the two required referral letters from current teachers. One was easy. Danny would ask Dr. Goldman. Danny had something on him. Danny had observed Goldman shouting, "Hump the host! Hump the host!" at an unofficial Theater Department party. Danny did not think he was merely quoting that famous line from *Who's Afraid of Virginia Woolf?* Danny saw Goldman disappear into a bedroom with the hostess and not come out for a long, long time. Goldman's beautiful young wife Mickey had, unfortunately, missed attending this soiree.

Goldman's beautiful young wife Mickey was a good friend of his former roommate, Dick; had taken some classes with Dick; and even had a drink with Dick and Danny once in a while. Danny knew Mickey would be all ears about the party.

Danny visited Goldman in his office and casually asked him to write a little something for his Peace Corps application. Goldman just laughed and kept saying, "You? In the Peace Corps?" over and over.

"Why'd they need a lousy lazy drug-bum actor in the Peace Corps?" Goldman chuckled.

Danny mumbled in his best Marlon Brando mumble, "Hump the host."

"What?"

Danny said it again, but in his Walter Cronkite voice, so it was *very* clear. Goldman heard it this time.

Goldman asked, "Okay, but how'll you know what I write in the letter?"

"Goldman, I'll know what you write, because I'm going to read it first."

"Danny, that's unethical."

"Goldman, shall we submit this ethical debate to your beautiful young wife Mickey for a judgment?"

Goldman changed his attitude fast. "Danny, you know I like you and wouldn't say anything bad about you. I was just kidding before."

"I'm still gonna read it, Goldman."

When Danny did read it, he came to admire what a truly gifted fiction writer Goldman could be, in the cause of peace and justice in the world and true friendship. This Peace Corps thing was going to be a lock, given the quality of Goldman's referral.

Danny needed one other referral and thought he'd go to the Religion Department for this one. Danny was the new darling of the Theater Department, but he had always been the darling of the Religion Department. Few Sunday nights went by without one religion professor or another dining, if not also wining, him in his family home.

Danny sought a referral from the hippest of the lot, Reverend Doctor Wilhelm "Call Me Willie" Kante - "like the philosopher but with an 'e.'" Willie sported some radical sideburns and had hair over his ears, although Danny thought he was a little too long in the tooth to be doing so. He wore a lot of paisley shirts, open at the neck, and a rustic primitively carved wooden cross hanging from a leather cord. He was genuinely hip, Danny thought, unlike the asshole youth minister who had failed to get Diana back. Kante taught some Reformation courses but mostly Social Gospel ones. Danny had been the star student in all of them.

Danny asked Kante for a referral letter, and Kante seemed very interested in giving him one. Kante asked Danny some of the same infinitely sincere questions that were on the 11-page form. In fact, Kante could have drafted some of the questions on the Peace Corps form. Fortunately, Danny was prepared for Kante's questions, having just written the answers to similar questions the night before. Danny used his pastoral counseling voice for his answers, giving them a ring, Danny thought, of extra sincerity beyond the content itself.

Kante said he would be most pleased to write a letter for Danny.

Danny asked, "When?"

Kante said the next morning at his office. He didn't have a typewriter or carbon paper at home. He told Danny to meet him at 10 at his office.

Danny met him instead, by accident, at 9:18 a.m. at the student post office. Kante was mailing a special-delivery letter to the Peace Corps. He said that he'd understood Danny to say that it had to be mailed today, and so, since he had the proper address in his files, he was getting a jump on things.

Danny saw a funny look on Kante's face. "Yeah, but I meant for you to give it to me so I could include it with my own packet," Danny said with some alarm. Danny had not been able to read Kante's letter first. Then Danny rationalized that he should have no cause for alarm. Kante was the hippest prof on campus, and he liked Danny, and Kante was into social justice as a way of life. Danny reminded himself that a lot of drug use at night could cause some paranoia in the morning. It was still morning.

Kante asked, "Are we still on for 10?"

Danny questioned, "Sure, but why? I thought 10 was just for me to pick up the letter?"

"No, Danny, I thought we could talk."

Shit, shit, shit. Shit. Danny recognized the real meaning of those words from his parents' phrase book. "Talk" usually meant "I'm going to fuck you up the ass." Now Danny *was* paranoid, and did not think it was the dope he had smoked the night before that was causing it.

"Okay, Willie, I'll come 'round," Danny said as casually as he could.

And Danny did go around to his office. Kante closed the door, asked Danny to sit, put on his fatherly smile, and said in his pastoral counseling voice, "I couldn't in good conscience fully support your choice of serving in the Peace Corps. You're a bright student - original in your approach to things, even - but not the stable and, well, frankly, sober individual our country needs to serve as a 'good-works ambassador' abroad. As much as I like you personally, and I do like you immensely, I think that if you go and serve your country in the military for a few years, as I did during the Korean conflict, you'll come back a more seasoned individual and more able to be of Christian service to the poor of this earth."

"You served in Korea?

"Not exactly. I was a chaplain's assistant at Fort Ord near San Francisco during that conflict." Kante got a faraway look. "Boy, does that city ever offer a lot of temptation. It was a hard job counseling the boys stationed there in a time of war. But that's not the point. I …"

Danny cut him off and involuntarily yelped, "The point is that you're trying to get me killed. I'm out of options here, Willie. What did you just do to me?"

"Control yourself, Danny. See, you're just demonstrating my point that you sometimes behave erratically. I followed my conscience on this call, Danny. And if you pray over it, you'll find you *do* indeed have options."

Danny couldn't speak to him again without yelling, so he was silent. He couldn't stay in Kante's office without crying, so he got up and left.

Danny went outside and fell back heavily against the sun-warmed bricks of the old chapel building. Danny smelled the lilac bushes that were coming off bloom and beheld the multi-green canopy of budding spring trees against the clean clear Iowa sky. Danny saw tulips beginning to open on the border of the parking lot.

Danny opened his mouth in a silent scream. A wall of anger, thick and high, blocked any tears; discretion blocked the scream. Danny retreated into numbness. He did numbness well.

Two weeks ago today, Danny's favorite cousin, Little Moose, who was declared "missing in action" before the school year started, was confirmed to have been shot dead at a place called the A Shau Valley. Danny pictured him there, with his insides hanging out, in a sea of festering mud, mouth open, with flies crawling over his eyes.

Danny knew he wouldn't have the guts to go home for the funeral. Danny was too frightened to see Little Moose's family. Danny had no idea what he should say to them.

Would he say to Little Moose's mom and dad, "My favorite memory of Moose is when me and the Moose-man used to sit around in his bedroom talking about his little sister Sally and about how big her tits were getting, then we'd jerk off together, and it's too bad we'll never have a chance to do that again?"

Danny wondered.

Danny wondered what he would say to Sally.

†††

Erwin Ernest Hagemyer III; age 19; 14 February 1968; small-arms fire; Vietnam; Church of the Nazarene; unmarried; Peru, IL; draftee

CHAPTER THIRTY-FOUR

It takes more courage to get out of a war than it does to get into one.~Mark Couturier

Her name meant "tender" in the most commonly agreed-upon interpretation of its entomological origins in the Semitic language group.

And this very young woman was tender and much more.

Lina laughed, and when she laughed, it was the music of a hand-carved wooden flute in the hands of a shepherd boy in the spring-green high sierra on a clear starry night, playing an accompaniment to a happy little stream rolling and rejoicing down a hill dotted with dozing sheep.

Lina laughed not just with her voice but also with her eyes and heart.

Lina said that, as a child, she had wandered the little dirt roads outside of her Iowa village in search of cows. When she found cows, she would stand on the fence and sing to them, until the herd came crowding to the fence and stared at her with their beatific bovine eyes.

Lina was a fine artist in oils, a gifted magic realist to be precise, and a superb draftsperson. She sculpted in clay and metal. She sang in the choir. She played saxophone in the band. She had been captain of her high-school basketball team. She had been captain of the swim team. She had the second-highest grade point average in the history of her school. She wrote fine poetry and even finer short stories. She fucked anyone she liked, and she liked most people. When she was 16, her parents and the local school authorities had exiled her to Zwingli College as a last resort. They couldn't understand her or control her.

She was 17 when Danny met her and in the second semester of her first year at Zwingli College. Danny was hallucinating his way through his eighth semester. Lina was flunking out of her second semester, after getting straight A's in her first. She had discovered drugs. She was working her way through fucking all the men in the leftist druggy raggedy-clothes "tribe" of which Danny was a charter member, and when Danny's turn came, she stuck with him and stopped fucking other people.

Her infinite gentleness and tender mercy were a balm to Danny's wounded soul, and her exotic beauty a treat for his eye. Although ethnically Swiss on both sides, she had the slant-eyed beauty and the very high prominent cheekbones of an American Indian or a Pacific Islander. Blue eyes with a lilac hint set off her lightly freckled skin and boy-cut nut-brown hair. Her smile was always warm and always genuine. She blushed easily; she laughed even more easily.

She said to Danny, "You seem normal to me."

After she said that, Danny fell in gentle love with her and she with him. This was not the earth-shattering addiction he had felt with Amy and Diana, but a sweet low-key romance with a warm person - a person who was amazingly talented in more ways than any one person should be. It seemed obvious to Danny that he should marry her. As she did not seem to object, they planned a wedding. The first part of the planning involved getting permission to marry from her parents. She was still a minor person under Iowa law.

Her father, owner of Noni's Notions, a dry-goods store in Lina's little home village and a naval veteran of the Pacific in WW II, asked Danny some serious and disturbing questions. Danny answered him with half-truths, white lies and a few big black lies. His future father-in-law pondered Danny's answers over his weak sugary tea at the oilcloth-covered kitchen table, and then deferred the decision to his wife.

Danny's future mother-in-law had defied her parents at the age of 16 to marry a young sailor, who had no apparent prospects and was just back from the war. She had seen this beardless sailor grow into his powerful dual role of notion-store owner and alternate village councilman, and she knew you couldn't always judge the man by the apparently poor prospects of the boy. No boy appeared to have poorer prospects than Danny, at this point. This made Danny all the more appealing to Mother Noni.

Noni (yes, her husband had named his store after her) was a true romantic, in the best of that dopey American tradition. She allowed that her daughter was in love, and what else did they have to know to give their permission?

Exactly.

After a counseling session with the local churchman and waiting 48 hours for a license, during which time Danny was exiled, along with the family dog, to a rollaway bed in the basement - presumably to allow his bride to regain, at least partially, her virginity - and after getting a negative result on their Wassermann test (there is mandatory testing for syphilis in Iowa), the happy couple was married in the presence of God, the bride's parents, her two brothers and one sister. The bride wore a purple miniskirt, and Danny wore the same sober suit he wore on the bus when he bought wholesale quantities of drugs in Iowa City or Madison. The bride carried a bouquet of silk flowers, courtesy of Noni's Notions. There were bows and ribbons galore in the church, also courtesy of Noni's Notions.

After the ceremony, the newly enlarged family gathered around the oilcloth-covered kitchen table. They drank punch made from pineapple juice mixed with ginger ale, decorated with floating lemon slices. They exchanged tentative, almost shy, best wishes to each other. They ate Triscuits heated under the broiler to melt the Kraft Cracker Barrel cheddar that cleverly hid little slices of pickle atop the cracker. Danny hated pickles and almost choked on the first one, but smiled and swallowed the thing, nonetheless. The couple left after the second round of punch. Noni packed them a lunch for the road. Danny hoped she had not put pickles on the sandwiches.

The couple was headed to Illinois to see Danny's parents. Noni had squealed to Danny's parents about the marriage, and hence, a stop in Illinois was not optional.

Danny's mother greeted the couple with stern politeness. Danny's father greeted them with silence, but not disapproval. He couldn't take his eyes off Lina. He smiled at her - almost grinning a few times. He seemed to want to say something to her, but never did, even though his eyes sparkled volumes.

The new couple spent their first night as man and wife together in the same single bed in the attic in which Danny had masturbated every night during his high-school years. Danny felt uneasy there with Lina. Having her in this bed somehow betrayed the warm, very personal and very private masturbatory memories that he cherished. He felt it defiled these memories, inviting a live woman into his once-sticky sheets. Danny couldn't get an erection. Lina didn't seem to mind.

In the morning, Danny announced they had to leave to visit some friends. Danny failed to mention that the friends were in Canada, and they would not be returning.

Danny's father said, "Here's a hundred bucks. Don't tell your mother. She's pissed off that you still owe her five from that stunt you pulled last summer - not getting her cigarettes and milk and coming back two weeks later without it.

"Treat that little girl good. Now that you're a married man, I hope you stop taking all those drugs. You know, even though I drink some, I know that drinking doesn't make me into a better man. Think about that."

"I will. Thanks for the C-note. I love you."

Danny kissed his mother because she insisted on it, but he didn't tell her that he loved her. Danny believed he did not.

Danny pointed the '55 Chevy Bel Air four-door, which he'd purchased for $300 the week before leaving Iowa, towards Detroit and the Ambassador Bridge into Canada. He had $110, a car that didn't burn too much oil, most of his worldly possessions in the back seat, and a gentle lovely woman beside him. Lina hummed and sang a lot on the ten-hour drive to the border. She sketched things she saw along the way with charcoal on a big artist pad on her knees. Her voice was always on pitch and her sketches, though sometimes very minimal, always captured what was most essential in her subject. Danny was in awe of her talent. Lina had fun sketching, sometimes giggling at what she had drawn.

CHAPTER THIRTY-FIVE

A rational army would run away.~Charles de Secondat, baron de Montesquieu

At the border, the first international border either of the two newlyweds had ever crossed, the border guard - a cheerful-looking, middle-aged man in a uniform at a little booth - asked, "What's your citizenship, please?"

They chimed out in unison, "American!"

He asked, "What's your relationship to each other?"

They both held up their ring fingers to show the wedding bands. "Married!"

"And what's the purpose of your visit?"

"Honeymoon!"

"Do you have any drugs or firearms?"

"No." Although Danny wished he had both.

"Have a pleasant stay." And he waved them through.

Danny noticed the border guard was not armed and wondered how Canada managed to keep the communists out. Danny thought, "What if I'd whipped out my dad's big Colt automatic? What would this nice man have done? Strange country, Canada ..." He knew American border guards had guns. Maybe the United States didn't let Canadians have guns. That was probably it.

Danny slowly fed gas to the 1955 Chevy Bel Air sedan. The car moved and stopped but did little else. Danny gave it gas slowly because the car had no muffler or tailpipe. The hopped–up straight-six engine burbled menacingly, but did not explode into a military jet roar the way it could have if Danny had pressed down the accelerator even a quarter-inch further. Danny didn't want to upset the citizens of this strange country within the first 10 seconds of arriving with a car that sounded like the loser of a demolition derby. The car also had no horn, no windshield wipers, no turn signals, no tail lights and no dashboard lights. It was safe to drive the old Chevy in the daytime, as long as it didn't rain. Danny wanted to make it to Toronto before the sun set or before it rained.

They were pointed straight at Toronto once they crossed the bridge at Detroit/Windsor. Danny had been disappointed to learn, somewhere in Michigan when he acquired a Canadian map, that Toronto was not a Canadian state but just a city - a much smaller target. Danny had a phone number in Toronto for two former students of Zwingli College. They had preceded Lina and Danny by a year. They were desperately serious political refugees. Danny and Lina were anything but. Danny and Lina were on a lark.

Danny's Toronto contacts were fellow members of SDS, Students for a Democratic Society, a thinly veiled commie front organization that later morphed into the Weather Underground. The Weather Underground furthered the cause of peace, equality and justice by organizing a few rather squibby bombings, botched bank jobs and bungled kidnappings. The Weathermen were politically astute but criminally incompetent.

Danny had actively participated in SDS at Zwingli, mostly by actively selling dope to members. Dick had participated by being the recording secretary. Danny ducked out of their seemingly endless meetings at the first sign of wrangling about whether they should change the system from within or without, or what strategy, they as cadre leaders, could use to make a real connection with the real workers and racial minorities, without alienating them by appearing to be guilty of intellectual elitism in the service of the inevitable universal socialist democratic revolution.

Danny much preferred the Zwingli College Black Panther meetings, at which Danny, as an honorary Panther due to his living arrangement with the heavily armed Marvin, was always more than welcome. Danny also dealt them dope. As most of the Panthers were from well-to-do suburbs and afraid to drive through the ghetto, they had a hard time scoring when they were home. They had come to depend on Danny.

The Panthers discussed almost nothing political; only how to get white chicks to fuck them. They drank wine, smoked Danny's dope and slapped each other's hands and said "brother" a lot. The revolution would presumably come of its own accord when they had figured out how to breed some good black blood into all the little blonde girls in this part of Iowa. Danny found the Panthers refreshing compared to SDS.

The Panthers found Danny refreshing too, apparently. They played a game using Danny. They allowed Danny to call them "niggers" in public while they laughed and joked with Danny, smiled and punched his shoulder. They did this to lure any unwary white boys within earshot into using the same word. When the other white boys used the word, hearing Danny use it, the Panthers made them pay dearly. Danny was their staked goat, as well as their dope dealer.

Danny liked the Panthers. They were certainly a fun bunch of guys. They didn't put up with a lot of backtalk from their women. The serious, sober and somber SDS types could learn a lot from these black princes about having a good time and also about keeping women in their place. The SDS let women talk at their meetings, and even appeared to listen to them. Panthers didn't even invite women. Danny rather liked women, but somehow women who were political were more offensive to him than men who were political.

The daylight lasted long enough, the rain held off, and the crippled Chevy made it to Toronto about four hours after crossing the border. Danny called and got good directions to his political friends' apartment. The political friends plied the newlyweds with strong Canadian beer and bland Canadian cigarettes. The two old ex-pats conspicuously used strange phrases in front of the new ex-pats to prove they were already assimilated, eh? They made the new couple sprinkle suspicious-looking brown vinegar on French fries, which they called "chips." They paid for the "chips" with what looked like Monopoly money, with some woman's picture on it.

"Wow, this is sure some strange place," Danny said, his mouth full of salty-and-sour fried potato.

Kevin, Danny and Lina's host, and surely the greatest unrecognized Marxist/Leninist scholar of his generation, said, "You two will have to get jobs to get your landed immigrant papers."

"What's that? What for?" Danny didn't understand the term Kevin used.

"Well, you have to work, don't you? And you can't work without papers. They'll kick you out eventually if you don't have papers and don't work."

"That's un-American!" Danny was outraged. "I don't have to work for awhile yet, anyway. I still have over sixty bucks in cash."

"Look, Danny, you have to work. And besides, it'll help you form a bond with the working classes in order to hasten the revolution."

"Fuck. Really?"

"Janey and I can get you a written job offer from a draft resister sympathizer at the place we work. You just take that job offer to the border, swear you speak English, and they'll let you in."

"But they already let us in."

"I know, but not permanently."

"Shit, Kevin, these Canadians sure have some strange ideas - first weird brown vinegar on the French fries, and now going across the border just to get back in again. There's sure a shitload of stupid rules up here."

"That's the way it works, Danny. We have to work within the system for awhile before we eventually overthrow it."

"Fuck, Kevin, how many times have I heard that shit about working within the system? Okay, we'll go get the job offers. What kind of job is it, anyway? Research or teaching would be good."

"It's working in a psychiatric hospital."

"Hey, I studied sociology. That'll be cool."

"I don't think they need sociologists over there. They need people to give enemas and change diapers and feed people. They'll start you on the geriatric ward. It's not that bad. After a while in geriatrics, you can ask for a transfer to another kind of ward. They even send you to school for free after you've proven yourself."

"Cool. Grad school?"

"No, you can learn to be a registered nursing assistant."

"Oh, a registered nursing assistant, huh? Get me the interview," Danny said sarcastically, but he had resigned himself to doing a few stupid things for a little while before he figured out what to do for real in this new land. Doing what Kevin and Janey suggested seemed reasonable in the short term. Political types were boring, but usually trustworthy.

CHAPTER THIRTY-SIX

We cloak ourselves in cold indifference to the unnecessary suffering of others--
even when we cause it.~James Carroll

D anny arrived exactly on time for his interview with the Head of Nursing Services at the hospital. Danny was still full of the work ethic that had seen his meteoric rise in the truck-stop business from junior attendant to acting temporary assistant shift leader. The Head of Nursing Services was a gruff old thing who had nursed in the English Army in WW II. Her hair was shorter than Danny's and her biceps were bigger. She didn't seem mean, though - just businesslike.

She asked Danny, "Do you have grade 10?"

"What's a grade 10?" Danny replied, truly mystified.

"Have you successfully completed grade 10 in school?"

"Tenth grade?" Danny was cluing in now. School, okay ...

She rephrased the question, "Yes, tenth grade. I forgot you're a Yank."

"Uh, I think I've completed grade 16."

"Can you prove it?"

"Yup, I have all my transcripts with me."

"Good, then, you have the job. Oh, are you willing to swear an oath of allegiance to the Queen and her heirs? Some of you Yanks aren't willing - you know, afraid of losing your citizenship or something."

"I rather like Her Majesty. Her heirs are pretty cool, too." Danny meant that. He was part English.

With that, Danny had his first job in Canada, working at one of the regional mental health centers for the Government of Ontario. His title was "probationary nursing assistant Grade 1." His new allegiance to the Queen and her heirs swelled his chest with pride, even if his job title left him flat.

The hospital tested Danny for tuberculosis and gave him a Wassermann test for syphilis, even though he told the nurse that in order to get his marriage license in Iowa, he had just passed the same test. After he passed his tests, the nurse gave him two snow-white starched uniforms - one of them two sizes too big, and the other one size too small. She told Danny to show up in uniform at 11 p.m. on Sunday to begin working.

Danny was assigned to the geriatric ward, just as Kevin had predicted - a job that entailed handling bodily fluids and solids, but was not dangerous. Danny figured that they sent him to this ward either as punishment for sins so bad he couldn't even imagine them, or to ease him into the mental health business by exposing him to patients who couldn't fight back.

Midnight shift was quiet - no feeding, no bathing, no diaper changes, no dressings, no enemas and no bed changes. If the afternoon-shift RN did her job at meds time, making sure the old folks didn't spit up or hide their sleepy-time pills, the crazy old farts would be comatose until the day shift came in.

The day shift was something else again, and Danny went on it after two weeks of midnights. Geriatric patients who qualified to end up in the back wards of a provincial institution were patients in pretty sad shape, capable of breathing and sometimes walking, but very little else. They were like full-sized babies, with their every need taken care of by the thugs on the ward. And the staff was mostly thugs. Danny would soon become a thug himself, much to his own horror.

The guys Danny worked with most often - Homer, Tommy and Satinder - were all British army vets from WW II except for Satinder, who was a peacetime British army vet. They hated Danny on general principle because he was a Yank. "You Yanks were two bloody years late getting into the fray. Buncha poofters." They tolerated Danny because he told them he hated Yanks, too. Danny had no idea what a poofter might be, but he gravely assented to hating them, too.

These blokes (Danny knew what a "bloke" was) seemed to hate the patients more than they hated Danny. Patient care for them was that irksome thing what stood between them and their smoke breaks, their tea breaks, their lunch breaks and their chat breaks.

Each day, the head nurse (herself a veteran of Queen Alexandra's Imperial Military Nursing Service) presented the blokes with "the list." From this list, they knew how much extra work they would have to perform beyond the usual feeding, diapering, shaving, dressing, barbering and bathing of the 16 men down the corridor. The list she gave them was the enema list. The blokes just called it "the list." The existence of "the list" or, sometimes, the size of the list, determined whether it was going to be a good day on the job, a tolerable day, or a very bad day.

The main enema list had the names of the recipients on it, but was broken down into three subcategories by enema type: fleet enemas (the easiest, just a little hand-held squirt bottle), the molasses enema (a half-pitcher of warm brown liquid, gravity fed, down a 3-ft. tube), and the 3H enema (high, hot and a hell of a lot, down a 6-ft. tube from a pitcher suspended near the ceiling, to increase the fluid pressure). The staff found giving enemas not just messy and disgusting, but also a waste of valuable time. The recipients of the enemas hated them, too. But enemas were necessary. It was logical that if you intended to feed gluey low-fiber food to ancient persons who did not exercise, you had to make sure the waste products from the food came out the other end.

The blokes faked the numbers on the "natural bowel movement" chart as much as possible and as often as possible to avoid having the head nurse put patients on the enema list. The tough old head nurse was wise to her staff's cheating ways and compensated for it by ordering periodic enemas for everyone, regardless of how many "natural" bowel movements the wily staff faked in the records. She had been in the Army and could spot a shirker a mile away. Except for Danny, all the blokes on his shift were expert shirkers, and resented Danny's lack of solidarity with their shirkiness. The three blokes Danny worked with were all proud union members, and strangely enough, all three were union stewards. The only person they had to represent on the ward was Danny; the nurses belonged to a separate union. The stewards all encouraged Danny to complain about something - anything - but having come up through the ranks of the Jones Oil/Gulf Oil system, Danny had few complaints. The work in the hospital was smelly and disgusting, but fairly easy compared to the work life he had experienced as an ambitious pump attendant. The union reps grumbled among themselves about Danny's failure to complain.

If Danny had a mind to complain, it would have been about enemas. An enema wasn't just the act of performing a simple and slightly uncomfortable procedure on a slightly frightened but, still, mostly co-operative patient. Oh no, on a geriatric ward, an enema was the act of performing an ass rape on a screaming, kicking, biting, irrational, beast-of-a-former-human who had to be subdued physically to allow the anal administration of large quantities of various noxious brews concocted by the head nurse. The blokes had to physically subdue the man/beast to administer the brew, and physically subdue him once again for the clean-up afterwards. Enema time was a time for muscle; the whole day shift was a time for muscle.

To keep on schedule and check off all the boxes on the daily duty sheets, the blokes were forced to resort to kicking and punching and twisting and literally beating the living shit out of these old guys - any shit they had left to beat out, after a three-quart soapsuds enema. The blokes did not have time to be gentle with the patients, or even be merely firm and forceful. The blokes had to deal with adults who had the intelligence of carrots and the temperament of wolverines. The beatings just made them meaner, but there was no alternative.

Danny's liberal humanitarianism was soon replaced by a grudging acknowledgement of the need for sheer brutality. Leaving patients un-bathed, unshaven, unfed, unshorn and constipated, with wet diapers, was not an option. Relatives would complain of "inadequate care." Doctors and nursing supervisors from the front office would raise hell at the least sign of "inadequate care." Relatives never imagined the brutality necessary to provide "adequate" care. The doctors and supervisors never went beyond the doors that led to the patient rooms and bathrooms, where all the brutality took place.

Only the blokes and Danny, now a bloke himself, knew what it took to get the job done - keeping the colons clear, the diapers changed, the stomachs full and the bodies washed.

After the enemas, bathing was the next worst thing. In order to encourage patients to cooperate or, more likely, to just quit struggling, blokes dunked patients' heads under water, put wet towels over patients' noses and mouths, pulled patients' hair and punched them in the guts. Danny was horrified by all of this brutality in the first few weeks when he was just observing and learning the job. Very quickly, however, he became one of the torture monsters himself.

When he went home and talked to Lina, he referred to himself as a concentration camp guard or a zookeeper. He did not go into specifics with her, as she was a far too delicate soul. He told Lina he wanted to get a tattoo on his front and backside that said, "I am a human being - do not abuse me," for when he got old. Danny didn't tell Lina that he would rather kill himself than let anyone drag him into one of the hells on earth known as nursing homes. He figured there was no use upsetting her; he was probably 30 years away from having to go into a "home."

The registered nurses and the doctors met several times a week, and did case conferences based upon the fancifully false information the blokes put in their daily patient notes. The professional nurses and psychiatrists ran a theoretical hospital ward that was only real on paper. The real geriatric ward was more like Hades than a hospital.

On the "real" ward, beyond the doors, Danny saw himself as a Nazi, or at least a Nazi collaborator, in his ill-fitting white suit which had shit and piss stains on it at the end of every shift and, sometimes, blood. Danny was afraid of quitting, because doing so might alert someone in the Immigration Department, who might then try to deport him for a lack of commitment to his work offer. Danny didn't want to disappoint his benefactor in the hospital personnel department - a person who believed she was helping to fight the madness in Vietnam by providing employment to Danny and other American draft evaders who needed a job offer in order to immigrate.

Danny also needed the money. Lina had not found a job yet. So Danny convinced himself that he was just gathering evidence of all the brutality he saw and participated in, in order to expose it to the proper authorities and get this place reformed someday or even shut down.

After several months of geriatric zookeeping, Danny still had not exposed the brutality to the press or the police. His goal of being a whistleblower extraordinaire was pushed further and further into the future, as Danny became inured to his role of geriatric concentration camp guard. His big exposé was just a rationalization he used to allow himself to continue being brutal.

After six months in geriatrics, Danny was offered a transfer to another type of ward, an "intermediate ward," just as Kevin had predicted. He accepted the transfer with relief. The "intermediate ward" was a collection of mixed nuts - young and old, long term and short term, and the somewhat violent and the not-so-violent. Danny's workmates here turned out to be younger and smarter, better educated and less brutal in general than the English army blokes. The inmates here were much more able to fight back than the geriatric cases, so the staff was much less inclined to start fights that might end with the patient winning. The patients never won on the geriatric ward. In some cases, these intermediate patients were together enough to articulate a complaint if they felt they had suffered physical brutality. Intimidation of patients, humiliation and threats supplanted physical violence on the intermediate ward - a different therapeutic modality.

Danny found interacting with patients on this type of ward much more stimulating than interacting with the veggies on the geriatric ward. This ward had a few sociopaths and borderline personalities. These nuts really knew how to spice things up. The sociopaths and borderline personalities were the poets and artists of the crazy kingdom - making bad poetry and bad art, but still hugely amusing compared to the puking, peeing and pooping residents of the geriatric ward.

One November afternoon shift on his new ward, after stealing the supper from a patient who was on a hunger strike, Danny was ingesting the nicotine from a disgusting-tasting, tinder–dry, unfiltered cigarette he had stolen from the supply cupboard. He had taken it from one of the little 1940s vintage white cardboard 10-packs the Red Cross supplied to patients from what must have been a nearly infinite supply still left in some government warehouse. World War II ended before the soldiers overseas had smoked all the cigarettes the Red Cross had warehoused for them. The Red Cross had been handing them out to mental patients for over 20 years. Smoking these cigarettes confirmed Danny's suspicion that cigarette tobacco does not improve with age, but the burn time was under one minute so there was less time available not to like it. Danny was drinking an equally disgusting coffee made from hot tap water mixed with WW II vintage instant coffee powder, possibly from the same government warehouse as it tasted a lot like the tobacco.

In the TV room with Danny were a dozen or so freshly medicated inmates. They were watching their favorite show, *Bowling for Dollars*. Don Carter had just thrown a nose hit, which left him with a 5-2 split in the final game frame of the PBA Open. The inmates were on the edge of their seats; they were all rooting for Carter. Just as he tried to come back with a spare on the split, a news bulletin flashed over the TV screen. A breathless announcer proclaimed that men had landed on the moon. The announcer further intoned that there would be live coverage to follow of men walking on the moon.

Everyone in the room was excited, but for different reasons.

The lounge exploded in comment.

"Lies."

"Ridiculous."

"Pile of shit ..."

"Fuckin' fraud ..."

"Don Carter was about to clinch the tourney ..."

"They can't fool me. No one can fly to the moon."

Some inmates threw old *Reader's Digests* and blue paper slippers at the screen. When regularly scheduled programming returned, the PBA Open was over; Don Carter may have won or lost. A game show came on that was too complicated for medicated persons to follow. All the denizens of the TV room got up and left the room in disgust.

Miss Burbricken, who was the senior-ranking member of the crazies, having been incarcerated for an astonishing 42 years, came up to Danny and whispered, "You know, they tried to fool us like this on Halloween the year before the war, on the radio, you know, but I didn't believe them then, and I don't believe them now. Only then it was big machines from space landing here, not earthlings going there ..."

Danny heard mumblings from around the pool table where some of the *Bowling for Dollars* fans had gathered. They were in an adjoining lounge, laughing about men on the moon, and walking around taking giant steps like they were wearing bulky spacesuits. Danny realized that he was the only one in the TV room who believed that men could fly to the moon.

Danny lit another Red Cross smoke and sat alone for a minute, pondering the nature of insanity. Later that evening, just before his shift ended, Danny watched the "astronauts" in silly plastic spaceman suits take giant steps through what conspiracy theorists would later contend were piles of wood ash in a London film studio, shot by Stanley Kubrick and paid for by the CIA.

Danny felt his work with the insane coming to an end. He felt the end coming sharply and all at once, in fact. He walked to the locked ward door. He opened it with his key. He left the door unlocked with the key in it, propped open with an orange plastic chair, hoping to facilitate the escape of at least some of the crazies. He went to the staff locker room and removed his ill-fitting white uniform. He threw his uniform in the garbage, took a shower, put on his street clothes and walked out of that place forever, thinking, "You'd have to be crazy to work in a place like that."

CHAPTER THIRTY-SEVEN

It is for us to refuse loyalty when injustice holds sway. ~Henry T. Laurency

Danny had permanently retired the broken old '55 hot-rod Chevy that he and Lina drove to the peaceful constitutional monarchy of Canada. He had parked it in the back alley of the house where they rented the upper floor. He had retired it, because even though it ran well enough, Danny knew that with no horn, no exhaust, no wipers, no brake lights and no turn signals, it would not pass the mandatory safety inspection required to license it in this land that Danny was finding to be overly bureaucratic compared to the American Midwest.

The poor Chevy sat for months, and Danny just forgot about it. Danny had a good used bicycle and bus tickets and legs that worked. He and Lina had no money for plates anyway, much less money to bring the car up to Ontario standards.

One day, in the too-early part of the morning, Danny heard a firm and insistent knocking at his door. Slipping on a pair of trousers and a T-shirt, he answered the door to find two large men in cheap suits scowling at him. They proceeded to walk right past Danny into the apartment without asking.

The bigger of the two big ones spoke. "Where did you get that picnic table?" He pointed to the picnic table Danny had built from a kit to serve as a kitchen table, in the absence of any real furniture.

"Huh?" Danny wasn't really thinking well this early in the morning, so he answered truthfully, "I built it from a kit."

"Are you sure you didn't steal it from the city?"

"Oh, no!" Danny thought. "These guys are cops. Where did I put that bag of dope last night?"

"Are you cops?" Danny asked ingeniously, knowing the answer.

"We ask the questions around here."

Yep, they were cops all right.

"It's too small and not the right wood and too new to be a city table, and besides, how could I have gotten it through that little door you just came in?" Danny said with the best debaterly logic he could muster at that ridiculous hour of the morning. The kitchen clock said it was only 10:35.

The big one rebutted, "You coulda taken it apart and put it back together in here, but that's not why we're here. Do you own a 1955 white-over-blue Chevrolet Bel Air, serial number IPJ66786-T-V-1955OOP-27243977-7?"

"Maybe; I'm not too sure about those last three numbers, though."

"Look, smartass, we know you own it, we just wanted to see whether you were going to lie about that, too."

"Too? In addition to what?" Danny was getting into the spirit of this debate.

"We ask the questions around here, remember? Do you know where the aforementioned vehicle might be at this moment?"

"Nope, but I can go look for it in the back yard."

"No, you can't go look for it while we're questioning you. Put your ass down on that stolen picnic table, and don't move it until we say so. Why don't you just go ahead and make a smart remark now? My partner, who is calmly standing there making a note of all of your lies, has, unlike me, a very short temper. Do you understand, you little coward?"

Danny nodded his head in agreement, in a cowardly fashion.

"That's better, kid. We understand each other now. We know where your car actually is, we just wanted to see if you knew or whether you were going to tell us some more whoppers. Your car's been impounded. We found it a week ago up on the sidewalk in Petticoat Park. Do you know any Indians? I'm warning you, we're going to check up on your answers very carefully."

"I just know this one guy, just to see him, not as a friend, who runs the Curry Palace over on Adelaide Street."

"No asshole, I didn't mean those fuckin' raghead camel fuckers, I meant wahoos - red fuckin' Indians."

"I don't think he has a turban or a camel."

"Shut the fuck up about towel heads and answer my question: do you know any red fuckin' Indians?"

"Nope, don't know any …"

"You'd better not be lying again. We have sworn statements from witnesses saying that they saw four stinkin' wahoo braves run out of your car after it jumped the curb. We can prove those wahoos are friends of yours, so you might as well admit it now and save yourself some grief."

"Do you mean my car was stolen?"

"We ask the questions around here, buddy. Do you think it was stolen, or did you just loan it to these four fuckin' loser redskins who jumped the reserve?"

"Officer, I'd like to report my car stolen."

"It's not 'Officer,' it's Detective Sergeant, and I don't take stolen car reports."

"Who does take stolen car reports? Does he?" Danny asked, pointing to the questioning official's silent partner.

"You're a slow learner, aren't you, kid? *We* ask the questions. How many more of you are there in town?"

"Huh? One. You mean with my name who owns a stolen '55 Chevy?"

"How many more cowards like you are hiding here from military service?"

"Hey, this is Canada. You don't have an army, do you?"

"Just answer the question. How many more of you are there? And where do you all meet up?"

"Do you have a warrant?" Danny just remembered some law show he saw on TV.

"We don't need a warrant. You invited us in to report a stolen vehicle. Just tell us your friends' names and where they live, and we'll just forget about the picnic table and your friends the Indians you loaned the car to, a car that was involved in a serious accident that destroyed city property. We can be your friends, if you co-operate, or we can be on top of you night and day for the rest of your life. That will put a cramp in your drug taking and all the other crap your type does here. Just give us some names."

"I don't have any names. I don't know anyone in this city, except the people I used to work with."

"Okay, punk, we don't have all day for this, we have to go now. Play it any way you like. But keep a good lookout, because we're going to be all over you like stink on shit."

"Hey, what about my car? I'm the victim of a theft. Don't you want to take a report?"

"We're detectives, asshole, we detect things. We already know who stole your car."

And with that, they left. Danny looked in the back yard and the car was gone. Danny guessed he should call the cops.

Danny called the cops and they said they would send someone around sometime. No city cops ever showed up.

Two weeks later, Danny was awakened even earlier by another bout of firm, insistent knocking. It was a different team of men in suits, but the suits were much more expensive and the men had better haircuts than the first two cops.

They showed Danny their identification: Royal Canadian Mounted Police. They asked very politely if they might come in to talk about his stolen car. Knowing he had little real choice in the matter, Danny ushered them in and offered them a seat at his picnic table.

Once again, it was the bigger one who asked the questions, and the smaller one who took notes.

"We understand your car was stolen awhile ago? That must have been quite a loss for you, being a new immigrant. We'd like to apologize on behalf of our country and of on behalf of ourselves personally. Immigrants built this country, and we're proud of that fact. Without good immigrants, such as yourself, we'd just be a cold place on a map and not a proud member of the international community."

This guy was a college graduate for sure. Danny couldn't wait for him to pitch the ball. Danny was sure he would put a really good spin on it. And he did.

"You know, Daniel - if you'll let me call you Daniel? I'm Brad, by the way, and my partner is Barney - we know you're one of the good immigrants. You and your wife are employable and you've signed up to complete your degree next summer, and you have no criminal record in the States aside from that little misunderstanding about the military. We need more good eggs like you who come here and contribute. But there are some immigrants who come here and just take, take, take. They want to destroy this civil society that has welcomed them with open arms.

"It's our job in the RCM Police to weed out these bad apples and to welcome the good ones like you. Often, the best way that we can suggest for you to show your appreciation for the welcome you've been given here is to help us weed out those bad apples. Frankly, Daniel, we need your help and aren't too proud to admit it."

"What help do you need from me, Brad?"

"Thanks for understanding, Daniel. My, you're really quick!"

"Yeah, that's me, Brad. Quick."

"Good. Good. Barney and I would like to drop around here every so often and see what we can do to help you adjust to this new country. And you can help by just telling us about your life a little and what you're doing, and what your friends and acquaintances are doing. We don't want you to lose touch with your home culture, so it'd be good for you to meet other Americans like yourself and tell us how they're getting along, so maybe we can help them, too."

Brad and Barney smiled and got up to leave. Brad and Barney held out their hands. Danny shook their firm, dry hands. It felt good to Danny to be one of the men who would help Brad and Barney build a better, stronger, and more secure Canada.

Just as they were going out the door, Danny called out, "What about my car? I do need your help. Where is it?"

Brad just looked puzzled and smiled warmly. "We don't know anything about that. Maybe try phoning your local police." And they were gone.

"Well, fuck," Danny thought, "I ask them for one simple thing and all I get is a warm smile and a dry handshake."

Eventually, Danny found enough time and dimes to stand in a phone booth that had an intact telephone directory, and call all the numbers listed for the city police to find out where, and if, his car was actually being held in an impound yard, as the first visiting officers had indicated.

After numerous calls, Danny found someone who confirmed the fact that the Chevy had been impounded. The nice person even told Danny where to find the impound yard. Danny rode his bike to the pound directly from the phone booth.

The man guarding the impound yard was not wearing a suit. Danny found that encouraging. The guard was wearing an old, tattered and too-tight police uniform. He didn't have a good haircut, and had not shaved for a day or two. Danny guessed that being king of the compound was not a highly coveted position in police society. But from the looks of it, this officer was not all that interested in impressing his police peers. He looked to Danny to be a lot more interested in retirement, his next drink, or at least a long nap.

"Hello, Officer, that's my car, right over there," Danny said, pointing to the Chevy.

"Okay. Whatcha want me to do about it?"

"I'd like to take it home. It was stolen. Check your records. See, I have the keys and the ownership right here." Danny had the keys and the ownership right there.

"Okay." And with that word, the guard seemed to drift off somewhere far away. He looked a thousand yards over Danny's shoulder at an empty street. He looked at it for a long time.

"So, can I get it, then?" Danny asked hopefully, praying the man was not having a seizure of some sort, or dying.

"Get what?" the guard asked, seemingly coming part of the way back to the same world as Danny.

"Get my car, Officer," Danny reminded him, pointing to the old Chevy again.

The officer came back a little more from wherever he had gone. "Oh, your car. No. You can't get your car until I check to see if you owe us any money for storage."

"Well, I'm sure I don't owe you any money for that. You see, the car was stolen," Danny politely explained.

The guard said, "Okay." Again. Then he stared off through the tiny dirty window of the wooden hut into the yard of the compound or some alternative universe - Danny couldn't say which for sure.

"So, can I get my car now?" Danny prodded.

"No." The old guy suddenly snapped back to reality and looked at a clipboard with a list on it. "It says here you owe us $880 to get it today. Tomorrow, it'll be $900."

"I only paid $300 for the car, and I only have $11 in the bank." Danny had a brilliant thought. "Uh, how much would it be if you bought the car from me, say for a dollar, got it out of impound yourself, and I bought the car back from you and gave you the fees? I'll bet you get an employee discount on impound fees. Or, if that doesn't work for you, maybe you could see if the department would like to buy it as a detective car."

"No."

"What do I do? I can't leave it here. I'm broke."

The officer said, "Give it away, and whoever picks it up will have to pay."

"Hey, do you want it?"

"Nope."

"Know anybody?"

"Nope. But you can always donate things to a charity or to the federal government."

This idea caught fire in Danny's imagination. "Donate, huh? And then they'd have to pay the storage fees?"

"As long as I run this operation, everybody who takes a vehicle out of here has to pay." He was a good bureaucrat.

"Well, then, it wouldn't be very nice of me to donate an old $300 car with no exhaust, no horn, no brake lights, no wipers, and no turn signals to the Red Cross or the Cancer Society and have them pay $900 to get it. That wouldn't be charitable."

"Charity has nothing to do with it. No money, no car, no exceptions. That's the law, son, and around here, *I'm* the law." He was a very good bureaucrat.

"I understand, Officer. Thank you." Danny rode off on his bike looking for a pay phone, his mind racing ahead of his spinning tires. Danny had some dimes left and was going to put them to good use.

For only five dimes, Danny found the right government office to get the proper forms to donate his car to the federal government. Danny rode his bike straight to the office.

The following week, Danny's new friends, Brad and Barney of the RCMP, came by. Danny was glad to see them. They seemed glad to see him, too.

Before they got too far into asking snoopy questions about Danny's fellow Americans, Danny interrupted them with a question: "Do you guys work for the federal government?"

The big one answered, "Daniel, we surely do, and we're proud to serve. Why do you ask?"

"Well, do you guys ever handle legal papers and stuff like that?"

"We sure do, Daniel. I am, in fact, a lawyer, and Barney here is studying law, but we've chosen to serve our country as policemen. We handle a lot of legal paperwork."

"Well, Brad, I know you guys were too busy catching bad-apple immigrants to help me get my car back, and I understand that. I kinda found the car on my own, and figured I really don't need it anymore and thought I might give it away to the federal government. It's been you and all the guys like you in the federal government who have made me feel welcome here, and I thought that I could help some by donating a car I don't need anymore."

"Gee, Daniel, you just pay your taxes and help us try to weed out those bad apples. That's more than enough thanks for us, but if you want to give us a car, I suppose that would be nice."

Danny whipped out the three-page form GC-RC-U7787-b, with his car ownership papers stapled to the front page. He handed the form to Brad. "There's an address on the back page saying where you can pick up the car."

"Well, Daniel, that's wonderful. We won't be able to get the car ourselves, but we'll pass this on to the admin people who do that sort of thing. Can we get on with talking about you and how you're making out here?"

"Well, not really, Brad. I've been having this crampy diarrhea thing all day today, and I feel it coming on again now. Sorry, but this is a really bad bug. Can you come back next week?"

"Sure thing, Daniel. I hope you're feeling better by then. And hey, buddy, thanks for the car. Speaking on behalf of the Government of Canada, you're a heck of a guy."

Brad and Barney did not come back the next week. Or the week after that ... Or ever again ...

CHAPTER THIRTY-EIGHT

It's not a matter of what is true that counts but a matter of what is perceived to be true. ~Henry Kissinger

A side from the moon landing, mental madness and having the Chevy stolen, the first year in Canada passed in a delightfully dull way - the dull way life should pass in a peaceful and sane country. Dullness to Danny meant a sweet and simple life that he could actually plan, with no draft to blow him off course. Dullness came to mean living in a country with no bullet holes in the road signs and no trash on the highways and no slums, at least in the city where Danny and Lina lived. Their part of Canada had no racial tension; their neighborhood had people in it from all over the world in all colors of the rainbow. When they passed each other on the street, people looked each other in the eye and said a cheery "good morning" in a variety of accents.

Marriage agreed with Danny as much as Canada did. There was just no woman to compare in any way to his wife. Danny found the contentment and rest with her he had never known with any woman before. Lina smiled her way through life, and worked on her art every day.

He was mightily impressed with her art. Lina had multiple talents. Her painting was going well. Her painting stunned everyone who saw it with its exquisite control and fine technique, combined with the vast imagination she showed in coming up with ideas for the images themselves. Lina began writing poems and short stories that showed yet another side of her genius. Two of her stories were published in local magazines for money. Two of her paintings were selected by the artist-in-residence at the university to be in a group show at the end of his term. She was teaching herself to play the soprano saxophone on a used plastic horn someone gave her. She played fast and she played accurately. She sounded like Bird himself, to Danny's untrained ear, when she played along with jazz records. She had perfect pitch.

She managed the twosome's meager unemployment insurance with a real nod to her Swiss heritage. She loved to cook. She was cuddly and sexy. Her smiling eyes and gentle musical voice lulled Danny into a state of peacefulness he had never known. They never had an argument, not even a little disagreement.

Sometimes she would paint for days on end with no sleep, or write for days in her journals in a neat tiny cursive. Those creative sprees worried Danny some, but Lina seemed to be doing good work, always seemed to be smiling when she did it, and didn't seem unhealthy as a result. She never even had a cold that Danny was aware of. At other times, however, she did the opposite. She would stay in bed for days and do nothing, but Danny figured that probably was just to catch up from when she didn't sleep. Danny never expected an artist to act normally. Lina was never irritable or out of sorts, whether working or in bed, so Danny went along with her somewhat odd behavior and loved her and admired her all the more.

The two avoided other Americans as much as possible, but it was not all that possible sometimes, as the other Americans spent much of their time cruising for other Americans, therefore finding Danny and Lina rather than the other way around. The other Americans seemed lost without a war to oppose and a government to overthrow. It never dawned on Danny to miss the war, and the government here was so dull and tried so hard to be benevolent, it would have been a shame to hang it.

At the end of their first year as immigrants, Danny and Lina moved out of their little apartment and into a clean and warm old house with another married American couple, Rob and Katy, and one nice unmarried Canadian female who called herself Melody, which may or may not have been her real name. She sang beautifully and often harmonized with Lina, who also had a good voice and loved to use it. A stray cat took it upon herself to join the five-person household, as they moved furniture into the house and had all the doors open. They named the cat Martha.

The five people and one cat lived in harmony for a few months, sharing the cooking and cleaning and an old car that belonged to Rob. The five were a good match. They simply liked each other and made everything they did fun.

Late in the fall, after a few months in the new house, Lina grew quieter and quieter, until she finally stayed nearly silent for nearly three weeks. She grunted and nodded and answered questions with one word, when she answered at all. She seemed distracted, and she seemed like she had something on her mind all the time. She got like that when she was doing a major painting or working on some linked short stories, but she was not doing any art at all during this particular silence. Usually when she "went dark," as Danny called it, it only lasted a few days, not a few weeks.

She even quit chattering to Martha the cat and petting her. Lina ate infrequently. She didn't respond to Danny's sexual advances, except in a mechanical way. Danny quit making any advances, as it was embarrassing for him to touch an unwilling person. She didn't answer Danny's questions about what was bothering her. Danny resorted to begging her to talk. Begging did no good. Danny badgered her to talk.

Badgering did no good. Lina seemed to look straight through Danny when he talked to her.

The morning of the day before Christmas, Lina finally spoke. "I need help getting my stuff into the car." During the night, she had piled her things by the front door.

Danny looked at the pile and asked, "Are you leaving me?"

Her look said "yes."

"I love you. I'm sorry if I did anything to make you angry." Danny said that even though she didn't look angry, and hadn't looked angry at any point during the last three weeks.

"Talk to me."

Lina looked briefly at her pile of belongings near the door and turned back to Danny and said, "I can probably get most of the things in the car myself." Her voice was mechanical. She stared at Danny's chest as she spoke. She had not looked him in the eye throughout her whole period of silence.

"It's okay. I'll help you." Danny picked up the two biggest suitcases and carried them to Rob's car.

Danny returned and saw Lina looking at some record albums. "Lina, you can take any of the record albums you want." Danny looked at Lina's pile of goods and noticed that Lina seemed very careful to take only her own things. She took some of the albums they owned in common, but she didn't take any of Danny's favorite albums. Danny knew that some of his favorite albums were albums they had bought together. She had left all the best music for him. Danny recognized her kindness in this act. It was her kindness that had been the sun around which all her other wonderful traits revolved. It was her kindness now that brought on Danny's tears. Lina never saw his tears, because she had quit looking at his face weeks before.

Acting on impulse, Danny grabbed Rob's fancy camera and shot a few rolls of black-and-white film of Lina's leaving. He shot it from every angle - close-ups, medium frames and wide establishing shots. Danny never processed the film but kept it with him for years, finally losing it in one of his own moves, decades later.

Danny heard through Katy, who drove the getaway car, that Katy dropped Lina off at a big commune-style boarding house full of university students and assorted hangers-on. Katy heard from a friend of a friend, later in the week, that Lina had moved into the room of a medical student. In February, Katy told Danny that the same person told her that Lina was pregnant. The medical student was the father.

Danny had avoided the communal house. He had even avoided the part of town in which it stood. But late in the night of the day that Katy told him Lina was pregnant, Danny walked to that part of town and stood outside the boarding house for hours in the snow. Danny had a 9-in. butcher knife in his hand that he had spent considerable time sharpening on a whetstone. Danny felt nothing, not even the cold. He had no thoughts. No plans ... He no longer wanted anything. When Danny saw the last light in the house finally go out, Danny threw the knife in the snow and walked home.

One week later, Katy crept into Danny's bed in the middle of the night and stayed until morning. Danny helped Katy wreck her marriage.

CHAPTER THIRTY-NINE

Repetition does not transform a lie into a truth.~Franklin D. Roosevelt

The phone rang. The voice on the phone said, "Daniel, it's your mother."

"Yes, I know," Danny said stiffly. He was waiting for a reprimand or command or criticism.

"Daniel, your father is sick."

"Okay." Danny was waiting for her to tell him how this was his fault.

"He's been sick for awhile, but I didn't want to tell you."

"How sick?" Danny was concerned now. She hadn't blamed it on him yet, so he was beginning to loosen up.

"Very sick … He's been in the hospital for five weeks. It's a brain tumor, and they can't operate."

"Shit." Danny felt a lot more than "shit." He felt the floor drop out from under him, but he was used to keeping his feelings under tight control around his mother. She used any feelings he dared show as a club to beat him. Danny loved his father. Danny could always conjure up the smell of the man in an instant, and his father's scent came to him now on a strong gust of memory. His father smelled like machine oil and tobacco and leather and wool.

"I think he's going to die soon." There was an emotion in his mother's voice that was not present in the usual set of emotions Danny was used to hearing from her - anger, frustration, and disappointment.

She sounded sad. That was new. She sounded human. Danny had no idea how to respond to this emotion in his mother. He had never encountered it before. So, he reverted to answering the way he always answered her, briefly and with irritation in his voice.

"Okay. What do you want me to do?" After saying this, Danny heard what sounded like a sob and was sorry he was being so harsh with this woman, but he knew no other way.

"Stay where you are, and don't come here. They'll arrest you if you come here. Your dad wouldn't have wanted that."

"*Wanted that?* You're speaking in the past tense." Danny was being punctilious. "Why? My father no longer wants things?"

"Well, he can't talk or write. He has a brain tumor. He's not in any pain." His mother's voice had gone flat; she was back in control.

"Okay. I think I have to hang up now," Danny said in an equally flat voice. Danny was about to shout or scream in agony or run full out at the wall and smash his head. He could not let his mother know he felt any emotion, especially pain.

"No, don't hang up. Tell me how you and your beautiful wife are doing. You dad would like to know. He still seems to understand things."

Danny thought, "God, she sounds human now. What the fuck is happening? I've never heard her being human before. I don't know how to deal with this, any of this." So he just said, "Okay. We're okay. I think I have to hang up now." And he hung up before she got in another word.

Danny sat on the sofa and stroked Martha the cat, thinking of nothing in particular. He felt nothing. He wanted nothing. He liked this cat.

CHAPTER FORTY

Repetition does not transform a lie into a truth.~Franklin D. Roosevelt

Two weeks later, she phoned again.

"Daniel, it's your mother."

"I know that. Why do you always refer to yourself in the third person?" Danny knew what this call was about from the time he heard the first syllable.

"Huh?" His mother was not familiar with that grammatical term. "Your father died last night. I was with him. He didn't suffer."

"Okay. What am I supposed to do about that?" Danny hissed. Danny felt hot anger wash over him like a wave of molten metal.

"Well, I thought you might like to know, but apparently not. Why are you always so snotty to me? Didn't you hear what I said?" Her whining criticism was comforting to Danny. He knew how to do this dance with her. They had been practicing it for years.

"Sure, I'm not deaf." Danny was playing his part. He was being the emotionless monster son that she always accused him of being.

Daniel's mother was pleased to confirm that he was doing the dance properly. "You're the most selfish person I've ever met. Your father loved you like crazy, but he didn't know you like I did - he didn't want to know what you were really like. He was always so 'above it all.' It broke his heart when you left. He was never the same. You killed him, you selfish piece of shit."

She went on, gathering steam as she ranted, "Just stay where you are, all cozy in Canada, with that little whore wife of yours, and forget I even told you. And don't come to the funeral. You're not welcome. Besides, not that I care anymore, but the FBI'll be there at the funeral to greet you if you do show up, and they'll put your cowardly ass in jail. My lawyer, of all people, just called me out of the blue and told me that. It'd serve you ri-"

Danny slammed the phone down.

Katy asked, "Who was that on the phone, Danny?"

"Just my mother with her usual load of shit. You want another beer?"

"No, I'm okay."

"Fine, I'll drink alone. It's better to drink alone than not drink at all." Danny sounded cheerful. He was not.

Danny called his cousin Billy a week later. Billy said he was at the funeral. He said it was nice. He said that the FBI was there, or at least he thought so - two guys in suits, tall and fit, with sunglasses, driving a gray Chevy sedan with tiny hubcaps and a dinky antenna on the roof.

"Fuck 'em, Billy, they made that trip for nothing. Fuck 'em all." Danny hung up without saying goodbye. Danny was choked up with grief and blinded by a vision.

In his mind, Danny could see those federal weasels in their suits, just waiting to pounce on a grieving son, salivating at the thought of a dramatic graveside arrest, and flourishing credentials and handcuffs in front of the gathered mourners. With luck, they would have to shoot the grieving son when he resisted or at least pistol-whip him. Danny knew that members of the FBI were exempt from military service. "Pricks …"

Two weeks later, Danny got a check in the mail for $1,800 US and an unsigned note in his mother's handwriting: "Your father wanted you to have this."

Danny cashed the check and gave $500 to Katy, whose husband had smacked her around and then abandoned her after she started sleeping with Danny. She could pay the rent for awhile. With the $1,300 he had left, Danny purchased a round-trip ticket to Paris on Air Canada. The remainder, not spent on airfare, went into traveler's checks denominated in French francs.

CHAPTER FORTY-ONE

When we fill our souls up with creativity, artistry and intelligence ...we have a better chance at avoiding the behavior that leads to destruction. ~Rick DellaRatta

Danny thought Paris was remarkable. It was remarkable because it looked just like Paris should look, and the people acted just like French people should act. Danny found the French brusque and aloof, but did not think any less of them because they were haughty.

Danny knew Americans were hated all over the world, except in Canada where they were merely quietly resented. He accepted the Parisians' disdain as his just desert for once having lived in that snake's nest of imperialism called America. Danny traveled with red cloth maple leaf flags pinned to his jacket and on the surplus gas mask bag he used to hold his personal items. The maple leaf flags were meant to indicate that he was not American, but Canadian. Most Europeans in tourist areas were wise to this trick. There was a big demand for maple leaf patches in American travel stores.

Danny took a small room in Le Quartier latin, off Boul' Mich, near L'île de la Cité - 19 rue Saint-Séverin, to be precise - and never stayed anywhere else in Paris, and never ventured beyond this neighborhood and central Paris the whole time he was there. The whole time he was there turned out to be much longer than he had planned, and much longer than he had the money to support himself.

The room he lived in had a lumpy bed with scratchy sheets; no pillows, just bolsters; and came with a bathroom conveniently located just down the hall and one floor below. Every morning, at 7, someone knocked at the door to indicate that the breakfast tray was ready just outside. On it were two small fresh baguettes, covered with a cloth to keep them warm, one ceramic pot of sweet butter and one ceramic pot of jam, and *un grand bol* of café au lait with a skin of boiled milk on top.

Every morning, after eating, Danny ran down the hall and down the stairs for his morning bout of crampy nervous diarrhea, followed by his always-losing battle to wipe his ass truly clean with the small waxed paper squares the French apparently believe to be toilet paper.

After his bathroom battle, Danny set off on foot to the Louvre, a 19-minute walk. Danny went to the Louvre every day, for almost the whole day, except Tuesday when the Louvre was closed for some obscure French reason. On Tuesday, Danny was forced to go somewhere else in the city. Danny hated Tuesdays. The only way Danny could maintain his grip and control, living alone in a foreign city, was to keep to a routine. Danny even visited the same rooms in the Louvre in the same order every day and stared at the same works, except Tuesday.

After four weeks, Danny's traveler's checks were just about gone. Danny rang up Air Canada to ask about a return flight.

"I am so sorry, Mr. Harper, but the Canadian air traffic controllers are on strike, and none of our aircraft are flying to Canada. If you wish, sir, we can fly you to New York or any other major Eastern Seaboard city in the U.S. and arrange for ground transportation to Toronto."

"Oh," Danny replied, not knowing what else to say. "Great," Danny thought, "I could fly to New York and get free transportation to the U.S. Federal Prison in Leavenworth, Kansas."

He asked, "When'll the strike be over?"

"Oh, I am sure it will be over soon, sir, if you would like to wait for a direct flight to Toronto."

"I'd like to wait for a direct flight to Toronto."

The next day was Wednesday. Danny went back on duty at the Louvre - a week behind on his rent and worried about spending money on food.

Danny was staring dolefully at some famous nude by some famous artist in the third room on the list of rooms he visited every day except Tuesday. He was disturbed in his artistic musings by two American-girl voices behind him - giggling and chirping in some awful New Jersey or New York accent. One was fat, and the other was skinny with a goodly dose of acne.

Danny changed his expression from doleful to soulful, as he saw a script appear before his eyes that, if read with skill, promised to solve his hunger problem. Danny said to the girls in his perfectly accented French, "This is his finest work with the female form, but it pales in comparison to the goddesses I have before me now in the flesh." Or something that sounded equally good to a non-French speaker.

"We don't speak French."

"I'm so sorry. I should speak English. You see, I'm a Canadian here writing a novel in French, and sometimes I slip into my written tongue without realizing it. I'll translate for you what I said in French. 'This is his finest work with the female form, but it pales in comparison to the goddesses I have before me now in the flesh.'"

That was not an exact translation, of course; Danny's accent was perfect but his vocabulary and grammar were very poor. The girls couldn't know that, so Danny felt confident.

The girls giggled. Danny had been right to feel confident.

Danny pressed his pitch. "Have you two had lunch? There's a passable café here, and I shall be honored to guide you to the good things on the menu, if you'll give me the pleasure of your company." Danny imagined this is how a suave Frenchman would speak to ladies, if it were translated into English.

He must have been right. The girls giggled a "yes."

During lunch, Danny regaled the American college girls with the story of the story he was writing about Napoleon's last days in exile on the Island of St. Helena before his mysterious death. Danny haltingly related, somehow bravely holding back his tears, that Napoleon's loneliness was akin to his own, because he, Danny, was also an exile in a foreign place. Danny told them how his wife had run off with a doctor, taking all of his irreplaceable manuscripts and leaving him penniless. The girls were quiet and hung on his every word. The fat one gripped his hand to give him support in his grief. The skinny one told him that they had never met a real writer before. Danny was sure they had never met a real actor before, either.

"I wish my dad was a writer, but he's just a dull old cardiologist, and he's never home," said the fat one.

The skinny one with the acne said, "Yeah, my dad's even duller; he's her dad's accountant."

When the bill came for the meal and the wine, Danny grabbed it and insisted on paying. He laid down a suitable sum in Canadian money, and the waiter just looked down his long Gallic nose at it and would not deign to touch it. Danny had been through this Canadian-money thing before with this same waiter. Danny knew the waiter would refuse this inferior non-French currency. The waiter did refuse the Canadian currency and most vociferously berated Danny in both good French and bad English, after his haughty stare failed to intimidate Danny into producing some real French money.

Danny loosely translated the waiter's diatribe to the girls. They were horrified at the way this mere serving person was trying to humiliate their soulful writer friend. Both girls whipped out their wallets, paid and left a much-too-handsome tip for the insolent Frog. The waiter stared at Danny. His Parisian mask of disdain cleared for a brief moment as he realized what was going on. He smiled knowingly at Danny, and left the scene with his tip.

Danny explained to the girls how horrible the people of this city could be. For instance, his landlady, just this morning, had threatened to evict him even though he was only a week late with his rent. She refused to understand that Danny was waiting for his publisher to send him an advance, and that he would pay her shortly.

"How long will you ladies be in town?" Danny asked with hope in his voice.

"Only two more days."

Danny looked deeply disappointed and said, "*Merde*, I'm so broke and so desperate dealing with these ignorant foreigners that I'd ask you for a loan, but I doubt my advance check will be coming any sooner than three days. I couldn't pay you back."

"How much do you need?" asked the skinny one with the acne.

"Maybe ?500 would see me through, but I refuse to accept it because I can't pay you back before you leave the city."

"How much is that in American?" The skinny one with the acne pressed.

"Oh, less than a hundred dollars."

"We don't need it back. Honestly, it's been real cheap traveling here, and our parents gave us a lot more money than we've used so far." They dug into their purses and gave Danny three twenties each.

Danny sighed, looked at the twenty-dollar bills, and gave a resigned Gallic shrug. "I'll accept this on one condition: that you give me your addresses in the States where I can mail you the money when I get my advance."

"Oh, don't be silly about paying us back! But if you insist ..." The fat one wrote her name and address on a slip of paper from her purse.

Danny grinned and lightened up, now that he had $120 US in his pocket. "Let's go celebrate, ladies. Let's forget all this talk about money and just be ourselves, young and feeling the love that this city is famous for. You know, here we can do anything we want - it's Paris! There are no rules when you're in Paris. Our fantasies can become reality here. I really feel things for both of you. I don't know what's come over me. Ever since I saw the two of you standing by that painting, my world hasn't been the same." Danny's world was not the same. He had $120.

The girls gave each other a secret look, and excused themselves to go to the washroom. They giggled the whole way there.

When they got back, Danny said in a conspiratorial voice, "I know a tiny place around here that has a fantastic selection of champagnes. I think we should go open a few bottles of good bubbly and get to know each other a lot better." With a bottle or two of champagne in him, Danny was pretty confident in his ability to get to know them better, in the biblical sense.

The fat girl and the skinny girl with the acne looked at Danny with trusting cow eyes. Danny knew he had found a way to climb out of poverty in Paris.

The days went by, the air traffic controllers' strike went on, and Danny met other American college girls. Danny bought a large hardbound notebook as a prop, so the girls he met at the Louvre had an aid to visualizing him as a writer. Danny spent a lot of time furiously scribbling notes for his novel on a bench in one of the more popular galleries in the Louvre. Danny actually wrote a lot of things in this book, but they were not in French and not about Napoleon.

Danny knew little about either. But he was writing whatever popped into his head, and having fun doing it.

Danny even wrote in the book when no girls were looking. He wrote when he was in that smelly little loo in the hall below his room every morning as he waited for his nasty daily bout of diarrhea to end. Sometimes he wrote three or four pages while his guts exploded. Danny told himself it was not like he was really writing, something he had promised himself never to do again after Amy left him five years ago. He rationalized that he was just scribbling down some notes about things in his life he didn't want to forget. He was not really *writing*.

CHAPTER FORTY-TWO

All governments suffer a recurring problem: Power attracts pathological personalities.~*Frank Herbert*

It was a soft and warm Tuesday evening - a spring-in-Paris evening. Danny had strayed to another part of the city because the Louvre was closed, and he had a day off from his work of hustling American girls. Danny decided to walk back to 19 rue Saint-Séverin along the Seine, as the Metro was often crowded at this time of day, and the subway maps confused Danny. They were all written in French.

Danny was walking, enjoying being near the river. He knew it was impossible to get lost walking along the river, since his room was only a stone's throw from its banks. Walking under one of the many bridges, Danny saw a lineup of good-looking, well-dressed guys about his own age leaning against the stone retaining wall. They looked at Danny with obvious interest, and one of them called something to Danny and started to walk next to him. Danny threw a vague smile his way but then tried to ignore him. He continued to walk beside Danny, chattering in French too swift for Danny to understand. Danny tried his best to answer the few phrases he recognized with short replies of his own. Danny's escort laughed and smiled, and tried to take Danny's arm. Danny had his notebook under that arm. Danny pulled away from his escort. The young man took a quick step ahead of Danny, grabbed Danny around the waist, and tried to kiss him. Danny's notebook fell to the ground.

Danny shoved the man, acting on defensive instinct. When the young man did not move much from the shove, Danny gave him a punch in the face with the heel of his hand. The man went down backwards like a felled tree, hitting his head on the pavement. Danny heard shouting behind him and saw two gendarmes running at him. When they reached the scene of the crime, one grabbed Danny, and the other one attended to the queer Danny had decked.

What followed, and it followed all night long in an overheated and under-decorated police office, was a French version of Kafka's *The Trial*. Various officials, all speaking rapid French, interrogated Danny at various times. They pointed to Danny's notebook and made menacing noises. None of his inquisitors acknowledged either Danny's overly precise English or his halting French answers, which, while perfectly accented, showcased Danny's weakness in vocabulary and grammar. Danny may have inadvertently confessed, in broken French, to high treason or serial murder, given his ineptitude in the language of Voltaire.

One of his inquisitors absconded with the notebook Danny had been using to write his fake novel. All of his inquisitors seemed inordinately interested in it, although Danny was not sure any of them could read English. Danny thought, "My writing is so rambling and incoherent, maybe they'll think it's secret spy code."

Danny kept pleading to be connected with the Canadian Embassy and pointing to the maple leaf flags sewn on his jacket. Finally, the police authorities, after apparently having searched for several hours to find the worst English speaker in the whole station, brought him in to interview Danny. This paragon of linguistic incompetence said to Danny, "M. Harper, the Canadians are not wish to be speaking to you.

You have one American passport. Your official American will be here soon. They will to speak to you."

"I'll bet they will to speak to me," Danny thought.

Danny waited for hours for his "official American" to be there "soon." He heard an eerily familiar voice speaking English in the next room. Danny was even more startled when he saw the speaker. The voice belonged to Richard Eric Webster – his former roommate Dick!

Danny was speechless when he saw him. Dick looked almost the same as he had on the last day of third-year classes when he told Danny he was transferring to Yale. Dick's hair was now a lot shorter. He was wearing tortoiseshell glasses and a suit that looked expensive, but it was the same Dick whom Danny had loved and depended on and looked up to like a demigod, or maybe even a whole god.

"How did you get here? What did they charge *you* with?"

"No, Danny, I'm not a prisoner like you. I'm here as a representative of your government, and I'm going to see about getting you home; the French seem pissed off that you were with one of their homo whores and beat him up when you were done"

Danny was so relieved he was on the verge of ecstasy and missed the remark about "homo whores". "To Canada? Wow, I'm going home to Canada!"

"No, Danny, 'home home' – to America."

"I'll be arrested."

"I know, and you deserve to be arrested. You refused to serve your country and you're a homo pervert. I know how you used to look at me all the time--mooning."

"But what're you doing here? Hey, you know I'm not a homo."

"I was asked to serve my country after I did my masters at Yale by some people who opened my eyes to the truth. I *chose* to serve my country."

"You joined the fuckin' CIA?"

"I really can't talk about what I do, or for whom I do it. I work here at the American Embassy. That's all you need to know."

"What about SDS? They let you into the CIA after you were in SDS and all that?"

"I never said I was in the CIA, but I can tell you that I got my job here because I was so good at keeping an eye on radicals back in college for the Dean. Who better to keep an eye on radicals than the recording secretary of the SDS chapter?"

"You were a fuckin' spy back then? For the CIA?"

"Let's not play games here, Danny. I have work to do with these French guys about deporting you. I don't think they want you around here anymore after you split open the head of one of their faggy citizens. And I'd really like a peek at that secret notebook of yours that the Frenchies seem so excited about."

Danny blurted out in anger, his eyes filled with tears, "You're a piece of rat shit."

Dick just smiled his enigmatic smile, shrugged and walked to the door of the interrogation room. He stopped in the doorway, turned, made his fingers into a gun, pointed the "gun" at Danny, dropped the hammer and smiled again.

A minute or so later, a Frenchman in civilian clothes, who did not identify himself, came in through the same door. He spoke to Danny in perfect and nearly unaccented English. "We will not deport you. You did a bad thing to a French citizen, and we will not tolerate that. But you are lucky we dislike your American spies here more than we dislike you. You are also very lucky your victim has a hard head, and a long criminal record. You must leave as soon as possible. Go back to Canada, my friend."

"I can't go back to Canada." Danny told him about the air traffic controllers' strike.

"Very well, you must telephone me every day, and update me regarding the strike. You must not change your address in Paris. You must take the first flight back to Canada after the strike is over." He gave Danny his business card. "Are we clear?"

"Yes, sir."

"Go." The man pointed to the exit.

CHAPTER FORTY-THREE

Most quarrels are inevitable at the time; incredible afterwards. ~E. M. *Forster*

Paris was the most likely city for the magic of love to explode into flower. Danny had not experienced any of that type of magic during his stay. He had given fine performances to several young women, but the goal of his performances was cash and not foreverafters - it was "take the money and run." Foreverafters were too risky. Danny's foreverafters took the form of the dream demons that, depending on his level of depression, assumed the shape of Amy, Diana or Lina, and sometimes the girl with one cold lavender eye and one cold blue eye floating in a sea of blood.

Danny was seated at "his" café, where he ate the same thing every day and nursed his old bottle of Ancre beer, when a stunningly beautiful woman walked directly to his table and asked to join him. Danny could not deny her.

"Do you speak English?" she asked in English.

"I speak a little, because I'm a Canadian."

She offered a few pleasantries in very good but heavily accented English. Danny listened and mulled over why he had lied to her about his native tongue. He didn't want to speak again until he was sure of what to say.

Danny felt provincial and inept in the shadow of her beauty and style, but had no intention of sounding inept when he did speak again. She was tall, and very slender. She had gray/hazel/blue-green eyes and a pale olive complexion, with straight jet-black hair down to her waist. Her eyes were ever so slightly slanted. Danny had never had a woman of this rather extreme beauty speak to him or be this close to him before. What truly unnerved him, though, is he had the odd feeling she was unlike any other woman he had ever met, but he could not put his finger on exactly why or how that was so.

Her name was Margrethe. "My name is not French, you see. It is Danish. You may call me Maggie. What is your name? You have not been so kind as to introduce yourself to me."

"It's Jim," Danny lied again.

"Well, Jim, when you are finished here, I would be pleased to have you walk with me. I have to stop by work. Come with me."

"Would you care for something to eat or drink?"

"No, I am content to watch you eat. I learn a lot about a man by watching him eat."

Danny was now self-conscious about his eating style, his pace and even how long he chewed. He waited. He was being judged, and he was sure he would screw it up somehow. When Danny had finished eating, Margrethe walked to his side of the little table and said, "Take my arm. You are taught how to walk a girl in Canada? No?" Danny stood and took her arm. If he thought he had never spoken to a woman who looked like this, he knew for certain he had never touched a woman like this. Recognizing his usual tenuous grip on reality, he wondered if she were really there.

Margrethe took Danny's arm and showed him how to hold hers, put him on the correct side of her, nearest the curb, and strolled with him off into the Paris afternoon - a tall, black-haired beauty in a midnight-green silk sheath with matching purse and pumps, with a scraggly, pretty-blond beach boy in a dirty T-shirt and a shapeless corduroy jacket with red maple leaves sewn on the sleeves.

Margrethe led Danny to the Metro and paid for them both. The couple got off on the Champs Élysées within sight of the Eiffel Tower. Danny had never been to this part of the city and found it quite intimidating. He had been hanging around the same neighborhood in Paris since his first day there. Margrethe led Danny into an elegant old building that had "Maison Dior" written in tiny gold letters on the door. Danny did not see the letters. He was focusing on Margrethe.

Inside, she motioned Danny to a chair, blew him a kiss, and went down one of the mirrored and carpeted halls. Maggie came back to him in the lobby nearly 30 minutes later, and apologized for being so long. "My fitting ran into unforeseen complicatedness."

"Fitting?"

"I am a model for this house."

"A model? What house?"

"This is the house of Christian Dior. I am a house model. I wear the creations to show how they look on real people."

"You're a 'Dee-Ore' model?"

"Yes, they like me because they say I am exotic. My mother is Vietnamese and my father is French. I live in France now because of the war."

"The war?"

"My mother's people have been at war a very long time with many different countries. One of these days we will win and there will be peace. My mother's people were fighting my father's people for a long time. I think sometimes I am always fighting inside myself this same war. I do not like being called 'exotic' here in France, and I do not like being told I am a 'big white ox' in Vietnam. What do you think of me?"

"I think you're the most beautiful woman I've ever seen."

Clearly disappointed, Maggie said, "*Merde*, men! You are all alike. You do not look first for a soul, you look only at what is outside."

Danny hung his head.

"Don't sulk, my pretty little boy. I will take you for a real French meal this evening, and you can look for my soul and I can look for yours."

Danny almost said, "Good luck finding my soul." But he had the wit, somehow, to keep his mouth shut. Instead he asked, "What time?"

They met again at Danny's café in the early evening. Danny had washed under his arms and between his legs, and had shaved, cutting himself in three places that, fortunately, scabbed over quickly. He'd put on his cleanest and best T-shirt. This time he took her arm, but still allowed her to lead. It was her city.

She led him to a brand new and very American-looking establishment, incongruously named Le Drugstore. It was a garishly decorated place, brightly lit and noisy, unlike the little traditional cafés Danny was used to in his little neighborhood. The food was pure French, and unlike anything Danny had ever shoveled in his mouth before. It was served slowly and in six courses, each accompanied by its own wine. Maggie ordered for both of them. The waiters kowtowed to her as though she were the Queen of France. When Danny ate alone, the waiters behaved as if he was dog shit. Maybe Danny was eating at the wrong places, or was male or American, or all of the aforementioned. Maybe Maggie was famous, as the restaurant was near the House of Dior, or maybe Maggie ate here often and was a good tipper. Danny wondered all these things, but was afraid to ask for confirmation.

Their conversation was neither deep nor broad. Danny told some small lies when Maggie asked him questions about himself. She said little about her own life. Danny was afraid of conversation with her. One minute he thought she was a spy, the next a dream, and the next, he knew she was real, but would go away if he said something stupid. They concentrated on eating and commenting on the food they ate.

The meal lasted slightly more than four hours. Danny was stuffed. Maggie ate all the food that was served to her. Where she put all that food in her tall and very slender body, Danny had no clue. Danny had a feeling the dinner was very expensive and when he saw the bill, he knew, if it had been a misunderstanding about her paying, he would be back in jail again. The meal cost more than it cost to stay in his nasty little room for a month. There was no misunderstanding. Maggie paid and left a tip so large that it alone would have fed Danny at his usual café for a week.

Danny took Maggie's arm, and they left Le Drugstore. Out on the street, Maggie hailed a cab, and one pulled over at once. She kissed him hastily on the cheek before climbing in. Danny stood there and looked at the tail lights of her cab wink in and out of traffic. No one would believe this story back home and rightly so; Danny didn't believe it himself. He stood in one spot looking at the curb where the cab had taken away this dream girl. He wondered if he could find his way home again on the Metro. He wondered if he would ever eat a meal like that again. Danny lived in a world of wonder. He did not wonder if he would see Maggie again. He knew he would not.

The following day, Danny was at his usual haunt, eating the same thing at the same time, and Maggie walked in and sat across from him. Danny was stunned. He thought she had deserted him like his mentally ill wife, like drugged-out Diana, and most of all like his first love, Amy. It had never occurred to him Maggie might come back. He was sure she had judged him and found him wanting in numerous ways.

She caught Danny scribbling in his notebook, even though there were no silly American girls to impress and hustle in this seedy little place.

"What are you doing, M. Jim? Writing your life story?" She giggled a little-girl giggle.

Despite the nice giggle, Danny took offense and barked at her, "I don't write!" as though she had caught him masturbating or stealing a piece of fruit. He slammed the notebook shut. "And you might as well know that my name isn't Jim, it's Danny." There was real anger in his voice and it surprised him. Danny was sure that, hearing the anger in his voice, she would go away. She seemed unfazed by it.

She asked, "If you do not write, then what are those marks on the paper that look like English words?" and she giggled again.

A well-aimed giggle from a pretty girl can turn away a lot of anger. "Yeah, that's writing, but it's just a lot of nothing." Danny's tone was not angry, just wary.

"If it's just a lot of nothing, then you can let me read it." Her logic was unassailable.

"No, you can't read it." Some anger crept back into Danny's voice.

"I will give you a kiss if you read it to me. I know you want to kiss me."

"Yeah, I want to kiss you, but you can't read it."

"Then you can read it *to* me, and I will kiss *you*."

The performer in Danny couldn't resist her offer. "It's just some stuff about why I don't write. I met this woman once when I was young …"

He read to her about his love affair with Amy. When he finished, Maggie was crying. "But that is so sad and that is so beautiful at the same time. Is that all true?"

"Yeah, it's true. And you can see why I don't actually write. I hate writing."

"Danny, or 'Jim,' you are lying. You are still in love with this woman, and you don't write because you are in love? You should write about love, and people like me will buy your books and cry. Do you want me to kiss you now?"

"No. Not now, not ever. I don't want to fall in love with you. I don't do so well at that. I just pretend to fall in love to get what I want. I fall in love for money. I'm a bad person, huh?"

"No, you are just a man. They are all like you, except you know what you are like. You are an artist, Danny, and artists have to know who they are before they can make art that is true. I still want to kiss you, but I will not fall in love with you. I have a wonderful husband and a wonderful lover, and I don't need one more of either."

"You're married?"

"*Oui.*"

"And have a lover?"

"*Oui.*"

"What're you doing here with me, then?"

"Is it wrong to talk to a handsome foreigner who looks so mysterious and can write well enough to make me have tears?"

"No, it's not wrong, Maggie."

"I have to go now and meet my husband. Do you still refuse my kiss?"

"Yes, Maggie, I still refuse your kiss."

She smiled and left Danny to his *steak frites* and his Ancre beer. She left him a small piece of paper with her address and telephone number on it.

Danny did not telephone her for two days. He did nothing but scribble in his notebook. He did not accost any college girls. He did not visit the Louvre. His money was running low, but that didn't matter. He didn't phone Air Canada to see if the planes to Canada were back in the air. He didn't care if the French put him in jail. He just scribbled. On the third day, he phoned. He phoned three times before she answered.

Knowing she had the key to something in his life, but not knowing what that key was, he blurted out in an embarrassingly desperate tone, "I have to see you."

She was busy and could not see him that day or the next, but agreed to meet him at his café at noon the day after that. He was at his usual table, with his usual meal sitting cold in front of him. He was on his third bottle of Ancre on a stomach that had been empty for a day or so. She sat next to him and not across from him. That was her way. She had sat next to him at Le Drugstore, too.

"Marry me." These two words distilled the essence of the hundred thousand thoughts he had had since he last saw her.

"I am married to a fine brave man. He is a hero of the Resistance."

Danny said something childishly stupid. "He must be pretty old, then."

"He is fifty. He was your age when he fought the Germans. They captured him and tortured him, but he escaped and fought them again until the end of the war."

Danny couldn't tell her that he had not fought against the evildoers in his own country who were busy destroying her home country of Vietnam. He couldn't tell her that he had run away from the whole mess. Danny hung his head and was quiet for a long time. Maggie would not break the silence, so Danny did. "Would you like a glass of wine?"

"Just one. I have a show this afternoon, and I don't want to trip over my shoes. Why do you want to marry me, you sad, sad boy?"

That was his problem. He was a boy. Danny realized that now. "I guess that was pretty stupid to ask you to marry me."

"No, it was not stupid. I know it came from your heart."

It had.

Danny was glad someone saw his heart. He had not seen his heart for a long, long time. His heart had been shattered and the pieces scattered since the day he saw the curtains missing from Amy's apartment windows. "I'm going home."

"Do you miss Canada?"

"I'm going to Chicago to fight in the war."

"I don't understand. Do you live in Chicago, too?"

Danny stood up and looked down at Maggie. He bent to her cheek with the intention of kissing her. She said, "No, please don't kiss me."

Danny looked at her for a few seconds more. "I have to go now." He put money on the table and walked away. When he was a short distance away, he turned to look back at her, but she had vanished. There was no wine glass on the table. It was as if she had never existed.

CHAPTER FORTY-FOUR

How far can you go without destroying from within what you are trying to defend from without?~Dwight D. Eisenhower

D anny walked to his room and telephoned Air Canada. The air traffic controllers were still on strike. The woman with the lovely French-Canadian accent on the other end of the phone recognized Danny.

"Mr. Harper, we have missed your calls the last few days. I hope you have not been ill."

"Not ill, thank you ..."

"How may we help you today, since there are still no air traffic controllers working in Canada?"

"I want to go to Chicago."

"That is not a problem, sir; we fly daily to Chicago from Orly."

"And can I get bus or train fare to Toronto to get home?"

"That should not be a problem, Mr. Harper, but you will have to wait a day or two and come in person to our Paris office to pick up your ticket to Chicago and train fare to Toronto."

"What's your name?"

"Monique."

"Thank you, Monique."

"You are welcome, Mr. Harper."

Danny flew to Chicago three days later. He had sold his travel camera and film to a girl from NYU he had met at the Louvre. She was on an art tour of Europe and her camera had been stolen. She paid him more than he had paid for the camera new, and Danny felt so guilty about taking advantage of her gullibility, he threw in the film for free and gave her a quick lesson in using the camera over champagne in his favorite bar. He had not taken a single photo in all his time in Paris and still had a good stock of film, so she really did get a good deal, if you didn't count the champagne she bought as part of the price.

Danny mailed a letter to Margrethe from Orly.

Dear Maggie,

Thank you for dinner. Thank you for being honest. Thank you for teaching me about myself. Thank you for making me feel good about writing again. Thank you for not allowing me to fall in love with you; I don't think I really know how to do that and not screw up. You're a friend who came into my life and made it a little better. Thank you. If I may, I'll write to you when I get to Chicago.

Danny (or Jim) ha ha

CHAPTER FORTY-FIVE

Dulce bellum inexpertis (War is delightful to the inexperienced).~Erasmus

The nameplate on the man's desk read Ralph Rolf, Assistant Chief Federal District Attorney. Despite the funny name, the man did not appear funny, and Danny had no interest in laughing. Danny was on a serious mission. He had waited five hours on a hard bench with no reading material with which to amuse himself in order to meet this man, who had agreed to see him after his last scheduled appointment of the day. Rolf looked like he did not have another appointment left in him. His shirt was wrinkled and his tie stained. Strain showed in his eyes, and his face looked as worn and wrinkled as his shirt. Danny guessed that he was quite old, about 40. Rolf did not stand to greet Danny and did not offer his hand. Rolf pointed to a chair without looking up. Danny sat where the man pointed. The chair he sat in was as hard and straight as the bench he had been warming for the last five hours.

Still not looking up from his papers, Rolf asked, "Are you Harper, the draft case?" as he opened a file on his desk that Danny presumed was his file.

"Daniel No-Middle-Initial Harper, sir …"

"Sir, huh? Maybe you *should* be in the Army."

"Not really, sir. I want to go to jail."

"Good luck with that. Let me tell you something before you start blabbing your whole sad, boring life story to me. I'll make it quick. In this noble democracy where I'm privileged to live and serve, there are approximately a quarter-million of you mostly white, mostly middle-class, fuckin' ungrateful college pukes under indictment for draft-related offenses. I have 17,017 such files to prosecute here in the Northern District, as of this morning, and tomorrow I'll surely have more. I have 37 assistants working under me. It takes 70 hours to prepare a prosecution and up to 300 hours if the case goes before a jury."

Rolph took a long breath and went on. "In the last year, we've been able to find the time to prosecute two draft files. You see, the other bad guys who break federal laws haven't been polite enough to stop offending long enough for us to use our precious time to throw all of you pansy-ass college pukes in jail, where you so richly deserve to be. We still have to prosecute forgery and mail fraud and corruption and conspiracy, and a multitude of other federal offenses." He swept his arms in a wide arc to indicate the ceiling-high shelves of hard-bound federal statutes that lay behind him, to his right and to his left.

"Are you dropping the charges?"

"Nope."

"I can't go to jail?"

"Not this century or even early into the next - not unless I get permission to hire about 2,000 more assistants. Get outta here, kid."

Danny had no more questions. Rolf turned his attention to the pile of paperwork on his desk. Danny felt, correctly, that the meeting was over. He left.

Danny wandered out onto the streets of Chicago, quickly emptying of homeward-bound workers. It was two hours past official rush hour and the Federal Assistant DA was still working at his desk.

Danny had failed in his mission to go to jail like a modern-day Thoreau. Danny could only think of one more alternative. Since the induction center would reject him as a draftee because he didn't have the proper papers to even get in the door, and since he had already *been* drafted and the Selective Service couldn't legally draft him a second time anyway, and since the federal justice system couldn't prosecute him for four or five decades, Danny decided to join the United States Marine Corps. Danny wanted to die, but didn't know it. He was so depressed that he failed to notice he was depressed - an unusual state of mental affairs for a young man used to taking his psychic temperature six times a day. An unusual and dangerous state of affairs ...

Danny took the elevated train back to the drab little room he rented at the West Side YMCA. He got off at his stop and wandered into the automat cafeteria next door to the Y to get something to eat. The automat was open 24 hours a day, and was never full and never empty. There were always some junkies in their eight layers of clothing sitting around staring at nothing, eating pound cake they dunked into coffee, long gone cold. As long as the food lasted, the cops who came in regularly could not throw them out for loitering. Tonight, Danny felt like one of those junkies - doing nothing, feeling nothing, going nowhere and waiting to be thrown out of life itself because he had run out of excuses to live. His last remaining hope of redeeming himself lay with the Marines. Surely they needed cannon fodder. Surely they would let him join up. Even if they wouldn't let him be a medic and he didn't have a chance to desert to the Vietcong in the field, at least he would be facing up to his duty to serve, to take his lumps, to finally be a man. To die with honor, since he had failed in his own mind to live with honor ...

The story Margrethe had told him about her old-geezer husband echoed in his ears. Her husband had fought for the Resistance against the Nazis, even going back to fight again after being tortured and escaping. Danny wanted to be such a man. He wanted to make a woman like Margrethe admire him and want to marry him. The Marines would make him such a man. The Marines also wanted to kill him. That was okay, too. Nothing mattered.

There was a poster near the entrance to the Y with a painting of a proud Marine on it, and the address of the nearest recruiting center stamped in a white space at the bottom. Danny intended to be at that address the next morning.

CHAPTER FORTY-SIX

The first casualty of war is not truth, but perspective. Once that's gone, truth,
like compassion, reason, and all the other virtues, wanders around like a wounded
orphan.~Ente Grillenhaft

The Marine Corps Recruiting Center nearest the YMCA was a storefront operation manned by a lone Marine gunnery sergeant. The sergeant looked a lot like the Marine on the recruiting poster, but a little older. He was a white person. The recruiting center was in a predominantly black neighborhood that had recently become home to a few Hispanics. In simpler terms, it was in the ghetto. Danny did not have to wait in line. There was no line.

The sergeant almost leaped to attention when Danny walked in. He quickly slipped a paperback book into an open desk drawer. In a thick rural southern accent, he boomed out, "Welcome to the Marines! I'm Gunnery Sergeant Clements. You can call me Bob, since you're still on civvy street. What do I call you?"

"Daniel No-Middle-Initial Harper, sir." Danny was wondering what sin this Georgia cracker had committed to be sentenced to serve in a recruiting center in the middle of a northern urban ghetto.

"You don't call a non-commissioned officer 'sir.' Bob will do. So you want to be the best? You want to be a Marine, part of America's shock troops? We're the pointy end of the stick poking into the commies' eyes."

"Yes." Danny was sure that Bob had been rehearsing this welcome speech for weeks or even years. Danny may have been his first prospect ever at this location, and this suited Danny's purpose well.

"Tell me about yourself first, Daniel. Then you can ask me all the questions you want."

Danny did tell Bob all about himself, and some of it was even true. Danny only lied about the things that couldn't be checked, and felt this was a reasonable amount of truth to tell the military representative of a repressive government.

Bob seemed impressed by Danny's oral resume. "So you're a good shot?"

"Yes. Like I said, I've been shooting a rifle since I was nine. My dad taught me. Killed a lotta squirrels."

"Great! You know, all Marines are required to qualify as expert riflemen before leaving basic, no matter whether they're going to be cooks or aviators or whatever."

"I heard that."

"You know, we're the elite - the best of the best. Don't be surprised if we can't take you. But from what you've told me, I don't think that'll happen. You're smart, you've got some college behind you, and you look fit enough. I'll be proud to send your info up the chain of command for review. You passed your pre-induction physical for the Army, I presume?"

"With flying colors. I got a perfect score on the intelligence test."

"One more thing, Daniel. The Marines get a lot of boys who try to enlist with us after they've been drafted. That's a problem, but it's a problem we can get around if we really want you. All the branches of the U.S. military are fighting on the same side, after all; Marines just fight a little harder. The thing is, it means some extra paperwork for my superiors. I'd like to be able to warn them about your draft status, if that will be a problem. You haven't been drafted, have you?"

"Yes, I've been drafted, but I'd much rather fight the commies with you guys." Danny felt a sense of relief that there weren't going to be any further impediments to his service. The Marines welcomed superior candidates who had already been drafted. Maybe when the Marines let him in and he deserted, the federal justice system would no longer snub him in favor of forgers and mail fraudsters. Maybe he could go to military jail, or be killed. Both appealed to him equally in the mood he was in.

"That's a real Marine, gung-ho attitude, Harper. We'll leave a message for you at that place you're staying, when we've checked a few things and cleared you. Oh, would you like a voucher for some chow? We have a deal with some of the local restaurants for guys who come in here and miss lunch." Bob pulled out two vouchers from a huge stack. Danny guessed that Bob didn't get much of a chance to hand out vouchers to guys here in the ghetto, since almost all of the guys in the ghetto already belonged to a gang, and Danny didn't imagine they had much desire to volunteer for Bob's gang.

Danny took the vouchers and shook Bob's hand. Bob's hand was very firm and dry, but Bob did not try to crush Danny's hand. It was exactly the right handshake for a recruiter. Danny fantasized that the Marines had a school for teaching just such handshakes to its recruiters. Bob was doing it all by the book.

Danny looked at the vouchers and decided to pass on eating at Cal and Sal's Chitterling Junction or the Emporium of Soul. He threw the vouchers into the street.

Days passed until finally, two weeks after his visit to the recruiting center, Danny found a message from Bob waiting for him at the front desk of the Y. The message said to come to the recruiting center as soon as possible. Bob had news.

Danny was elated. He was on his way to an adventure, maybe even death in Vietnam, or at least, a trip to the Federal Prison at Leavenworth. Somewhere - anywhere - was better than hanging around a rundown YMCA and eating at an automat surrounded by junkies. Danny couldn't wait to hear what Bob had to say, so he caught the EL to the recruiting center and hoped it would still be open when he got there.

Danny made it. The center was still open. Danny rushed in the door, and stood in front of Bob's desk in an "at ease" stance he had seen once in a war movie. Bob looked up from some paperwork and stood as well, but he did not seem to be at ease. He had bad news.

"Daniel, sit down." Bob indicated a metal folding chair. "I have bad news. Are you aware there's a federal indictment against you? My superiors didn't see fit to tell me the nature of the crime for which you've been indicted, and I don't want to know." Bob held up his hand in a "stop" gesture so Danny would not be tempted to tell him the nature of his problem. Gunny Bob was nothing if not discreet.

Bob continued, "This indictment is a problem for my superiors. They say we can't let you join until this indictment goes away. But the good news is that as soon as it goes away, the Corps will be happy to have you. I have that in writing. My assessment of a man as having the right stuff to be a Marine is seldom wrong, and my superiors have confirmed that." Bob let the news sink in. "Do you want a voucher for some chow?" The stack of vouchers on his desk had not gone down appreciably in two weeks. Bob handed two vouchers to Danny and smiled.

Danny smiled back and said, "Bob, it's been a pleasure meeting you. I'll get right back to you once this little problem is squared away."

But Danny knew that by the time the problem went away, he would be too old by several decades to get into the Marines, if what the Assistant Chief Federal DA had said about the size of his caseload was accurate. Danny had run through plans A, B and C, and had no plan D. He was alone in a strange city but still had some of the money Air Canada had unexpectedly dropped on him as compensation for not being able to fly him back to Canada. When that was gone, he would have to get a job. Danny did not want to get a job. He was writing all day long these days. He still had an Air Canada return flight voucher to anywhere, but he wasn't sure it was transferable if he needed to sell it. Thought piled upon morbid thought, and the thoughts led nowhere - the very definition of depression.

When worried, Danny usually turned to drugs, but he really hadn't been doing a lot of drugs in Chicago. Partly, it was to save money, but mostly, the junkies in the automat popped up in his mind every time he thought about buying some speed or weed. Danny did not want to end up joining them for coffee and pound cake. Danny didn't even have much of an urge to turn to booze.

Danny's only stash consisted of some peyote buttons, and they had been around a long time. It never seemed like the right time to use them. Danny knew they were a special key to the "doors of perception," but Danny had only used them once before with mixed results - lots of vomiting and a just a few odd visions. Danny respected drugs and was not truly a "recreational" user, although drugs were certainly a recreation at times. Danny had had too much religious training not to think, even after years of using drugs, that every high was an opportunity he could and should use to gain some spiritual insight. Kids from Christian colleges were like that - Danny more than most.

As he walked the broken ghetto sidewalks back to the EL station, he decided now was the time to consult the ancient gods who had, in their mercy, inserted their wisdom into these cactus buttons. Danny no longer had a clue what to do other than consult the gods.

Danny saw an older Negro man whose eyes, to Danny, spoke of many sorrows. He was sitting on the steps of a row house. He was balancing a brown bag on his knee that looked like it was covering a half-gallon bottle - probably malt liquor. Danny stopped and held out the Marine chow vouchers to the man. The man looked at the vouchers and took them without a word. He then held out his giant jug of malt liquor at arm's length, offering Danny a swig. Danny took a long, deep pull of the fortified beer. Danny wiped the top of the bottle on his sleeve before he handed it back to the seated man. The man took the bottle back and held it up in a gesture of salute.

Before getting "buttoned up," Danny wrote to Margrethe.

Dear Maggie,

I'm still in Chicago. It seems I'm not of much use to this country in any way. I may go back to Canada or back to Paris. I have return airfare anywhere Air Canada flies. I have my rent paid for the rest of the month and could stay here as well. I don't know yet. I hope this finds you healthy and happy. You'll never know what you've done for me. It was probably just a little natural thing for you to cry at the story I read to you about Amy, but I'm now writing every day - nothing special, just stories I like ... Some of them are even true! May I send some to you? I have to find a Xerox machine somewhere; some of them are kind of long to copy.

I hope you're in good health and happy. I miss you, even though we only met a few times.

Danny

CHAPTER FORTY-SEVEN

All the gods are dead except the god of war.~Eldridge Cleaver

Danny took the peyote. He walked around the little park across from the YMCA. He threw up three times and felt like throwing up six more. He had a quart of beer in a brown paper bag to wash his mouth. Danny was not alone in the park. He was surrounded by junkies and winos. He felt at home in this dissolute crowd. Danny lay on his back on the most stable-looking picnic table he could find. He settled in to see what the gods had in store for him. He closed his eyes.

There is a small prop plane over thick jungle canopy in North Vietnamese airspace. Above and behind this plane are two American carrier-based F-4 Phantom jets. They are bristling with a full load of air-to-air missiles of two different types: radar-guided Sparrows and heat-seeking Sidewinders. Each missile has different capabilities. The Phantoms are also armed with 20-mm automatic cannons. The carrier pilots have a choice of weapons to bring down this lumbering old prop plane. The pilot of the prop plane is unaware of their presence and is not taking any evasive action.

The Phantom pilots, using hand signals to maintain radio silence, agree on a plan to bring down this old Chinese hand-me-down two-engine passenger plane, designed before WW II by the Chinese and built by the French under contract. The Phantom leader decides they will go in for a gun run, because guns are a much more personal way to kill the enemy than using a missile at great distance. The enemy plane is traveling at a sedate 160 knots on the straight and level at 4,000 feet. The Phantoms are at 20,000 feet, and desperately trying to stay as far over their official stall speed of 135 knots as they can while still flying slowly enough not to overtake the enemy plane. None of the carrier pilots trust the official stall speed of 135. They know that F-4s in various configurations can stall anywhere from a low of 140 knots to a high of 180.

The American flight leader wants to put the enemy pilots into a panic by attacking the lumbering unarmed plane from the rear and throwing some cannon rounds with tracers to starboard and port of her wings, deliberately missing, just let its occupants know who is boss of this airspace before he rips them apart.

The Phantoms go in on the target in single file, flight leader first. If the flight leader for some reason misses killing the target because he is teasing them, his wingman will finish the job. Flight Leader Rollins comes in on a fast dive from above on a perfect tail approach. He deliberately misses, as planned, with his first two bursts. He intends to terrify the enemy pilots and whoever else is in the plane. He is making a statement to the effect that he, Lt. Richard Rollins, call sign "Big Dick" because of his diminutive stature, is the hottest fuckin' naval aviator in the fleet despite being the shortest naval aviator on the ship. Rollins' third burst blows off both of the plane's wings, and the ugly Chinese air machine becomes a ball of expanding orange gas. Big Dick's wingman stays in perfect formation and they fly over the ball of fire.

They resume their patrol, climbing back to 20,000 feet.

Danny heard a gruff voice saying, "Move along, asshole, or I'll move you myself." Two of Chicago's finest were standing over him, billy clubs in hand. Danny fingered the divot on his head from his last close-up encounter with this police force in 1968. Danny staggered to his feet, still seeing crazy puzzle pieces of jungle in his vision. Danny grabbed for his brown-bagged beer, and one of the cops deftly smashed it with his club just before Danny could reach it. Danny saw this in slow motion.

"Pick it up, asshole. No fuckin' littering in city parks."

Danny knelt down to pick up the wet bag, and threw up again. One of the cops whacked him in the neck with his club and when Danny woke up, the cops were gone and it was night. The puzzle pieces of jungle had been replaced by random bursts of yellow light behind his eyelids. Danny's head throbbed, and he had bad stomach cramps. He limped home to the YMCA and resolved to leave Chicago as soon as possible. He felt a compelling urge to see Margrethe, but did not know why. He looked at his face in the mirror when he reached his cell. It was covered in blood.

The next morning, when he went downstairs, the desk man had a letter for him. It was from Margrethe. Danny felt a cold chill run down his spine. He felt the one cold blue eye and the one cold lavender eye from the suicide in the shower staring at him, again from behind his back. Danny opened the letter even though his paranoia advised him against it. Danny suspected the peyote had not yet cleared his system.

Dear Danny,

I am sad today. My brave husband was killed on a diplomatic mission to a provincial capital in the north of my home country. American jets shot him down as he flew in an unarmed passenger plane that was carrying the sick and wounded. I am sick of war and sick in my heart. He was the only man I ever loved and the war has taken him, too, as it took my father and mother and my oldest brother. I cannot work. I cannot eat. I can only cry for the best man I ever knew whom I will never see again.

I do not know why I write this to you. You are a stranger. My friends do not wish to see me cry anymore but I cannot stop. I will never love again. I am dead with my Philippe in the jungle.

Margrethe

Danny became calm. He felt nothing. All desire disappeared. His pain floated away like a wisp of smoke. The one cold lavender eye and the one cold blue eye staring at Danny from behind his back winked out like streetlights at dawn. He knew the eyes were gone for good.

He used the telephone at the front desk to connect to Air Canada. He went to his room. He finished the chapter he was working on. He knew these words would be the last words he would ever write in the United States of America. He packed his few possessions and caught the EL train downtown. From downtown, he took a bus to the airport.

END

EPILOGUE

Reprinted with the kind permission of <u>Rolling Rock Magazine</u> ©
Issue # 187, 22 May 1975

THE FALL OF SAIGON/ SPRING IN PARIS—Daniel
Harper/Paris Correspondent for <u>Rolling Rock Magazine</u>

The American phase of the war in Vietnam is over. For now...
For the United States... America got its ass kicked. I cannot think of a
more delicate way to phrase that.

My friends here in Paris and my wife, who is half Vietnamese and
half French, tell me their Vietnam War has been over since the fall of
Dien Bien Phu in 1954 when the Viet Minh kicked the asses of the
French Foreign Legion in a pitched battle. The war against the French
colonists started in 1883 with only minor interruptions during the two
World Wars.

The Vietnamese are a persistent lot. No one told the Americans,
or maybe someone did, and the Americans were just too arrogant to
listen. "We're different from all other nations and exempt from the
lessons of history."

I am not going to harp on abstractions regarding the immorality
and waste of war. Far wiser men and far better writers than I have
covered that ground over and over again, to no apparent effect. I
more a storyteller than a literary lion. And I have a story to tell. It is

about my wife and me and our chance meeting with a young U.S. Marine Captain named Wayne Nelles, in Paris one gentle spring night. The Captain was a highly-decorated combat veteran from the look of the medals on his chest that include the Navy Cross, the Silver Star, two Navy Commendation Medals for valor, and three Purple Hearts. He has given me permission to use his real name and rank, because he "no longer gives a sweet fuck" about his career in the corps. To quote the Captain again, "What's the worst they can do to me; cut off my hair and send me into the jungle?" He laughed when he said that, but there was no real mirth in his voice.

Nelles immediately seemed a very bright and well-educated man, with a writer's vocabulary and sensibilities. He also seemed a deeply angry man who was loathe to display it. He was wounded in ways and in places that might never heal. When we met him he was drunk, not roaring drunk, but quietly, silently, inertly drunk. He was in full uniform. He was staring at my half-Vietnamese wife, Margrethe, in our favorite café just off off Boul'Mich—such staring not being an unusual occurrence, since my wife still works as a house model for Dior. She approached him, sensing his inner turmoil, because that's the kind of person she is. She's a born healer and this man looked like he needed some. They spoke in low tones for a few minutes, then, she motioned me over to his table.

I identified myself as a reporter, because it isn't fair to purloin a story under false pretenses. The first thing he said was, "I won't talk about the Corps or the war." And he proceeded to talk about nothing else.

"Where's the gold, sir, or the uranium or diamonds?" He asked, seemingly out of the blue.

Then he went on, after leaving the question hang in the air for a good while, as he stared at Margrethe, "A black kid from Georgia asked me that question about an hour before he died in my arms. He meant what were we Americans doing there, if there was nothing to steal. Fuck, I couldn't tell him. I didn't have the heart to bleat some horseshit about communism and capitalism. I don't believe that crap myself. And the kid didn't know jack shit about communism anyway, except that white people told him it was bad. And the gooks that killed him that day and tried to kill me every day weren't fighting to the last man in muddy those holes of theirs for Marx; they were dying for their land—a land that had no gold or diamonds but had something more precious—their ancestors and their families."

I remarked on his remarkable speech with a quote from Alan Watts "Wars based on principle are far more destructive...the attacker will not destroy that which he is after." Surprising to me was the fact that Nelles was familiar with this quote. He expanded on that quote by saying, "All wars are immoral, probably even WWll and the Civil War, if you really study the guts of 'em, but not all wars are irrational. Stealing is fucking rational." He banged his fist on the table for emphasis, "But that poor black kid knew there was nothing to steal in that fucking jungle. It was not rational to be there. Europe was a prize to be won in WWll and the South in the Civil War, but there wasn't shit to steal in Vietnam. It's immoral to steal, but it's not irrational." He banged the table again. "You get what I'm saying, Mr. Rolling Rock Reporter? My war wasn't moral or rational. How the fuck am I supposed to live with that?"

Nelles sounded as if he had memorized the speech or had written it down somewhere.

I opened up to him with my personal thoughts, a standard reporter tactic to encourage the source, but still hoped he wouldn't judge me, "That's why I didn't fight over there. Aside from being a coward, probably."

"Fuck "coward" and "brave" and all that "definition" shit. There's only "alive" or "dead". They gave me medals for bravery when I was the most cowardly. They wanted to court martial me when I was brave. Fucking accountants running that war—adding machines in uniforms safe in the rear… "Brave" would have been shooting the colonels and generals, not the Gooks."

He looked at my wife. "You been over there? In the war?"

"No. I was born here." She paused and gauged if the soldier could handle her next thought. "The Americans killed my husband when he was on a medical aid mission in the North. Shot down the plane he was in--full of wounded children…"

"I'm sorry m'am."

"It's okay, Captain Nelles, you didn't do it."

"I would have." Nelles said softly, not looking up from the empty bottles of Ancre beer in front of him.

"I know, but you didn't." Margrethe said in an even softer tone.

Nelles began to cry. If he was a quiet drunk, he was an even quieter weeper. His expression never changed in the slightest. Tears rolled down his scarred cheeks from eyes that never blinked. Water over stone…

I asked, uncomfortable with his tears "Do you want another drink?"

"Sure. This French piss have any alcohol in it? I can't feel a thing", Nelles said in a faux hearty tone."

"I'll get the waiter's attention. I have to go to the can." I said, and I left the table.

When I came back, I saw Nelles and Margrehte in a tight embrace, their lips together and their mouths open. Nelles was moaning, as if in pain. I sat down quietly and said nothing, just watched. There were fresh drinks on the table. When they paused for breath in their passion, Nelles saw me and froze like a jack lighted deer. After a few beats he said, " I gotta go now."

Margrethe said, "Sit."

I seconded the motion. Nelles did as he was told and was quiet. He didn't look up from the table. Margrehte put her hand on Nelles' hand and said, "Drink."

Nelles drank.

I drank.

Margrethe drank.

Made in the USA
Charleston, SC
23 April 2012